In the FALCON'S SAFETY

DENISE LUPINACCI

Fulton Books, Inc.
Meadville, PA

Published by Fulton Books 2021

ISBN 978-1-64952-922-0 (paperback)
ISBN 978-1-64952-923-7 (digital)

Printed in the United States of America

Dedicated to my daughter, Daniella, who inspires me by dreaming big and working hard to make it happen.

A special thanks to my son, Nicholas, who shares my love of reading and was willing to read my book several times… despite my genre, pushing me to do better. He is always willing to talk about grammar, character building, and plot.

PROLOGUE

1714 Scotland

The journey was starting to get monotonous as the trees that lined the path seemed endless. Deep into their third day of traveling home, the Duncan family were still in good spirits from the Highland games they enjoyed with the MacKay clan. Mary Duncan's mother was a MacKay, but she married a Duncan. From the time Mary could first remember, they had made this journey every year. Fond memories of playing, watching the festivities, jesters, and minstrels with cousins is how she remembered it. A carefree time. It was an excitement not usually found in the lowlands.

Mary's father died some years back, and her mother later remarried a prominent MacKay highlander whom she had known as a child. Being married to a man with such a high status gave Mary the privilege of staying at the castle when visiting with her family.

Mary and her younger sister, Elizabeth Duncan, continued the tradition of going to the games every August. They made a holiday of it with their two small families, often going up a couple of days before the games started to visit with their mother and leaving a couple of days after the games had ended. It was something that both families looked forward to every year.

Mary's husband, Robert Duncan, sole heir to Laird Duncan, looked to the sky to determine how much daylight was left. He reckoned they had but two or three hours at the most to prepare the camp and cook. Had it just been him and his soldier companions, he would have ridden on for another hour, or perhaps even longer, not caring if he was setting up by moonlight, but with his family, he kenned he needed extra time.

"We best be pulling off to set up for the night while we still have enough light," Robert said to his brother-in-law, Ian.

As Robert changed directions, Ian Duncan, Elizabeth's husband, followed, guiding the two horses pulling the cart down a path that split the forest in two, just enough for a cart to go through. With the sun low in the sky, the cover of the trees made everything darken. They rode for another half hour along the small path until they came to the large clearing that rested below a mountain. As soon as they exited the woods, it was as if the sun came back out, no longer hiding among the branches of the trees. It was a peaceful sanctuary that lay hidden a good distance from the main path. The clearing edged a wide river flowing gently some ways before winding around the mountainside. It was a perfect place to set up camp, a little heaven on earth.

As soon as the cart came to a stop, Mary's daughter, Anna, jumped out of the wagon, her brownish-gold braids flying up until her feet hit the ground. Anxiously waving her hands in a gesture to jump, Anna called, "Come on!"

Her cousin, Lizzy, gazed down with big hazel eyes behind straggly blond hair as she gripped the edge of the cart. Though slightly taller than Anna, jumping from that height scared her. Reaching her arms out to her father, Ian scooped down and picked her up, placing her on the ground with a kiss on her forehead. As soon as her feet touched the ground, Anna grabbed her cousin's hand and pulled her along.

"Let's go throw rocks in the river!" Anna said to Lizzy as she pulled her along so she'd keep up with her.

"Don't go into the water!" Mary called to them.

Anna shrugged as she turned her head for a split second, not slowing down at all. Once at the river's edge, the girls bent over, picking out different rocks. Once they had enough to fit in one hand, they straightened. Anna threw the first rock. *Kerplunk.* The girls giggled as they took turns seeing who could make the highest splash.

Robert and Ian unhitched the cart from the horses as Ian's son, James, cared for the horses.

Ian grabbed his bow from the seat of the cart, digging around until he found his quiver and arrows.

Robert unfastened his bow and quiver from his saddle and casually swung them over his shoulder before securing his pistol under his belt in the front. Walking over to his wife, he gave her a kiss as he rubbed her belly, which was already starting to show. She had to bend her head a good bit to look up to him since he stood a whole head taller. Her lips curved to a beautiful smile as he winked at her before turning toward the woods to join Ian.

Anna's older brother, Robbie, was tasked with getting the fire started. Though only eight years old, Robbie could build a fire as well as any adult. As the oldest son of the future laird, Robbie always shadowed his da, learning and familiarizing himself with tasks at an early age, including building fires.

He dragged fallen branches from the edge of the woods to the camp and started breaking them up, arranging them into three piles, larger pieces, small sticks, and twigs. Laying the twigs on a pile of dry kindling, he pulled out a piece of flint from his pocket, striking it against his dagger, creating sparks that flew into his pile of kindling. After a few strikes, the kindling caught. Dropping his flint and dagger, he bent down low to blow on the pile that started a small stream of smoke. As he blew, a flame burst out. He sat back, slowly feeding the fire with more twigs before adding the small sticks. Soon he had a nice fire going. He went back into the woods to gather larger pieces of wood.

Mary put wee Willie into the cart to keep him from roaming. With the help of her sister, Elizabeth, they pulled out a canvas from the cart, despite Willie pulling on it in a playful game of tug of war. After setting it up as many times as they had, both tents were raised sturdy on flat ground in no time.

Within half an hour, the camp was completely set up, horses fed, and a nice fire was going. James and Robbie were now sword fighting with sticks in the clearing between the camp and the river while Mary and Elizabeth sat by the fire, watching wee Willie bang on a pot.

Losing interest in throwing stones, Anna headed toward the base of the cliff lining part of the river. She turned her attention to a specific rock on the side of the cliff. Picking up a slender stick long enough for her to reach the rock, she began to trace the outline of the rock, clearing away the sediment that had built up around it. Just as the rock started to loosen, Lizzy joined her.

"Come on, Lizzy. Help me stack some rocks so I can reach," Anna ordered.

Without questioning, Lizzy helped her gather several large flat rocks, a couple requiring them both to carry together. After stacking them one on top of the other, Anna stood on them as they wobbled under her feet. Balancing herself by putting one of her hands on the side of the cliff, she reached up with the other to dislodge the rock. Unable to get it to move, she extended her other hand, finally wiggling it out.

It fell to the ground with a big thud, and both girls giggled. Standing on her tippy-toes, she reached into the newly created hole and pulled out a beautiful blue gemstone. She jumped down to show Lizzy.

"Wow, that's pretty!" Lizzy said.

The girls looked at it in the palm of Anna's hand for a bit before taking off to the campsite.

"Look what Anna found!" Lizzy screamed. "She dug it out of the cliff."

Anna held the unusually shaped but perfectly polished blue gemstone to show it to her mother and aunt.

Huffing, bent over, and trying to catch her breath, Lizzy explained again, "She dug it out of a hidden spot in the cliff."

"I hid it there the last time I was here," Anna explained.

Her mother exchanged a confused glance at Elizabeth before turning back to Anna. "Anna, this is the first time ye have ever been here," she replied.

"Nooo," Anna said, waving her empty hand, clearly frustrated with being misunderstood. "I hid it before I was killed," she stated matter-of-factly as she plopped the jewel in her mother's hand.

She promptly grabbed Lizzy's hand, turned her around, and led her to watch the boys playing with their makeshift swords.

Mary studied the stone in her hand. The brilliant blue stone was polished smooth and cut into a diamond shape with two smaller, equal sides, creating one perfectly square corner and the other two longer equal sides, forming a longer and finer point.

Mary turned to Elizabeth who looked shocked as she made the sign of the cross. "She's bewitched," she mumbled as she stared at Anna.

The men came back after another half hour, each carrying a duck, as they chatted lightly. Handing their kill over to the women, Robert told Mary and Elizabeth about the half-burned stone house they had seen in the woods. The roof and one of the outside walls had collapsed. It had been left empty and exposed to the elements for what looked like decades.

CHAPTER

Twelve years later

The chill in the air made it hard to want to get up, but even as the sun showed its first rays of light, it started to warm up. The chilly night was unusual for August, even for the Highlands.

The castle would be reached in half a day's ride, and that was enough for everyone to ready themselves with great speed. Before long, the tents were taken down, horses fed, saddled, and hooked up to the cart. Robert and his brother-in-law, Ian, loaded the final sacks into the cart.

They hadn't made this journey to the MacKay's Highland games in six years. That was when Anna's grandmother fell ill. Anna's mother, Mary, and Aunt Elizabeth were escorted to the castle prior to the games to care for their ailing mother. Not being able to leave for an extended amount of time, Anna's father, by then, Laird Duncan, stayed behind in Dundee with Robbie, Anna, and Willie. Ian was deep in a critical point of putting a roof on their newly built cabin, so he stayed behind, as well with his son, James, and Lizzy. A couple of weeks later, they all headed to the MacKay's Highland games and joined Mary and Elizabeth.

Though Anna and Lizzy did not live far from each other and their families spent most Sundays together, they had grown very distant through the years. But that year, the trip was different. That journey had felt like the first couple of times Anna remembered making the journey. The two girls played and laughed together. Perhaps it was because her aunt was not there, but it was like it used to be when they were wee lasses.

That had all come to an end when they arrived four days after Anna's grandmother had died and one day after the funeral.

The games had begun the very next day, but Anna's mother dinna spend much time with them at the festivities as she normally did. Anna's da accompanied Anna and Willie to the games a few times but spent a lot of time with his wife as support.

That was the same year Robbie met the young lass Mary Ellen. Her family had been sitting on a blanket beside Anna's as they watched the games. Robbie had chosen his favorite champion and was cheering him on when Mary Ellen boldly told him that her dad was the best of the competitors and would come out way ahead of his favorite. Sure enough, her dad went on to the next round and Robbie's champion did not. Not only did he move on to the next round but was also the top competitor in one of the categories. After that, Robbie and Mary Ellen were together every chance they could.

Once again, Lizzy had stuck by her mother, barely speaking to Anna.

This trip was no different, though Anna dinna expect anything else. She was used to it by now and dinna mind much. Lizzy was more interested in material things and gossip while Anna preferred being outdoors and was more thoughtful. Anna was much too excited about the festivities to be bothered by Lizzy's indifference to her. Not only were they going to see the games once more, but her brother was also getting married.

Thinking of the last time they had visited the MacKays made Anna think of her mother. She had died in childbirth six months after Anna's grandmother passed. They had been concerned about the pregnancy because her last one had been complicated and the babe was born dead. Her mom had barely survived.

It had been a hard year. How she missed her mom and the time they spent together chatting over tea or walking through the gardens. She would send Anna out every morning to pick fresh flowers for the afternoon tea. On occasion, they would have company, but usually, it was just the two of them. They would talk about all different things, but her favorite was when her mother would tell her stories about growing up in the Highlands. After she died, afternoon tea became too hard to do, even with company.

That was when Anna started spending more time with her da and brothers. He brought her along everywhere and taught her most of the things he taught her brothers. Not everything, though. He would not teach her to wield a sword. She supposed it was the memory of the battlefields and how the men treated the camp women, but besides that, she could hold her own with a bow or rifle. They would occasionally take hunting trips, the four of them, until Robbie left to train under Lord Reay, the MacKay chief, at age fifteen. They would take turns making the kill, gutting, cleaning, and preparing the meal over a campfire.

Thinking about it now, she wondered what her mom would have thought about the idea of her trading in her tea dresses for hunting trousers.

Turning her attention back to the present trip, she finished brushing and braiding her hair as the cart trotted along.

Her hair had lost the gold she had once as a wee lass, which left her with beautiful brown curls that went halfway down her back when braided. Left loose and curly, her hair fell past her shoulders. Her eyes were a vivid blue. People often comment on how striking they were. Other than her eyes, she felt she was quite average, not one who would be remembered for her beauty, but not unattractive either. She was not one who was caught up in her looks, so it did not bother her much. She would prefer someone spending time with her because she had a kind heart as opposed to her beauty.

Once her hair was braided and she had finished eating her biscuits, she asked to stop and finish the trip on her horse.

Robbie was getting restless the closer they got to the castle. He had only been gone a little more than a week, to escort them to the MacKay lands and gather the remainder of his things from home, but he was anxious to get back to his bride-to-be. He kept urging his horse a little faster.

"Why don't ye run along and announce our arrival?" her da said to him.

Robbie turned, grinning from ear to ear. "Aye. I'll let them know ye are almost there," he said as he put his horse into a canter. Da turned to Anna and Willie with eyebrows raised, which was greeted with laughter from both of them.

Within the hour, they were pulling up to the castle. Servants greeted them, bustling around to help them down, care for the horses, and carry their trunks inside. They were led to the hall where they awaited the presence of the Lord and Lady Reay.

The hall was much bigger than the hall at their estate. The sunlight shown through large windows on one side of the room, illuminating the tapestries hanging on the other wall. The gold threads glistened in the sunlight. Twice as many tables filled the hall as would fit in theirs. There were three fireplaces, one on each of the far ends of the room and one behind the head table. The room made their hall back in Dundee look like a common dining room.

After a short while, the lord and lady appeared. They had aged a bit, but it did not take away any of their elegance. They welcomed them with pleasantries before calling for servants to have their rooms readied.

Robbie joined them in the hall once he had located his bride-to-be. The last time Anna had seen Mary Ellen, she had been a young girl, now she was a grown woman. She had light brown hair with some wave to it, her eyes a light brown, and she had a button nose. When Mary Ellen smiled, her eyes smiled too.

Anna dinna really know much about Mary Ellen, except for what Robbie would tell of her when he came home for the holidays, but chatting with her now, Anna was excited to have her as a sister-in-law.

After pleasantries were exchanged, they were led to their rooms. Anna and Lizzy were sharing a room between her aunt and uncle, and her da and Willie. Lizzy pushed her way inside the room to claim the space she wanted, ordering the servants where to put everything. Anna sat down on her bed before leaning back and taking a deep breath. She closed her eyes as she waited for Lizzy to get the room in the order that she wanted it. Once everything was in the place to Lizzy's liking, Anna got up to unpack her belongings.

CHAPTER

The wedding took place the day after they arrived. Anna's da had a new dress made for her for the occasion. It was green satin and had brilliant blue trim, which complemented her eyes. She couldn't remember the last time she had the occasion to dress up quite this nicely. Though they held a high status, Anna's family rarely had formal occasions. The Duncan clan was small in comparison to other clans, like the MacKays, and were very familiar with their tenants. They often checked on families in need and kenned the families well that were under their care.

Despite the familiarity with their tenants, they were highly respected as the laird's family, and they all played the part when required, and Robbie's wedding certainly required it. So she let down her hair, letting it fall behind her, the loose curls on her back felt different from the braid she was accustomed to. She always braided her hair to keep it from tangling when she rode her horse. Making two small braids on either side of her face, she pulled them back, tying it back with a blue ribbon.

Aunt Elizabeth joined Anna and Lizzy in their room, her portly form swallowing up what little space there was in the room. Using both hands, she gently moved Lizzy's hair so it lay on her back. Walking around to face Lizzy, she secured a red rose on one side of her hair.

"There, now ye are perfect," Aunt Elizabeth said. She paused for a bit to admire her daughter all dressed up before saying, "Come now, it's time to go."

After her mother turned to leave, Lizzy did a childish spin in her yellow skirts before batting her hazel eyes at Anna and following her mother out the door like a baby duckling following the mother duck.

How I miss my mother, Anna thought.

Anna straightened out her skirts and pinched her cheeks to bring some color into them and gracefully headed down the stairs. As she descended the stairs, her da and brothers came out of the hall to wait for her at the bottom of the stairs. They all looked so dashing. She smiled down at them. Robbie's eyes sparkled, and with a big grin on his face he said, "Ye clean up nicely, little sister. Ye even let down yer hair."

All of a sudden, she felt self-conscious, as if all the eyes in the room were on her, but she held her head up high, keeping her composure.

Robbie went up a few steps to meet her halfway, offering his arm for her to grab onto and escorted her to their da and Willie. Grinning, her da reached into his pocket and pulled out a brilliant, rather large, blue stone, which complemented her dress perfectly. It was in the shape of a diamond, but two of the sides were shorter than the other two. The longer sides narrowed to a finer point than the point opposite of it. He had the stone fashioned into a necklace at the long narrow point. Holding it up by the ribbon, he let the stone dangle in front of her eyes. At the sight of the stone, a feeling of warmth and belonging came over her. Not being a materialistic person, jewels and frills had never flattered her much, but this stone was different. Its beauty radiated as if it called to her like no other object had before. It was beautiful, and she wanted it.

"It's beautiful!" she exclaimed. "Where ever did ye get it?" she asked as she cupped it in her hand, pulling it closer to get a better look as he continued to hold it by the ribbon.

"Ye found it when ye were no more than five or six," he replied as he turned her around so he could tie it around her neck. "Do ye not remember?"

A strange feeling came over her that she could not explain as he asked the question. She shook her head and looked over to her aunt when she heard her gasp. Her aunt had the look of horror on her face as she made the sign of the cross, but for some reason, it did not seem to bother her. She felt a connection with the necklace, like it was meant for her. Anna turned back to her da as she fingered the gemstone. Either he did not seem to notice her aunt's reaction, or if he did, he ignored it as he smiled at Anna.

"It suits ye beautifully," he said quite pleased with himself as he clasped his hands behind his back and rocked from tippy-toes to heel, admiring the final touches he had made to her dress.

Anna put her hand on her da's offered arm as they turned and regally made their way toward the main entrance. Elizabeth and Lizzy made to go through the door, but without saying a word, Ian held up his arm in front of them, stopping them to allow Anna's family to go first. The butler opened both of the massive double doors, allowing the four of them to proceed together in a single line. They descended the stone steps down to the cobblestone road with Anna's hand on her da's arm and the other on Robbie's. Willie walked beside her da. Ian, Elizabeth, and Lizzy followed close behind.

As they walked toward the church, Anna could hear her aunt mumbling. She could not hear what she was saying, but she could feel her cold stare on her back. She was determined to not let her aunt get the best of her today.

Anna looked at Robbie. "Ye look very handsome," Anna said to him, fighting the urge to shoulder bump him in her sisterly way. He looked back at her with a broad smile, a smile that was identical to her da's smile. He looked fine in his ceremonial Duncan tartan, his long dark hair pulled back and tied neatly with a black ribbon. He strutted with the confidence of a well-trained soldier, but his manners were that of a gentleman.

A handsome man in MacKay ceremonial kilt stood at the entrance of the church, smiling at Robbie as they approached.

"Brodie, let me introduce my father, sister Anna, and brother Willie," Robbie said.

"It is a pleasure to make yer acquaintance, Laird Duncan," he said as he graciously bowed before turning to Anna, taking her hand in his, and placing a kiss on it. "My lady."

He turned to Willie and bowed.

"Brodie is one of my good friends," Robbie explained.

"It is a pleasure to meet yer acquaintance," Anna's da replied with a bow.

Anna did a quick curtsy.

Brodie turned to Robbie, extending one hand toward the side of the church, and said with a smile, "Are ye ready, then?"

"Aye," Robbie replied. As he was walked away, he turned his head toward his family with what seemed like a bigger smile on it than he had before, if that was even possible.

Robbie and Brodie entered the church from the one side and Mary Ellen and her dad from the other. Her white gown was satin with a skirt that ruffled more fully than an average dress. A ring of fresh white flowers crowned her head. She made a beautiful bride.

The church was small, allowing no more than thirty people comfortably. There were some relatives of Mary Ellen's, but most guests were men that soldiered with Robbie and their wives.

After the ceremony, they all went back to the great hall. Lord and Lady Reay did not attend the ceremony or banquet, but the banquet was exquisite just the same. The head table was set up for Robbie, Mary Ellen, and their immediate family. Venison and wild boar were served on platters of vegetables piled high with pitchers of ale at every table.

Once most of the people got their fill to eat, a fiddle was brought out, and Robbie, Mary Ellen, and their families started the dancing until everyone joined in. After a few jigs, they sat back down and watched as the guests danced and came up one at a time to congratulate the newly married couple. Introductions were made, and many a man complimented the beauty of Anna, who graciously thanked them.

Some guests she had met before on their previous journeys, but they had changed so much that Anna had to be reminded of their acquaintance.

Lizzy sat with her parents but seemed to be enjoying a constant flow of men that stopped by to reacquaint themselves with her parents. She had no trouble gaining their attention and often danced with everyone else.

Anna was asked several times to dance, and though she loved to dance, she graciously declined and chose to sit with her family.

As more drinks were served, the men got louder and louder. After a couple of hours, the bride and groom departed, and shortly after, Anna and her family did as well.

The celebration went well into the night, despite the fact that the guests of honor had retired.

CHAPTER

T he next day started late as most folks at the wedding had stayed up late to celebrate. The Duncan family spent a considerable amount of time reacquainting themselves with family and getting to know Mary Ellen and her family.

With Mary Ellen being her parents' only child, Robbie and Mary Ellen would be living at her father's estate in order for Robbie to learn the ways of running a large estate while he was not soldiering. Mary Ellen's father had difficulty getting around due to injuries acquired on the battlefield, so he was eager to begin his lessons.

The following day was a bustle of activity for the servants who were busy with preparations for the games. Hundreds of people would be coming to participate in the festivities, and though not many would actually come to the castle, a lot needed to be done.

With everyone so busy, Anna decided to go to the gardens. The gardens were well-maintained. The rose bushes wound up on trellises taller than she. She could smell the roses as she walked along the path that weaved through the garden. Along the outside of the rose garden were statues graced with flowers of every color and size.

"Would ye like to go for a picnic?"

Anna turned to see her da and Willie on their horses and her horse saddled and ready to ride.

"Would I?" she exclaimed as she went up to her beautiful white horse, Butterfly, and patted her face.

She had the horse from the time it was small. Very few people had ridden her, and she had a special relationship with Butterfly. She often talked to her as if conversing with a person. When she was lonely or sad, it was Butterfly that she would confide in.

She quickly mounted Butterfly, and they were off, following a path that went through a field of purple heather until they reached the woods. They walked along the edge of the woods for a while until they came to a narrow path that weaved through the thick forest and down to a beautiful river.

Dismounting their horses, her da laid a blanket down with a basket full of cheese, bread, and apples. She immediately picked up an apple and gave it to Butterfly.

"That's why I got an extra one!" Willie exclaimed.

They all laughed.

"It's beautiful here," Anna said, taking in the scenery. The trees lined the other side of the river, giving shade to half of the river. The water was so clear ye could see the fish swimming.

"How did ye ken it was here?" Anna asked, turning toward her da.

"Yer mother had shown it to me," he replied. "We would sometimes sneak down here when ye wee ones were being occupied by others, and we would picnic here in this spot."

Her mother always loved flowing water. She would love to take the kids by the stream near their house to watch them fish or swim. Sometimes she would pack a lunch, and they would picnic there all day. After her mother died, Anna would go to the stream by herself when she was missing her. The sound of the running water and the birds chirping would remind Anna of her. When by the stream, she could almost feel her mother's presence. It now was her favorite place to go when she wanted to be alone.

As if reading her mind, her da said, "Yer mother would be proud of the young woman ye have become." Then he turned to Willie and ruffled his hair with a big grin, saying, "And the lad ye've become."

"Aw!" Willie exclaimed as he made an attempt to straighten out the mess he was sure his da made of his hair.

They were quiet for a bit while they ate their meal, watching the fish in the water, and listened to the sound of the breeze going through the woods.

"I received a lot of comments from people saying how much ye look like yer mother did at yer age," Anna's da said to her.

Anna looked up at her da and smiled.

"Ya could have been twins, ye ken," he added.

After a few minutes went by, Anna commented, "There was an older woman who said Ma bought a horse from her."

Her da chuckled as he put a piece of cheese in his mouth. "Ahh. I've heard that once or twice."

Anna and Willie both shifted positions so they were facing their da, looking at him as if waiting on their bedtime story.

"One year, when yer mother was about yer age," he began as he turned to Willie, "they had come up for the games, but she and yer aunt Elizabeth stayed on for a few extra weeks with their cousins. She stayed with her aunt Isabelle and uncle John. That was her aunt Isabelle that ye met. Her husband died a few years back."

He cut a piece of cheese and handed it to Anna. "They raised horses, ye see, and during that time, one of them gave birth to a filly, which yer mother fell in love with."

He chuckled as he cut another slice of cheese and handed it to Willie.

"When yer grandparents came to take them back home, yer mother refused to part with it. Yer grandparents made an offer for the filly, purchasing it, but the filly was much too young to part with its mother. It was decided that they would come back in spring to claim the horse."

He ate another piece of cheese and laughed. "Apparently, yer mother drove her parents crazy all winter long talking about the horse."

He looked at their horses thoughtfully and said, "Actually, that would be Butterfly's grandmother. Yer mother loved that horse. I guess that is where ye got yer love of horses from."

Anna looked at Butterfly and smiled. She remembered when Butterfly was birthed. She had pretty much claimed her as hers from the moment she saw her, much like her mother did with Aunt Isabelle's filly.

Anna picked up another apple and brought it over to Butterfly while Willie got up to skip stones in the river. After coddling Butterfly for a bit, Anna went over and joined Willie.

Skipping stones was something they had always done from the time she was little. At first, she would merely throw stones in the water, imitating her da and Robbie, but once she got older, Robbie showed her how to pick out the right smooth, flat stone, hold it just right, and throw it parallel to the water. She practiced every chance she got until she was able to do it.

Robbie was so proud of her the day she showed him she could do it. She laughed to herself as she remembered how happy she was that he was proud of her.

After a couple of hours, they headed back. People had already started to arrive, and the grounds started to fill up with tents and the smell of campfire. Everything was buzzing with excitement. They walked around through the encampment, her da stopping to talk to old acquaintances. After several hours of socializing and sharing food with others, they returned to their rooms to retire.

CHAPTER

4

Lizzy pulled the curtains back a bit to let some sunlight into the room. "Ohh," Anna moaned as she rolled onto her other side so the sun wasn't directly in her eyes.

"I'll no miss the beginning ceremony because ye overslept," Lizzy declared as she readied herself, not trying to be quiet at all.

After brushing her long blond hair, she put a bow in it and spun around, allowing her skirts to swirl before turning to the door. As Lizzy opened the door, Anna could hear folk talking down the hall, confirming that, indeed, most folks were up already.

Once left alone, Anna gave a big stretch before resuming her curled-up position in bed. She lay there, contemplating getting up and closing the curtain but did not budge. As the sounds of the crowd in the distance started getting louder, she convinced herself to get up and ready herself.

Anna got dressed quickly, splashed some water on her face, and put her hair in its usual braid.

As she descended the stairs, she noticed that most everyone had already headed out to claim their spot for the games. Anna grabbed some biscuits, cheese, and an apple, which she put in her pocket, before heading out the door. She made her way to the game lands, maneuvering her way through the spectators until she found Mary Ellen, Lizzy, and Mary Ellen's cousin Agnes.

The bagpipes started playing, indicating that Lord Reay had arrived. He addressed the crowd, welcoming everyone, and announced the beginning of the games. The crowd cheered as the first event, the caber toss for men over thirty-five, began. The competitors would balance the small end of a long log, run, and toss it. The crowd would roar after each person's turn.

Lizzy questioned Mary Ellen and Agnes on the details of every competitor. She even went so far as to ask about their marital status if she was really interested in them.

Anna watched the games, not participating in the conversation of the group. At one point, she had a sudden urge to look around. Anna's attention drifted past the group to where her brother Robbie was talking with friends. At that moment, one of the men Robbie was talking to looked up, and their eyes met. Anna's heart jumped. She had a sense that she kenned him, but she was sure they had never met. She was mesmerized. It was as if he could see the deepest part of her soul.

She forced her attention back to the others, but she could not rid herself of the feeling that his single look had penetrated her soul. At one point, Mary Ellen looked up at her.

"Anna, are ye all right? Ye look like ye've seen a ghost!"

"Yes. Yes, I'm fine," she said as she pulled out her wrapped-up biscuit and cheese from her pocket. "I have not had anything to eat yet." She broke off a piece of cheese and put it in her mouth.

She tried to concentrate on the game, or even the conversation within her group, tried to act like she was somewhat interested in it and the games, but she couldn't shake the intensity in which those eyes looked at her.

The caber toss had come to an end, and the winners were being announced. There would be a break between games to allow time to set up for the next event, which would be the younger lads. Lizzy and Agnes decided to go to the gardens for a while, and when they turned around, they nearly bumped into Robbie, his friend Brodie, and *him*. She could immediately feel her heart beating heavy in her chest.

"Good morning," Mary Ellen said to them as she smiled pleasantly.

"Mary Ellen," they both greeted her, "good morning to ye."

"Anna, ye remember Brodie from the wedding?" Robbie said.

"It's nice to see ye again, Brodie," she said with a quick curtsy.

"Ms. Duncan," he said as he gave a small bow. He turned to Lizzy and did the same before turning to Mary Ellen and Agnes with a much less formal greeting.

"And this is Alex Boswell," Robbie said to Anna and Lizzy. "The three of us soldier together," he continued turning back to Alex as he put an arm around Anna's shoulder and drew her in for a squeeze saying, "and this, Alex, is my bonny little sister, Anna."

Anna straightened herself from the sisterly squeeze she was in. Alex smiled at her with the darkest brown eyes she had ever seen. His dark brown locks went just past his broad shoulders. "Ms. Duncan," he said with a bow.

"And this is my cousin, Lizzy Duncan," Robbie said.

Alex turned to Lizzy and bowed. "Ms. Duncan."

Anna was very thankful for the immediate change in his attention. She just looked at him, speechless. *What is it about this man?* she thought.

"Ye may call me Lizzy," she said with a giggle and a curtsy. "Will ye be competing in the games?" she asked, clearly taken by Alex.

"We will be competing, but not 'til the morrow," he replied, "in the evening."

"Oh, how exciting!" she exclaimed. "We were just heading over to the gardens for a walk. Would ye care to join us?" she asked with a broad smile and a tip of her head.

Alex agreed before turning to Anna who started backing away. "Will ye be joining us, Ms. Duncan?" he asked as he offered his arm.

She shook her head as she backed away more, clearly uneasy. She had a hard time speaking but finally choked out her answer. "No, my brother, Willie, is competing in the youth games next. I dinna care to miss it."

He hesitated as if he may change his mind about going, but Lizzy stepped in front of Anna and grabbed his arm, which he had offered Anna. "Oh, that is too bad," Lizzy said. "Perhaps she can join us later."

Alex looked at Anna with what appeared to be a disappointment in his eyes as Lizzy turned him toward the gardens. Lizzy gave Anna a smirk before flipping her hair over her shoulder and turning around. Agnes and Brodie turned toward the garden themselves and followed.

As they walked away, some of her uneasiness dissolved.

"What was that all about?" Mary Ellen asked as she watched Lizzy walk away babbling to Alex.

"Oh, that's just Lizzy," Robbie said with a shrug.

"She is not verra fond of me for some reason," Anna replied. "I dinna ken why."

Robbie put one arm around Mary Ellen and another one around Anna and gave a howl as the games proceeded. "She's always been that way," he said to Mary Ellen.

Turning his head toward Anna, Robbie gave her a little squeeze and said, "I ken it's because ye are so much bonnier than she."

Anna looked up at him with skepticism. He nodded as he gave her a wink to reaffirm his comment.

Her da joined them to watch the youth's caber toss. The logs were not as large as the adults, but they were equally as hard to balance and throw for the lads as the larger ones were for the men.

Willie had been practicing for weeks ever since they had made plans to make the journey. He was very young when they last attended the games, but their da showed him how to balance and throw the log.

There was at least a score of lads competing. Willie was third to compete. He beat one of the lads before him, but not the other. Willie was in third place when the last lad got up. As the boy balanced the log, he was a bit off-balance but got it under control, ran, and tossed the log. It went end over end, almost vertically, moving him into first place and pushing Willie into fourth.

They waited for Willie as he strutted over, a half smile on his face and a shrug of his shoulders as he saw them. "I *almost* came in third. Did ye see?"

They all cheered and patted him on the back.

"Ye did a great job!" Robbie said as he tried to ruffle Willie's hair, who ducked under his arm to get out of the way of it.

Willie excitedly talked about the competition for several minutes before Anna asked, "Can we walk to the stables and check on the horses?"

At home, she would check on her horse three or four times a day when she could. She would pet her and talk to her. Sometimes when she was washing and hanging clothes and no one was around, she would bring the horse over and talk to her, telling it how she felt about things she dinna wish to tell people. Her da would tease that if he'd allow it, he was sure she would have it living in the house with them.

They walked to the stables while Willie continued on about the competitions.

They arrived at the stables, but nobody was outside the barn, so they walked in and called out. The stable boy popped his head out from the other row. "Hello. Can I help ye?"

"We just came to check in on our horses. Is that all right?" her da asked.

"That's fine," the boy replied as his head immediately disappeared again.

They walked over to the stall where her horse was. "There ye are, Butterfly," she said as she reached into her pocket and offered her the apple she had stashed earlier.

The others checked on their horses briefly and then waited for her outside the barn. After a little while, Da called to her, "Come along, Anna, we can stretch them in a bit."

Robbie and Mary Ellen went along their own way while Anna, Willie, and their da found a grassy area to sit. Da left to purchase food from the people selling items along the cobblestone road. Anna took pleasure in watching the people walking by, children laughing, and lovers strolling through the rows of people stretched out on the grass. Her da came back with plenty of food to eat. They spread the food out on the blanket while they watched the last few competitors in the shot put. The men would take turns throwing a huge stone to see who could throw it farther.

After a brief break, the women shot put event started but with smaller stones. Partway into the women's event, they decided to walk around through the crowd to enjoy some of the other festivities, dancers, storytellers, and jesters performing.

After supper, they headed back to the stables for a ride. While the stable boy was getting Willie's horse ready, Anna put her saddle on Butterfly and started to secure it. As soon as the stable boy saw, he started yelling at her, "Are ye mad, lass? Ya gonna get me in trouble! Get!" His arms came up as he waved her away.

She quickly moved away from the stall. "I'm sorry. I dinna mean no harm." She left the barn and waited with her da and Willie. Her da looked at her with a look, as if to say, "*Ye ken better than that.*" She looked down to the ground, drawing in the dirt with the tip of her shoe, embarrassed.

They took the horses back down the same small path through the woods to the river and walked upriver along the bank. There they passed a few couples trying to steal some quiet time away from everyone, and a little further down was a family playing in the river, no doubt trying to cool off from the heat. They moved on until they found a spot of their own.

Anna looked up and pointed to a falcon flying above the river. "Look!" she exclaimed.

The bird was coming toward them lower than one would expect of a falcon. It soared over the river and turned to perch on a dead tree right across the river from them.

"It's beautiful," she said. A sense of serenity came over her as she watched it.

"It's a peregrine falcon," her da said.

Anna studied the bird. It was dark gray with almost a blueish tint and a white belly with a dark gray V on its chest. The V almost looked like an arrowhead. It seemed to be looking right at her. She was captivated by it, having a hard time pulling her attention away.

"Did ye hear me?" Willie asked her.

Anna turned to look at Willie.

"Ye should see if it's not too late for ye to compete in one of the women's events," he repeated.

"I dinna want to compete. I've never even tried any of the events," she replied as she did a quick scan of the shore. Finding what she was looking for, she picked up a smooth flat rock and said, "Unless it was an event for skipping stones!"

Willie immediately got up and said, "I'd still beat ye!"

"Oh yeah?" Anna said as she threw her first stone, skipping it five times.

They played for another half an hour, both having a score of seven skips when their da said, "It's about time to leave."

As they turned to mount their horses, the falcon took off flying right over them, even lower this time. It was as if it kenned they were in awe of it and wanted to show off. Each wing spanned the length of a man's arm. The underside of its wings was white and lined with dark stripes.

"Wow!" escaped from all three of their lips. A calmness came over her that she couldna explain.

They made their way back for the last of the competition for the day. Immediately after the last event of the day, the crowd dispersed. They waited a bit as the crowd rushed back to their camp.

Robbie, Mary Ellen, Alex, and Brodie caught sight of them, so they all walked back together. She dinna dare look at Alex for fear he may see all the way down to her soul. She dinna ken what had come over her.

"We looked for ye this evening, but we couldna find ye," Robbie said.

"We took a ride to the river," her da said.

"We saw a beautiful falcon along the river," Anna said. "It was verra…," she paused to think, "impressive."

"A squirrel would impress ye, Anna," Robbie chuckled as he put his arm around her, giving her a squeeze. Once they reached the castle, they said their goodbyes and departed for the night.

Anna was fully expecting Lizzy to be there, but to her surprise, she was not. The servants had left clean water in the basin that she used to clean up with. Just as she was getting in bed, Lizzy entered the room, not trying to be quiet at all.

"Oh, I had a delightful day!" Lizzy said as she spun around with arms opened before bringing them in to cross over her chest. "Alex is the most handsome man I've ever seen," she declared with another swirl. "We walked through the garden, and he told us all about the castle." She paused turning to Anna with a smirk. "It is such a shame that ye missed it." The tone of her voice gave away the deception of her words.

"I canna wait for tomorrow!" Lizzy exclaimed.

Anna closed her eyes as soon as Lizzy was done cleaning up and blew the candle out. Anna dreamed of the beautiful falcon she had seen.

CHAPTER

5

The second day of the games started much like the first. Robbie, Brodie, and Alex joined the women on a blanket as they watched the morning games. As soon as she saw Alex, Anna became verra uncomfortable and Lizzy, flirtatious.

They all chatted among themselves as Anna listened to their soldiering stories. As Brodie was talking, Anna reached for a piece of cheese in the basket at the same time Alex did. Their hands brushed against each other. Anna felt a tingling that started where they touched and spread to her whole body. She immediately pulled her hand away and looked up to see Alex pull out a piece of cheese. He held out the piece of cheese to her with the most handsome smile she had ever seen.

"Milady," he offered.

Her heart was beating so hard in her chest she was sure everyone could hear it pounding over the talking of the crowd. Although feeling uncomfortable, she put on a formal smile and took the piece of cheese from his hand, trying not to touch him in the process.

"Thank ye, sir," she said. *What's gotten into me?* she thought.

"Alex," he replied to her.

"Alex," she whispered as she looked into his eyes. The brown of his eyes was so dark it was hard to see where the color ended and the pupils began.

"So are ye competing today, Alex?" Lizzy asked, breaking the spell and pulling his attention to her.

"Aye. Robbie, Brodie, and I will compete this afternoon. If we move on to the next round, we will, two days from now as well."

"I have no doubt that ye will." She smiled at him.

"It all depends on whom he is first paired up with to start," Robbie said as he leaned to the left, giving Alex a good push with his shoulder.

"I dare say, I willna be losing to the likes of ye," he chided back.

They all turned their attention to the games as the crowd cheered for the new champion of the hammer throw. Robbie let out a screeching whistle as the onlookers cheered.

"There is a minstrel performing this evening in the hall," Alex said, turning his attention back to the group before focusing on Anna.

"Oh, that sounds like so much fun!" Lizzy blurted. She turned to Agnes. "What think ye?"

"Sounds exciting!" Agnes replied.

Alex turned back to Anna. "Would ye care to join us?"

"I would be delighted," she said with a graceful tip of her head and a smile before reaching down to get a drink as a distraction from looking into his hypnotic eyes.

They chatted their pleasantries a bit more before Anna announced that she would like to go to the stables.

"Ye and that horse." Robbie smiled and winked at her. "I dare say if she had a choice between the horse or a family, we'd all be discarded."

Normally, she would have swatted him, but in the presence of everyone, she simply turned and glared at him briefly before replying, "Well, my horse has never hung my doll from a tree after dragging it through the dirt!" she declared.

"Ack. That doll kenned where ye hid my wee wooden sword. I was just trying to get it out of her."

"I dinna hide yer sword. Wee Willie took it. He would hide it under his bed so he could play with it when no one was watching."

"And ye never told me?"

"So ye could torture him instead? Nay. I wouldna do that to the poor lad any more than I would tell da why my doll was soiled. I dare say ye would have gotten a thrashing for that one."

"I owe ye a great debt," Robbie said as he placed his fist over his heart.

"I believe ye can make it up if ye would be so kind as to escort me to the stables," she replied, standing up.

"Mary Ellen and I would be delighted to go," he said with a smile as he got up and offered his hand to assist Mary Ellen up.

"I would love to see yer horse. May I join as well?" Alex asked as he rose.

A jolt went through her as his words came out. She turned her head to him with a smile, but she felt uncertain. Her intent had been to get away from him, from the feeling she had in his presence, as if he somehow could read her every thought. She considered blurting out *no* but kenned it would be impolite.

"Aye. That would be lovely," she barely whispered, briefly lifting her gaze to him so as not to be rude.

He stood a whole head taller than she, requiring her to tip her head back to look at him. She looked down at his offered arm and paused before placing her hand on it. It was as if a fire came out of his arm into her hand, running up her arm before spreading to the rest of her body. She tried to ignore it by clenching her teeth as if it was painful, though it was not. Not painful but…desirous.

As he turned her toward the stables, she caught a glimpse of Lizzy glaring at her. She immediately felt uncomfortable knowing she would have to share a room with her for a few more nights. It was not as if she had suggested it.

"So ye like horses, aye?" Alex asked.

"I like my horse," she replied.

"She likes *all* animals," Robbie blurted out. "I dare say she likes them better than man himself."

"Is that so?" Alex glanced at her.

She opened her mouth to reply, but Robbie started before her, "She will sit for hours watching the birds, otters, deer, squirrels. Ack, me da would always worry she'd be attacked by a wild boar."

"Which I have successfully killed while hunting if ye recall. It is not as if I am unarmed, ye ken," she pitched back at her brother, not liking that he made her out to be some careless girl.

"I ken." He smirked at her, pleased he had gotten a spark out of her.

"Well now, how impressive," Alex nodded as he commented.

She shrugged, not caring to discuss anything more about herself with someone who made her feel that uncomfortable.

"And what about ye?" she asked. "Boswell. That is in the Lowlands. What brings ye to the Highlands?"

"My mother is a MacKay, so I was sent out to train with Lord Reay, much like yer brother."

As they made it to the stables, she made sure to greet the stable boy. "Good morning, sir."

"Would ye be riding today, milady?"

"No, not today, sir. We just came to check on our horses. May we go inside?" she asked.

He nodded and moved away from the door to let them by. They walked past the stalls until they came to Robbie's horse. She greeted him with a pet and sweet words. From the corner of her eye, she saw Robbie jokingly jab Alex with his elbow, giving him a smirk. Without turning, she made a fist and whacked him in his chest and was presented with an "Oomph!" before a hardy laugh was released.

Mary Ellen's horse was in the stall next to Robbie's. They stopped so Anna could give him some attention before moving on to the end of the row where Anna's horse was.

"There's my Butterfly!" she exclaimed as she petted her horse's snowy-white hair and snuggled her face against its cheek. Butterfly snorted, shook her head, and sniffed at her hand. She laughed and pulled out an apple from her pocket that she had grabbed that morning before leaving the castle.

"Butterfly," Alex said with a curious smile. "How ever did ye come up with that name?"

"I dinna ken," she replied, keeping her attention on the horse instead of Alex. "It was the first name that came to mind. I had thought of several other names, but for some reason, I kenned it had to be Butterfly."

He nodded with the most genuine smile as if approving of her answer. For some reason, his approval made Anna feel good. She turned back to her horse with her cheek against its cheek to hide her smile.

They lingered there only a couple of more minutes before she asked Alex, "And where is yer sturdy steed?"

"I believe he's in the other aisle," he said as he led them to the other row and down a few stalls. He stopped in front of a big black stallion.

"He's beautiful," she said as she stroked the stallion's neck lovingly. He watched her intently as she did so. She put her fingers through its thick black mane.

"What's his name?" she asked.

"Thunder," he replied.

She contemplated it for a few seconds as she continued to pet the horse. Finally, she nodded and repeated its name quietly, "Thunder."

They stayed but a couple of more minutes before turning back to the festivities. They walked past food vendors along the cobblestone path selling meat, as they cooked over the fire. Other vendors sold bread, cheese, fruit, and ale. They purchased a variety of food from different vendors and brought it back to the others who were still on the blanket.

"Oh, perfect!" Lizzy exclaimed. "I'm famished."

They ate as they watched the competitions. Lizzy filled them in on what they had missed. Halfway through the event, the men left to ready themselves to compete.

The girls sat around talking while watching the games. Anna used this time to get better acquainted with Mary Ellen. Lizzy seemed to talk only of Alex or the latest gossip she'd heard. Anna was grateful when her da and Willie spotted her and joined them.

Upon the end of the event, there was an intermission so the field could be readied for the next game. Two midgets came out dressed as soldiers and picked up one of the logs used for the youth caber toss. They took turns pretending to balance it vertically, wobbling it around as they ran and tossed it, watching it plop to the ground not far from their feet. The children all giggled and cheered.

Once the next competition was ready to begin, the announcer came out shooing them off the field. The two jesters grabbed their logs and dragged them off the field, pretending to struggle.

A drum roll sounded as the men prepared for the caber toss. There were three men before Alex, two who successfully threw the caber end over end.

As Alex stepped up, Lizzy jumped up and down. "Alex is up!"

The previous competitor walked the long log up, so it stood vertically in front of Alex, standing at least three times his height. Lizzy got quiet, and her hands flew to her cheeks as she watched Alex crouch down to grab the log and stand up, balancing it.

Anna watched as there was a jerk inside her chest. There was something familiar about him that she couldna place, his posture, perhaps, or the expressions he made. She could not pinpoint it. Anxiously, she watched as he balanced the log and started to run. Secretly, she hoped that he did well, and when he threw it end over end, she felt a bit of pride.

That's odd, she thought as she clapped. *Why do I care how well he does?*

Lizzy jumped and grabbed Agnes's arm. "He's so fine!"

Brodie stepped up after two more men and successfully threw it so it flipped over, but it was leaning a bit.

Robbie was one of the last couple of competitors of the event. He started with good balance and flipped the caber over almost perfectly vertical, jumping into second place, pushing Alex into the third spot.

Anna felt a hint of disappointment. *What is the matter with me? Robbie should be the one I want to win*, but deep down, she kenned she wanted Alex to take it all.

As the men moved the logs off the field, an announcer came on the field on horseback, calling out to the crowd, "Are ye having fun yet?"

The crowd cheered as he rode in front of them, carrying the MacKay banner with the MacKay crest, an arm with its outstretched hand holding a dagger. The arm was encircled in a belt with the words "MANU FORTI" (with a strong hand) written at the top. The crowd cheered.

He made a second pass, yelling, "Are ye ready for some more?"

"Yes!" the crowd called out, getting even louder. By the time he made it off the field, the log had been removed, and the stone was in place for the stone put.

The same men competed. Anna felt her chest tighten when Alex stepped up to compete. As he lifted the stone, his muscles flexed, displaying his sturdy build. An image of Alex holding her in his strong embrace made Anna's heart beat faster. She shook her head as if to rid herself of the image.

Alex turned away from the field as he positioned himself and paused before he turned back around quickly and released the stone, throwing it. His form was direct, not dramatic like some of the other competitors who spun around completely, trying to get more momentum. He had speed and strength without the need of additional spins.

Lizzy screamed as the stone landed further than the rest. Anna's smile widened, and she gracefully clapped, ignoring that her insides felt like bursting.

Alex went over to the side and was greeted with a slap on the back and a few words from Robbie and Brodie. Anna was almost transfixed on him as the next competitor prepared to throw. At one point, Alex looked in their direction, and her heart skipped a beat. She immediately turned to watch the throw. *He couldn't possibly have kenned I was staring at him, not in the middle of the crowd*, she thought. She kenned he could not have, yet she felt the heat rise to her cheeks just the same.

Brodie's throw was one of the top three distances until the man before Robbie jumped behind Alex's throw.

As Robbie's turn approached, he turned toward Alex and called out a few words as he walked onto the field, laughing. He got into position, his broad shoulders almost as large as Alex's. He threw the stone, and it landed halfway between Alex's marked spot and the last place marker. He looked down to the ground, shaking his head, but when he raised his head, he was clearly laughing.

Anna watched as her brother walked over to Alex and Brodie, grabbing the offered canteen as they obviously were teasing him.

During the intermission, Anna's da left to acquire some food. A vendor brought the dried meat and bread to the competitors on the field. Barrels of water were stationed not only by the field for the competitors to drink from ladles but throughout the grounds for the spectators.

By the time her da came back with the food, the maide leisg event began. One participant would sit on the ground across his opponent with their soles against each other's. Both men would hold on to a stick between them, trying to pull his opponent off the ground.

The men were randomly picked to compete against each other. After a couple of rounds, Robbie took his position across his opponent. Both tugged on the stick, it pulled first toward Robbie, then toward the other man, then back to Robbie's side until Robbie pulled his opponent up.

Brodie and Alex both won their first round. In the second round, Robbie was paired up with Brodie. Even from a distance, Anna could tell the exchange of words was between friends as opposed to rivals.

After a bit of a struggle, Robbie succeeded in lifting Brodie off the ground. Brodie laughed as he held out his hand to help Robbie up, slapping him on the back as they walked off the field.

Alex's next opponent was quickly pulled up. Another round was played, which decided who would play the winners of tomorrow's rounds. Robbie and Alex both would be moving on to play again in two days.

The men made their way back to the group following the end of the maide leisg, which was the last event of the day.

"Ye did so well!" Lizzy waved as she called out to Alex as he rejoined the group.

"Ye all did verra well, lads," Anna's da said as he stretched his hand out toward the remaining food on the blanket. "Sit and have a bite to eat,"

"Thanks," Robbie said as he plopped himself beside Mary Ellen, giving her a kiss as he grabbed a piece of bread.

As Alex sat down beside Robbie facing Anna, she felt her heart beat faster. He looked at Anna's tense expression and asked, "Were ye not impressed?"

Anna immediately took a breath, realizing she had been holding it. She gave him her well-trained smile as she lifted her canteen to him as if to toast him, "Verra impressed."

Several people stopped to congratulate the men on their games and others to just visit. One particular man, whom Anna recognized as one of the other competitors, came over to the group.

"Aah, Bruce," Robbie said. He introduced Bruce to the group before saying, "Bruce will be joining us for the minstrel performance this evening."

"It is a pleasure to meet ye all," Bruce said as he bowed.

"And ye as well," Anna replied.

"Oh…I canna wait," Lizzy declared.

"Well, let's be on our way," Robbie said as he stood up and offered his hand to help Mary Ellen.

Brodie helped Agnes up while Bruce reached down for Lizzy's hand to help her up. She hesitated, turning her head toward Alex who was offering Anna his hand. She turned back and put her hand in Bruce's, allowing him to help her up.

"Ye'll escort Anna and Lizzy back to their rooms when it's over," Laird Duncan ordered Robbie.

"Yes, sir, I'll return them back immediately following the show," Robbie answered.

As they walked back to the castle, they conversed about the day of events pleasantly. Anna did not say too much. Just the touch of her hand on Alex's arm made her tingle all over. She'd never felt like this before with anyone. As if this new feeling wasn't uncomfortable enough, Lizzy kept throwing cold looks at her.

They made it to the grand hall as most folks were arriving. As they took their seats, Lizzy maneuvered around so she was between Bruce and Alex, who was beside Anna. She chatted with Alex, ignoring Bruce completely until the minstrel came out.

The minstrel sang a ballad of a man who was in love with a fair lady who was promised to someone else. It was a love that matched no other. They had planned to be secretly married, but the betrothed found out. He kidnapped and imprisoned her before hunting down her lover.

Her lover was not a skilled warrior like her betrothed, but seeing his beloved imprisoned gave him the strength to prevail. Her lover was victorious in killing the man but was mortally wounded in the process.

She tended him for days, not leaving his side. She held him in her arms as he took his last breath. The thought of living without him was too much and the woman took her own life.

As the story was being told, Anna was completely aware of Alex next to her. At one point, she looked up at him. She could barely see him, as the room was darkened for the performance. He turned, and their eyes met, sending chills throughout her body. She immediately turned back to the performers.

Her reaction to the story and the man beside her gave her a sense of foreboding. *This is absurd*, she thought as she tried to concentrate on the story and not the man beside her, but her thoughts kept drifting back to him. *Perhaps he is some type of warlock and has me under a spell of some sorts.* She shook her head. *No, that's silly.*

After the performance, Robbie and Mary Ellen escorted Anna and Lizzy to their rooms. The crowd was thick, but most of the people were headed outside to their campsites, so once they reached the hallway, they were able to move more freely.

As soon as the door to their bedchamber closed, Lizzy turned on Anna. "Was that yer scheming to bring Bruce to escort me so Alex could escort ye? Ye ken I favor him!"

"'Tis not like that at all," Anna replied. "I had no idea they were bringing someone else." *As if I need one more issue with ye*, she thought.

Anna filled the basin with the fresh water with rose petals that the servants had left and quickly washed up and made ready for bed. Pulling back the covers, Anna slipped into bed as Lizzy took her time readying herself. Lizzy dropped her brush and huffed, muttering several times. When finally done, she blew out the candle and got into bed…and noisily tossed around for another several minutes, huffing and puffing.

When all was quiet, Anna promptly fell asleep.

And she dreamed of Alex.

CHAPTER

Robbie, Alex, and Brodie had guard duty from midnight until midmorning, so Anna, her da, and Willie broke their fast with Mary Ellen and her family in the morning. They leisurely ate, enjoying the company of each other, unlike most folk who were anxious for the festivities to begin.

Instead of going immediately to the games after their meal, the three of them went to the stables to take the horses for a ride. As they waited for the stable boy to ready their horses, the bagpipes blasted, and they could hear the crowd in the distance cheering, announcing the next competition.

As soon as the boy brought the horses out, Anna presented Butterfly with an apple before mounting. The scent of heather filled the air as they walked through the field to the wooded path that seemed much more worn with tips of branches broken from the number of people that traveled it to get a break from the activities. Once at the river, they walked downstream. The river was wide and peaceful in some spots and rough, narrow, and winding in others. They walked casually for a good hour until they found a spot where the riverbank was large. The river had a deep, peaceful pool where several fish swam.

Anna slid off her horse and grabbed a plaid, spreading it out along the bank. They sat on the plaid for a long while, enjoying the quietness away from the roaring crowd.

Willie got up and walked along the river's edge to look for stones. He picked up one and threw it low to the water and horizontally. It skipped across the water four times. He made a face and leaned down to pick up another stone and threw it. It wasn't long before Anna joined him. Her da leaned back on his forearms, watching them with a smile.

"Lord Reay was verra impressed with how well ye competed," Da said to Willie.

Willie stopped in mid throw and turned around with eyes spread wide open. "He was?" he asked.

"Aye," he replied. "He asked if ye'd stay to train under him."

"He did?" Willie dropped the rocks in his hands and darted over to his da. "And can I?"

"Well"—his da contemplated for a long while, which Anna was sure was just to make Willie more impatient—"I suppose I wasna much older than ye are now when I went to train."

Willie smiled and hugged his da. "Oh, thank ye!"

"Aye," his da said. "But I'm going to miss ye," he whispered, but Willie dinna hear him. He was already back at the edge of the woods, picking up more stones to throw as he jabbered on how excited he was.

"Look!" he stopped mid throw and pointed up across the river to a falcon that landed in a large tree. "I think it is the same one we saw the other day. It must have a nest in that tree."

"We went the other direction today," Anna said as she looked up. "It sure seems like it is looking directly at us."

"It must ken that ye like animals," her da chuckled.

She turned her head and smiled at her da with a twinkle in her eye.

"Aye," she said before turning back to the falcon, smiling as she did so, studying it. It gave her the same spellbinding feeling she had last time she saw it. Its eyes seemed locked with hers. She was fascinated with it.

"Haa! That one skipped six times!" Willie called out, bringing her back to their little game.

Anna looked down to search for the perfect stone as she walked along the water's edge slowly before stopping to pick one up. She turned to Willie with raised eyebrows and a big grin, took aim and released it, skipping along the water six times. They continued skipping stone for quite some time. Constantly aware of the falcon's presence, Anna would occasionally look up at it. It still seemed to be watching her.

"There. Nine skips!" she declared as she turned to Willie. "I win!" She fluffed his hair.

"Aw!" He jerked his head away and stroked his fingers through his hair in an attempt to fix the mess she had made of it.

"It's time we head back," her da said as he rose.

"Aye," they both replied as they turned to their horses.

Willie and Da mounted immediately and waited for Anna to caress Butterfly as she normally did.

"Come on. I'm getting hungry," Willie said.

"Ye are always hungry," she said with a smile as she made her way around the side of her horse. She put her left leg in the stirrup, shifted her weight, and began to swing her right leg around just as she heard a loud snap. The under straps of the saddle broke. The saddle shifted toward her as she fell back and landed on the ground with the saddle on top of her. Her head hit a large river rock and knocked her out.

"Anna!" her da dismounted, running to her. He picked up her saddle from atop her and tossed it to the side. He knelt and gently turned her head to inspect it.

"She's bleeding," he said as he unwrapped his neckerchief and wet it in the river, using it to clean the blood off her head. "Anna. Anna, do ye hear me?"

Willie rushed over in a panic to see his sister's still body. His da handed him the neckerchief. "Rinse it out," he ordered.

He gently pulled her onto his lap.

Willie put the now-red-stained neckerchief into the water. As the water flowed through it, a stream of blood was carried downstream with the current until it completely dissolved in the river. He squeezed it out, bringing it back to his da. His da wiped the wound down and applied pressure to stop the bleeding.

"Tether her horse to mine and secure her saddle to one of the horses. I must stop the bleeding, and we will go."

Willie worked quickly to do his bidding, then knelt beside him. "It's done," his voice etched with concern. "Is she going to be all right?"

He did not answer but said, "Take off yer neckerchief."

Willie unwrapped it and handed it to his da who folded it and replaced his with it. He handed his neckerchief back to Willie. "Rinse it out again and squeeze as much water out as ye can."

Willie brought it back, and his da opened it up, wrapping it around her head, using it to secure the other one in place.

"Get on yer horse, and I'll hand her to ye until I mount." He carefully rose as Anna was cradled in his arms. Cautiously, he handed her up to Willie. Once mounted on his horse, he edged his horse alongside Willie's and transferred Anna over, cradling her.

"I need to take it slowly. I want ye to ride ahead and get some help. Find the healer. Ye ken where the path is to lead ye back to the castle?"

"Aye, sir," Willie quietly replied, though his expression said otherwise.

"Then go. Quickly."

Willie kicked his heels into his horse and took off. He would make it back in less than half the time since they had ridden there at a leisurely pace.

He followed the river upstream but was going so fast that he would have missed the path leading back to the castle except for the fact that there were two men coming out on the path to the stream at the same time. He almost collided with them.

He brought his horse to a stop in front of them, instantly relieve to have recognized them.

"Whoa! What's the rush?" Alex asked.

"Alex. Brodie. My sister has fallen from her horse. She's injured!" Willie said.

Alex turned to Brodie. "Go notify Robbie and find the healer." He turned to Willie. "Where is she?"

Willie turned to point, and Alex took off with Willie on his heels. As they reached Anna and her da, they slowed to a stop. "Laird Duncan," Alex said. "Brodie and I were going to the river when we saw Willie. I sent Brodie to get Robbie and a healer." He glanced down at Anna, cradled against her da's chest. "What happened?"

Laird Duncan stopped beside them. "Her saddle strap broke as she was getting on her horse. It threw her off, and she fell, hitting her head on a rock. It knocked her out. She was bleeding a bit, but I got it to stop."

Alex turned his horse to walk beside the laird. His heart tore at him every time he glanced at her. *God, please don't let anything happen to her*, he prayed.

*****

They walked at a pace that would not jolt her around. When they reached the castle, Alex slipped down from his horse and held his arms out to take Anna from her da. "Where's her room?" Alex asked.

"No, take her to my room," he said before turning to Willie and saying, "Tie the horses up."

Brodie and Robbie were just coming up the hill with the healer. Her da turned and led Alex up the castle steps, not waiting for them.

She was so small in his arms, so fragile. He wanted to press his cheek against her head and whisper reassuring words in her ear, but he just held her tight against his body as he carried her up the stairs. She made small moaning noises as he ascended the steps and Alex took comfort in hearing them. Her da looked back at her without missing a step as he made his way to his room and opened the door.

"Lay her on the bed," he said.

Alex slowly lowered her, relinquishing her to the bed as Robbie and the healer entered the room.

"Let me take a look at the lass," the healer said as she sat on the edge of the bed and unwrapped the makeshift bandage. Using the water from the basin and a clean cloth, she proceeded to clean the area from the dried blood, which was now caked in her hair. Anna let out quiet moans as the healer cleaned her wounds.

Brodie and Willie entered the room as the healer continued to clean her head as she moaned a bit more. Willie edged up, clearly worried. His da put his arm over his shoulder to both keep him back so the healer could do her work and to comfort him.

"It does not look that bad," she said. "The bleeding is done, and the wound is not that big."

As the healer was putting fresh bandages on, she gave instructions on propping her up and giving her broth to eat when she wakes.

Alex backed up to stand beside Brodie and whispered so only Brodie could hear, "Let's go take a good look at that saddle before anyone else does."

Alex and Brodie excused themselves. "We will tend to the horses."

They went to the horses and led them to the trough. While the horses were drinking, they inspected her saddle. It was a well-made saddle that looked well-maintained. The broken edges of the under strap had been cut with a sharp blade most of the way. Someone had tampered with it.

Alex's chest tightened as a fury started to overtake him.

"It looks like the straps were cut some and tore the rest of the way," Alex said calmly, not giving any indication of the turmoil inside other than to look around to see if anyone was watching them.

"Aye," Brodie agreed after inspecting them himself, also looking around clearly on guard.

"Get Robbie. I'll head to the stables. We need to question the stable boy," Alex said as he mounted Thunder and gathered the reins of Butterfly and the horse of Anna's da before heading toward the stables. Brodie and Robbie caught up to him just as he approached the stables.

"Take a look at this," Alex said as he grabbed the strap of her saddle. Robbie slid off his horse and grabbed the end. "Who'd do such a thing?" Alex asked, looking back to the castle, then scouted the grounds, which would normally be empty but was now lined with tents.

"I dinna ken," Robbie said as he looked around to see if anyone was watching. "Let's ask the stable boy."

As Robbie started to enter the stable, Alex raised his hand to indicate stealth as he handed the reins to Brodie. He quietly walked down the first row, stopping for a bit to stroke a couple of horses.

Alex could hear the stable boy in the other row, but he dinna look up. He took his time there, looking back at the door where Robbie and Brodie watched.

He moved down the row a couple of stalls and did the same, growing angry the longer he went unnoticed.

After a couple of minutes, he walked the rest of the row and casually turned to the next row. The stable boy stood up, dropping his knife and wood he was whittling. "Sir, ye startled me. I dinna hear ye come in."

Robbie came around the other end of the row. "Ye are not being verra attentive lad," Alex said sternly.

"All was quiet, so I was whittling a bit, 'tis all," he said as he hurried to the door to tend to their horses. He stopped as he saw Butterfly saddleless.

"This is Lady Duncan's horse," he said as he moved to grab the reins. "Why is the saddle off? She's already been told she is not to be putting it on and off while here. She'll be getting me in trouble."

Alex put his one arm on the horse, blocking the boy from going any further and grabbed the end of the saddle strap with the other hand to show the boy. "Ye've not been doing a verra good job at watching the stable," he said. "Who else has been in there?"

The boy's expression changed to terror as he looked from the strap to Alex's face. "No one, sir. I swear to ye!" He looked at each of the men.

"Ye dinna even look up while I walked around stopping to fiddle around the horses. Anyone could have easily done this in that amount of time," he said as he held up the strap.

Hearing the commotion, the stable master walked out from the corral. "What seems to be the problem?" he asked.

"The strap on my sister's saddle has been cut most of the way. It snapped as she was mounting the horse, and she fell, hitting her head on a rock. It knocked her out," Robbie said. "She was a good distance from the castle."

"I swear I dinna see anyone near the stalls," the lad declared, looking up to the stable master then back to Robbie.

The stable master whacked the boy in the back of the head. "Ye need to be alert at all times when ye are here, especially when there are so many horses," the stable master yelled. "Everyone needs to wait outside for their horse."

"Aye, sir. I am sorry. I will be more careful." He looked at Robbie all forlorn then to Alex who was glaring at him. "I truly am sorry, sir."

"There is another stable boy who was here earlier today as well. I will have someone fetch him and question him right away, sir," the stable master said as he grabbed the reins of the horses and handed two of them to the stable boy to take back into the stalls as the others turned back toward the castle.

"Any idea who would have done this?" Alex asked Robbie as they walked back to the castle. "Is there anybody who has ill will toward her?"

"I dinna ken," he replied.

"What about Lizzy?" Brodie said. "She does not seem verra fond of Anna. I saw the looks she gave her last night when Alex was escorting her to the hall. They were not too nice."

"She's our cousin. What does she have to gain?"

"Just the rest of the days here at the games with Alex's undivided attention, that's what," Brodie replied.

Alex turned and glared at Brodie.

Brodie shrugged. "She's made no attempts at hiding that she favors ye," Brodie said to Alex.

"Not a chance of that happening," Alex mumbled.

They arrived back at the castle and went upstairs. Robbie did a quick knock on his da's door before opening it himself and entering. As they walked in, they were all pleased to see she had her eyes opened and she was sitting up in the bed.

"There's my little sis. Ye gave us quite a scare," Robbie said. "How are ye feeling?"

"My head hurts, and I'm a bit dizzy."

"The healer says she should stay sitting upright and not sleep for several hours," her da explained. "And she's to stay in bed for two days."

Anna mumbled her displeasure.

"My lady, I am pleased to see ye are awake," Alex said as he bowed to her. "I must be on my way, but may I call on ye later to see how ye are doing?" He paused to glance at her da. "If that is okay with yer father?" he turned back to Anna who smiled, then to her da who nodded.

"That would be nice," she said.

"I'd like to thank ye for yer help," her da said.

"It was the least I could do," he bowed.

"My lady," Brodie said as he bowed and left the room with Alex.

Robbie followed them out the door to the top of the stairs and turned to them. "Keep alert. Maybe ye might hear something in the village or at the games. And let me know what the other stable boy says."

"Aye," they both said as they turned toward the games.

*****

Alex and Brodie walked around the encampment first. Despite the games going on, there were still many people around the camps, taking a break from it all. They occasionally stopped to talk to people in an attempt to discover any clues as to who may have done Anna harm. Not finding anything suspicious, they moved onto the games.

"There ye are, Alex. I was hoping I would see ye. Would ye like to join us?" Lizzy said as she scooted closer to Agnes and patted the newly made space for him to sit.

"Not now. Thank ye, though," Alex replied blankly.

"I haven't seen ye all day. Are ye getting ready to compete?"

"I do not compete today as I had guard duty 'til morn," he said. Watching Lizzy and her mother's reactions carefully, he said, "Anna had an accident today."

"Oh? What happened?" Lizzy asked curiously.

"She fell off her horse," he replied.

"Really?" she said skeptically. "I dinna think she's ever done that. She's practically one with that horse. She willna let anyone near her horse."

"With all the festivities going on here and she'd prefer the company of that horse instead of the games and people," Lizzy's mother said, "there is something wrong with that girl."

"Her saddle strap broke," Brodie said.

"Oh, that's awful. Is she okay?" Lizzy asked, sincerely concerned.

"She bumped her head. They moved her to her da's room. She's to stay in bed for the next couple of days," Alex replied.

"Oh really?" Her eyebrows raised. "Well, that is too bad. She will miss out on all the excitement." She looked almost pleased, he noted.

"We need to be on our way," Brodie elbowed Alex and bowed. "Ladies."

Heading toward the village, they discussed Lizzy and her mother's reaction.

"Lizzy looked pleased when we told her Anna would be in bed for a few days," Brodie said.

"Aye," Alex agreed, "but she did seem a bit concerned with news of her injury." He thought for a moment before continuing. "Lizzy is more jealous, her mother though…she really seems not to like Anna."

They walked through the village that seemed abandoned compared to a normal day. Most people were at the games, but there were some shops open, the bakery for one. They were making loaves of bread to sell to all the spectators. The scent of fresh bread poured out the opened door and windows, drawing them in. Alex stopped to purchase a loaf. He ripped the warm loaf in half, handing one of the halves to

Brodie. They ate it as they finished their search of the village before heading back to the stables and castle.

*****

Back at the castle, they found Robbie in the great hall with several other soldiers waiting for their meal. Alex and Brodie took seats across from him and waved to the servant girl for some ale.

"What'd ye find?" Robbie leaned toward them.

"Nothing," Alex said. "The other stable boy saw nothing, so he claims. But even if he did, he most likely wouldna say for fear of punishment."

"Aye."

"Lizzy seemed genuinely concerned when we told her Anna had gotten hurt, but yer aunt…" Alex paused.

"What?" Robbie asked.

"Well, it just seemed like she was disgusted that Anna left to ride her horse instead of watching the game. What does she have against Anna?" he asked.

Robbie shrugged. "That's just my aunt Elizabeth," he replied.

"Lizzy looked almost thrilled that Anna would be tied up for a couple of days," Brodie added.

"Aye, but like ye said, Lizzy is in competition for Alex's attention. Nay, I do not think it was her," Robbie stated.

"Then who?" Alex asked.

"I dinna ken," Robbie shook his head. There was a couple of minutes of silence.

"How's Anna?" Alex inquired.

"Bored and tired," Robbie replied. "But she needs to stay awake a bit longer. The MacKay had a chess set brought up, but she's growing bored of it."

"Chess, ye say? She plays chess?" Alex asked.

"Aye, but don't bother playing with her. She beats me four out of five times," Robbie declared. "I think she lets me win once in a while so I don't lose face." He chuckled as he shrugged his shoulders and took a gulp of ale.

"Has she eaten yet?" Alex asked.

"No. I was going to bring her up something when I was done and send my da down to eat. He's been up there all day."

"I can bring some food up for her if it is all right. Ye can both have a break," Alex suggested.

"Aye. But consider yerself forewarned if ye decide to play chess with her," Robbie declared.

CHAPTER

7

Alex knocked on the door of the room of Anna's da with one hand as he held a tray of food in the other. He heard the chair scrape across the wooden floor and heavy footsteps before the knock was answered.

"Laird Duncan." Alex bowed. "Robbie thought ye may like to join him downstairs for the evening meal. Would it be okay if I dined with Anna?" he asked as he held up his tray of food. His heart pounded at the thought of seeing her again.

Her da paused to contemplate. He looked down at the food and up to Alex. "Aye. A little change of company may do her good," he replied.

Her father moved the chessboard from the table beside the bed and placed it on the chest of drawers so Alex could put the food down.

Her da turned to look at Anna. She was looking at the tray of food to avoid looking into Alex's eyes. Her da turned back to Alex.

"Perhaps we can play a game of chess afterward," Alex suggested as he pointed to the chessboard.

"Aye." Her da smiled and patted him on the back of his shoulder. "That's a great idea." Her da chuckled, thankful to get a break from chess but still unsure about leaving his daughter in a room with a man no matter how honorable and close he was to his son. He turned back to Anna to see her reaction. "Are ye fine with dining with Alex?"

"Aye, Da," she said, noticing his hesitation. It was not that she felt unsafe with Alex. It was quite the opposite. She felt safe with him, but she couldna understand why she was so smitten with him as if she was a schoolgirl.

"I'll be fine." She was thankful for the distraction even though she was uneasy around him, but the thought of a new opponent in chess outweighed her anxiety. She enjoyed chess, and it was easy for her to ignore the happenings around her when she was concentrating on the game.

Her da walked toward the door, tossing one more look her way, which she returned with a small smile before he left the room.

Alex took one plate of food off the tray and placed it on the table where Anna could reach it. He scooted the tray to the other side of the table and poured her a glass of water before sitting down in the chair.

"How are ye feeling?" he asked.

"Bored," she said as she looked at her food, consisting of a steamy bowl of broth, roasted grouse, some fresh bread, and strawberries for dessert.

"At least they let me take the bandages off my head. My stomach hurts where the saddle fell on me, and I'm a little sore where I bumped my head, but I dinna ken why I have to stay here for two days. I'll go crazy." She blew on her broth before sipping it without looking at him.

After a moment of silence, she looked up from her food and asked, "Why were ye not at my brother's wedding since ye two are so close? Brodie was there."

"I had gotten news that someone had ransacked my father's house a few weeks prior to the wedding. My father and brother were returning from a tenant's house late and encountered a couple of men unexpectedly who knocked them out as they were heading back from the stables to the house," he said as he cut a piece of grouse. She stopped her eating and looked up at him, suddenly sympathetic.

"The butler and maid were forced into a closet as the men ransacked the house. My father dinna come to until early the next morn." He forked the piece of meat and put it in his mouth.

"How awful," she replied. "Who did it?"

He shrugged his shoulders as he finished chewing and swallowed. "I dinna ken. There were two men with hoods over their faces."

"Are yer da and brother okay?"

"Aye."

"What did they take?"

"We dinna find anything missing."

"That's amazing." She picked up a piece of bread and took a bite. After swallowing, she asked, "Did they have to stay in bed for two days?"

He chuckled. "I dinna ken. I doubt it. I arrived almost two weeks after the fact."

There was a knock on the door. Alex raised his eyebrows to Anna before turning toward the door, his hand resting on his dagger as he opened the door cautiously. A servant stood in the hall.

"I was checking to see if the lady needs anything," she said as she peeked in. Alex swung the door open all the way so she could see that Anna was all intact. She turned back to Alex and looked him over before turning back to Anna again. "Is there anything I can get ye?"

"No, I'm fine." She smiled, "Thank you."

The servant did a quick curtsy before turning to leave. Alex closed the door as he turned with a big grin on his face.

"Ye ken that she will be here every five minutes, even if ye are my brother's best friend," she said.

They both chuckled.

After they finished the meal, Alex swapped the tray with the chess set, and they both set up the chess pieces with no conversation.

Anna started with her knight. Alex followed with a pawn. After a couple of more moves, the servant came back and took away the tray.

Alex watched Anna as she thought over every move. *God, I can watch her all day*, he thought.

"How did ye learn to play chess?" Alex asked midgame as he took one of her pawns.

He smiled as she studied the board a few seconds to plan her strategy and moved her bishop. She looked up with a smile and said, "My da taught me. After my mother died, I started spending more time with my da and brothers."

She looked down to watch his next move, more to distract her from the feeling his smile had on her. *He is so handsome. Is that why he makes me feel this way? No, looks have never made me feel this way before.*

The game continued much in the same way; he would ask a question, and she waited to answer until her move was done. Her answer was always short and to the point never giving any extra details.

Alex smiled, completely content watching her contemplating her every move.

Robbie walked in as Anna made her last move. "Checkmate," she exclaimed.

Robbie gave Alex a hardy whack on the back of his shoulder as he laughed.

Alex stood up with a smile and gave Anna a bow. "My lady, that was a very good game. I look forward to playing another, but I must bid ye good eve."

"Thank ye for the company," she responded.

"Any time, milady."

"Anna," she said. "Ye may call me Anna."

"Or Annie," Robbie blurted out right before a pillow hit him smack in the face. "Or not." Robbie shrugged his shoulders and turned to Alex, laughing.

Alex turned to Anna. "Anna," he said, bowing once more before leaving.

As soon as the door closed behind Alex, Anna looked at Robbie. "I canna stay here two days," she said.

"Ye have only been in here but a half a day," he said. "Ye ken what the healer said."

"Where will da and Willie sleep?" she asked. He looked around and shrugged.

"Well, can ye at least leave the room while I take off this dress and ready myself for bed?" she asked.

"Mary Ellen will be up any minute. She can help ye."

"Oh, for heaven's sake."

"What if ye get dizzy and fall when ye are standing up?" he said.

"Really?" she spat as she started to get up. Just then, a knock came on the door. Robbie quickly answered, letting Mary Ellen in before swiftly leaving so Anna could not say anything else.

"How are ye feeling?" Mary Ellen asked as she walked over to Anna just as she rose off the bed. "Can I help ye?" She reached for her.

"No!" Anna snapped.

Mary Ellen snatched her arms back but did not move. Her expression was a clear shock.

"I'm sorry, Mary Ellen. I dinna mean to snap, but I have been in this bed most of the day with someone watching me constantly. Really, I'm fine."

"They are just worried about ye. Ye hit yer head pretty good I heard."

"I ken that, but I'm not a fragile lass that cries over a snagged nail."

"I think they ken that as well, but they are worried ye'll have a dizzy spell. Ye need to sit and rest."

Anna huffed at that as she shed her dress, leaving just her shift. She walked to the basin and washed her face.

"Robbie talks about ye a lot. He would be devastated if anything would happen to ye," Mary Ellen said as she walked over to the basin behind Anna.

"I ken that," she said as she walked over to the window with Mary Ellen in tow. "I would be devastated if anything happened to him."

Realizing Mary Ellen was going to follow behind her every step she took, she gave in and walked over to the bed, pulling back the sheets.

She sat down in the bed and pulled the sheets over her legs. "He's fond of ye too." She smiled. "It is nice to have ye as a sister."

"Aye," Mary Ellen replied. "I have always wanted a sister." Once Anna was settled in bed, Mary Ellen went back to the door and opened it to find Anna's da with his fist raised to knock and Robbie leaning back against the wall on the other side of the hall. She turned back to Anna. "Good night, Anna."

"Good night, Mary Ellen."

CHAPTER

8

The servant came the next morn with some porridge, biscuits, jam, and tea. Anna got up and moved to the chair. "Ye are not really going to make me stay in bed all day, are ye?" she asked her da while she cut her biscuit open and spread some jam on it.

"How are ye feeling?" he replied with another question.

"I feel fine," she said. He looked at her disbelievingly. "Really," she stressed.

"Well, perhaps we can go to the hall or sit outside. I don't want ye to go all the way down to the games in case ye get overheated or dizzy," he said. "And ye are most definitely not riding today."

"What happened to my saddle? I heard a snap before I fell. It was not worn. I checked it before our trip here."

"I ken," he paused. "I wasna going to tell ye, but…" He paused again. She stared, waiting for his response. "It appears that someone tampered with it."

"What?" she exclaimed, instantly frightened. "Why… who?"

"I dinna ken. The stable boys swear they dinna see anyone. That is why I want someone with ye at all times."

Anna nodded, worry etched across her face. She finished eating in silence as she pondered the situation.

Robbie, Mary Ellen, and Willie stopped by after breaking their fast.

"How are ye feeling this morning?" Robbie asked.

"Physically fine," she said. Not wanting to get Willie worried, she did not mention her concern about the saddle. "I wanna see ye compete today."

"Ugh, ye can see me tomorrow perhaps, in the finals," he said.

"Oh, ye are that sure of yerself, are ye now?" she asked.

"Ye doubt me?" he said with a smile. "There will be jesters in the hall tonight after the games. Perhaps we could all go to watch it together."

"Yes!" Willie exclaimed. "Can we go?" he asked as he turned to his da.

"That sounds like a great plan," he said.

After a bit, they all went out to the back of the castle where the cook's garden was, close to the house. Da laid down a blanket for them to sit on.

"I wanna go watch the games," Willie said. "Can I go?"

"We can take him with us," Mary Ellen offered. "He can stay with me and my parents while Robbie is competing."

"That's fine," he said, turning to Willie. "Ye mind yer brother and Mary Ellen."

"Yes, sir," he replied. Turning to Robbie, he said, "Let's go." Immediately, he started heading down the path.

Robbie chuckled. "I guess we'll be on our way." He grabbed Mary Ellen's hand, and the two of them strolled behind Willie.

Anna and her da sat by the garden for quite some time, watching the servants coming and going, gathering vegetables and herbs from the garden. Another garden contained strawberries and raspberries and was lined with fruit trees.

She enjoyed sitting outside. She spotted a squirrel jumping from tree to tree and watched the birds digging for worms.

Other birds chirped at each other as they appeared to play a game of *ye can't catch me.*

On occasion, the roar of the crowd in the distance could be heard over the birdsongs.

She looked up at one point to see the falcon land on a tree once again, facing them. She smiled as she watched it looking at her for some time. "There's something about that falcon that's just..." She paused.

"What?" her da said as he looked up at the falcon.

"I dinna ken. It's..." *A sense of peace,* she thought but kept to herself, "mesmerizing."

"Ye canna take it home with ye, lass," he said with a laugh. She glanced at him with a smile before turning back to the bird.

"Perhaps it's the MacKay's hunting bird," he said.

"I dinna think so," she said, watching it for a little longer before it flew off.

She enjoyed being out in the morning, but the rest of the day dragged. After lunch, they went back to the room to rest and play some more chess.

They ate their evening meal in the hall, which they shared with only a few people due to the games, but it provided some distraction to pass the time away.

When the servants started moving tables together toward the front of the room to make a platform for the jesters to perform on, Anna and her da walked outside and found a spot to sit and watch as the people started to trickle in. They could tell once the games were over by the groups of people heading back to their tents.

Robbie, Mary Ellen, and Willie came back with Alex, Brodie, and Lizzy. Lizzy was clearly talking to Alex as she was looking at him, hands flying around as she talked. He seemed uninterested, but he smiled at Anna when his eyes locked on hers, giving her butterflies in her stomach.

"How'd ye do?" Anna asked Robbie as they approached.

"I made the finals," he said.

"And Alex here took first in two events," Lizzy said as she linked her hand onto his arm as if he had offered it to her.

"He got lucky," Brodie said to Anna. "I lost my footing on a bump in the ground."

"Oh yeah?" Robbie slapped him on the back. "Alex beat ye fair and square."

He turned to Anna. "Are ye ready to go to the performance?"

"Aye," she said as she got up and added, "Let's go."

They made their way up the stairs and into the main hall just as it was starting to fill up.

Willie picked the first row, and he and his da moved in as far as they could. Mary Ellen and Robbie moved in next to them, Robbie pulling Anna in beside him. Alex followed, getting the last seat in the row.

"Aah," Lizzy huffed. Brodie went to the next row and moved in toward the middle. As he went to sit down, he noticed that Lizzy had plopped herself directly behind Alex, so Brodie moved over to sit by her.

The performance consisted of song, dance, and fire-breathing acts. After the fire-breathing act, two jesters jumped up on the tables and started juggling apples. After a while, one of them put down the apples and came out juggling three knives. The crowd cheered.

Not to be outperformed, the other one left and came back with three knives of his own. Then one of the jesters threw one of his knives to the other, who caught it and tossed it up with his other knives, not missing a catch or toss. An intake of breath was heard from the children. The jester with the four knives tossed one knife back to the other in the same fashion, gaining a clap from the crowd. They continued that way for a couple of minutes before one jester dropped one of his knives and kicked it up to the other, who caught it and tossed it in the air with the other knives without missing a beat. The crowd gave out an "ooh." They did it another time and received an "aah."

Lizzy leaned forward so her face was close to Alex's. "How exciting!" Anna heard Lizzy say to Alex.

The jesters did it a third time, just as Alex's hand came in front of Anna's face, catching a knife.

Anna sucked in a breath as Robbie turned just in time to see Alex lower the knife in his hand to his lap. He quickly looked back at the jesters who still had three knives each, then back to Alex as he pulled Anna out to the aisle and proceeded to leave the hall with Robbie in tow.

"Where are ye going?" Lizzy asked, looking between Alex and the jesters, then back to Alex again. She started to get up, but Brodie grabbed her arm to keep her put. Everyone else was focused on the performance.

"Oh my god! What just happened?" Anna exclaimed, frightened. She looked at Alex who was now bleeding. "Ye are hurt!"

"Come on!" Robbie grabbed Anna's arm and led her up the stairs to his da's room. Alex followed as he took his neckerchief off and wrapped his hand.

When they got to the room, Robbie walked Anna to the edge of the bed. He sat her down as she stared blankly, shocked. He turned to look at Alex, blood seeping through his wrapped hand.

"Are ye okay?" he asked.

"Aye. It'll be fine." The blade had cut him between his thumb and index finger before he caught it by the handle. "It dinna come from the stage. I saw it coming from the corner of the room."

Anna had gone completely white.

"What!" she exclaimed. Her chest suddenly felt like someone was standing on it, and her hands began to shake. "Someone is really trying to kill me!"

Robbie gave Alex a look and shifted his eyes to the base of the bed. Both men put their hands on their swords, and Robbie quietly pulled his out as Alex walked closer to the bed.

Anna was still mumbling her disbelief and did not notice them until Alex pulled the blanket up from the edge of the bed as Robbie thrust his sword under the bed, moving it from side to side in a swift motion, sure to injure anyone who might be hiding underneath.

"What…what are ye doing?" Anna said as she pulled her legs up and scrambled to the middle of the bed.

"Anna, we are just making sure no one is hiding under yer bed!" Robbie said as he sheathed his sword.

"But…why? Why is someone trying to kill me?" she asked.

The sound of heavy footsteps rapidly approaching were heard in the hallway. Both men drew their swords. Robbie went to the side of the door, and Alex stood guard in front of Anna.

The footsteps immediately stopped at the door. With his sword held high, Robbie yanked on the door as his da stumbled in and fell.

"What the devil!" he yelled as he looked up at Robbie then at Anna with terror on her face as Alex stood guard in front of her, his hand bandaged, and his shirt bloodied.

"Mary Ellen said ye left. What the hell happened!"

Robbie helped his da off the floor, poked his head out the door, and looked down the hall both ways before closing the door. He moved the chair by the fireplace to the edge of the bed for his da to sit in before explaining what happened.

"I dinna see it," Robbie said. "It was only after Anna gasped did I turn to see the knife in Alex's hand in front of her face before he took it down."

"A roomful of people and only one person saw it?" his da spat.

"Barely, sir. I only saw it from the corner of my eye. I dinna see who did it. It was just a swift movement, and I reacted."

"I am indebted to ye, Alex," her da said. He looked down at Alex's hand wrapped in a bloodied neckerchief. "Are ye hurt badly?"

"I'll be fine, sir," he said.

Alex pulled the dirk from under his belt and studied it for a bit, flipping it over before handing it to Anna's father. "It is not the same as the knives the jesters were juggling. Theirs had broad-curved blades, a scimitar of sorts." Alex gestured to the knife in the Laird's hand, "This is a Highlander's dirk."

"Aye," the laird said. "There are no markings on it to identify the owner. Do either of ye recognize it?" he asked as he got up, handed the dirk to Robbie, and sat on the bed.

He pulled Anna into his embrace as she stared blankly at the knife in Robbie's hand.

"There, there," he said.

She turned her face into his chest.

Alex's heart went out to Anna as he watched her hug her father. He wanted to hold her, protect her, comfort her. He turned his focus back to the dagger in Robbie's hand.

Robbie shrugged his shoulders as he handed the dagger back to Alex. "Nay, I dinna recognize it."

Alex looked at it thoroughly, flipping it over. He did not recognize it, but as he held it, his chest got tighter as his anger grew.

The sound of people below the opened window broke his concentration.

"The performance must have ended," Robbie said. "I'll go get Willie and the others." Before heading out the door, he turned to Alex and pointed at the open window. "Close the window."

*****

Robbie weaved his way through the crowd, leaving the great hall until he found the others.

"Where did ye go, and where is Alex?" Lizzy asked.

Robbie pulled Brodie aside and whispered to him what happened as he continually looked around, but nobody seemed to be eyeing them. He instructed him to look around the hall, behind tapestries and corners on that side of the room to see if he could find any clues as to who did this.

"Aye," Brodie said before turning to the ladies and bowing. "I bid ye both good night."

"Come along," Robbie said to the group, giving Mary Ellen a look to not ask questions.

He dropped Lizzy off at her room.

"But…but where did Alex go?" she asked.

"Anna was feeling ill, and he helped me escort her up to my da's room."

"Anna…," she mumbled, and she went into her room and closed her door not too quietly.

*****

He dropped Willie off with his da.

"Are ye ready to go?" he asked Alex.

"Aye," Alex said as he turned to Anna and bowed. "Milady." Then he turned to Laird Duncan. "Sir."

Her da nodded to him.

"I'll be back in the morn to break bread with ye," Robbie said to his family as he closed the door.

Once in the hallway, Robbie turned to Alex. "I had hoped that the saddle incident had been a boy's prank, or perhaps, I hate to say it," Robbie whispered as he made the sign of the cross and continued, "meant for someone else, but it seems that is not the case."

"Ye cannot think of anyone who has an ill wish on her or yer family?" Alex asked.

Robbie shook his head in frustration. "Nay. And it is not as if she is heir to the Duncan clan. That falls on me."

"What happened?" Mary Ellen asked.

Robbie briefly filled her in as they left the castle.

"Perhaps a suitor that had been turned down?" Alex suggested.

"Nay, despite her being of age to marry, she had not shown any interest in anyone, and my da wouldna force her to wed someone she didna want to."

"So perhaps yer father has turned suitors away without her knowing? It's possible that if a suitor was turned away, he may feel threatened if he thought his rival may gain her dowry," Alex proposed.

Robbie thought for a while as they walked. "I'll consult with my father about that, but I'm sure he would have mentioned it to me if someone had asked for her hand in marriage."

CHAPTER

9

Robbie and Mary Ellen showed up early, but everyone was ready. Robbie pulled his da to the side. "We looked the place over last night but dinna find anything," he whispered. "I talked to Lord Reay," Robbie continued. "I have arranged for Brodie to escort ye home on the morrow. Alex and I would go as well, but we both already just got off leave. Alex and Brodie are like brothers to me," he explained. "I'd trust them both with my life."

"Aye," his da whispered back. Turning to everyone else, he said, "Are we ready to go downstairs?"

"Aye," they replied as they got up and made their way downstairs.

Brodie and Alex were already at a table when Lizzy and her parents came in. Lizzy waved as she saw them.

"Let's sit with Alex," she said to her mother as she led the way.

Brodie looked at Alex with a smirk on his face, which Alex returned with a grump. Lizzy sat herself down beside Alex.

"Good morning," she said to him.

"Good morning," he replied as he immediately passed a basket of biscuits to her, then one of fruit as well in hopes to fill her mouth so she would not talk as much. Brodie coughed to hide his laugh as Alex kicked him hard under the table.

"Aww," Brodie blurted.

"Are ye all right?" Lizzy looked at Brodie as if he had three eyes.

"Aye."

"Here's Alex and Brodie," Willie said to the group as he made his way to the table and plopped down beside them. The rest of the group followed.

Lizzy caught sight of Alex's bandaged hand and asked, "What happened to yer hand?"

"Just a cut," Alex said as he lifted it briefly, easily closing his fingers into a fist and opening it again as if to show her he had full motion of his hand.

"But the competition," she started to say with obvious concern.

"I wouldna make a verra good soldier if a cut disables me," he replied bluntly.

"Aye," she said. "I suppose not."

"Do ye mind if I watch the games with ye as I am not competing today?" Brodie asked Anna and her da.

"I would welcome the company," her da said.

Robbie and Alex ate quickly and left to prepare for the competition. Lizzy and her parents left shortly after to ensure the best spot.

The rest of them ate slowly, enjoying each other's company. Willie told Brodie how he would be staying to train, and Brodie told stories of when he first started training.

After a while, Willie looked at his da and asked, "Can we go now?"

"Aye, let's go," he replied as they got up and headed out.

People were starting to fill in, yelling greetings to some and stopping to talk to others. They found a good spot and laid the blanket down. Anna could tell Brodie and her da were more on guard than relaxed, enjoying the festivities.

Their mannerisms kept last night's events fresh in her mind, which she would just as soon forget.

Mary Ellen kept up a polite conversation with Anna between Willie filling in all the competitors, pointing out which ones were his favorites.

Finally, the bagpipes began, indicating the beginning of the games. The crowd was more intense with their cheering as they were in the final competitions and were now familiar with the competitors.

There were only ten men competing in the finals in each category. Alex and Robbie both competed in the caber toss, which was the first event.

Robbie was the third competitor. He flipped the log over, end to end, standing it up vertically and falling on the twelve-thirty mark, jumping into first place.

There was one competitor between Robbie and Alex. As the caber was being walked in to stand directly in front of Alex, Anna felt the excitement within her. She anxiously watched as he bent his knees to pick up the log.

As he picked up the log, he could feel the pressure on his cut. He clenched his teeth as he stood up, ran, and tossed the log. It successfully flipped end over end, but not completely vertically, and it fell at the ten-thirty position.

He shrugged to Robbie, as if admitting defeat before walking the caber up vertically for the next competitor, who did an almost perfect toss, moving Robbie into second place.

Robbie's hands went to the top of his head and from a distance seemed to exclaimed, "Aw!" though he appeared to be smiling nonetheless.

Alex slapped him on the back of his shoulder as he chuckled as well.

Anna watched the exchange between the two of them and smiled. Just the sight of him made her heart leap.

The game ended with Robbie coming in second place. Since Robbie dinna compete in any more events, he rejoined the group, but Alex stayed on the field to wait for the maide leisg event.

As the other games were going on, Anna caught herself watching Alex a couple of times instead of the games. She would casually focus back on the events, hoping nobody noticed. The thought of being found out made her heart race, and she felt her face heat up.

The maide leisg was the last event. Each of the ten men was paired up with another. Alex easily beat his first two opponents. In the third game, Alex was paired up with another man who also won both of his first two games.

Anna felt her heart beat faster as his rival appeared to be getting the better of Alex when, finally, Alex gained the strength to pull the man up.

A rush of excitement came over Anna as Robbie and Willie both let out a "Yeah!"

The man shook his head in frustration but held his hand out to help Alex up.

After a couple of more rounds, Alex was still undefeated, coming in first place.

The crowd immediately started to disperse at the end of the games, but they waited on the blanket for Alex to rejoin the group. They did not even get up to fold the blanket, and Anna kenned it was so people would have to walk around it. Anyone could easily slip a knife into someone walking in a crowd, and no one would be any wiser.

Once Alex arrived, the crowd had died down.

"There is a banquet tonight for the winners and their families," Robbie said.

"Well, let's get back to the castle and ready ourselves," Da replied.

They went back up to their room to rest for a bit and ready themselves.

Anna decided to wear the same dress she wore for Robbie's wedding at the banquet. She unbraided her hair and brushed it so her soft curls flowed down her back before putting on the necklace that her da had given her.

Robbie and Mary Ellen were waiting at the bottom of the stairs when the three of them came down. They walked in together and found a seat, leaving one open for Alex.

The people in the hall were loud with excitement from the games despite the formalness of the banquet. Rounds of drinks were served, adding to the intensity of the group.

After a few minutes, Alex came over and sat down. "Ms. Duncan, how beautiful ye look." The softness of his voice and the sincerity in his eyes made her feel like a princess. She could feel her heart beating fast, and her stomach was in knots.

He was all cleaned up. He had a commanding presence about him, looking more like a laird than a soldier. His hair was brushed neatly and tied back with a black ribbon. The MacKay tartan was draped over his broad shoulder, secured with a brooch that she did not recognize. It was not the MacKay crest, but perhaps it was the Boswell brooch.

"Thank ye," she stammered out, not knowing what was the matter with herself.

As he sat down, his eyes shifted down to her necklace. "What a beautiful stone," he said. "Where ever did ye get it?" he asked.

"My da gave it to me to wear for Robbie's wedding," she replied as she touched the stone hanging from her neck that felt very warm to her touch. "Apparently, I found it when I was a wee lass."

Alex smiled slowly, the most beautiful smile she'd ever seen, and he raised his eyes back to look into hers. "It's a lapis lazuli," he told her. "Some folk say it has special powers. They call it the stone of knowledge."

As he talked, she could swear she felt the stone getting warmer where it lay against her body.

"How does it work?" she asked.

"They say that the one who possesses it has a strengthened awareness and an increased level of intuition, that is if one can elevate their spiritual energy to that of the stone," he proclaimed.

"Hmm," Robbie let out, giving Anna a look that he thought Alex was crazy.

"Aye." Alex looked at him. "That's what people say."

Everybody immediately got quiet as Lord Reay and his wife proceeded to the head table.

Trays of venison and pheasant were served to each table with potatoes and turnips, decorated with fruit. A constant flow of wine and whiskey made its rounds as well.

After the meal, acknowledgments of the winners were made. Several of the folk left shortly after the announcements of the winners. Most would leave at the crack of dawn for their journey home, but the majority of them were on MacKay land and did not have but a two-day travel at the very most, unlike Anna's family who would travel four days at the least.

They stayed only a little while longer before heading up to their rooms to retire for the night.

*****

Keep running. They can't find me. Not yet.

She stopped to gasp for air and look behind her. I think I lost them. I've got to keep moving. I can't stop...can't stop.

*****

"Anna, Anna...wake up!" her da called as he shook her.

She opened her eyes and sat up, trying to catch her breath. Her da held her.

"It's okay, lass. I've got ye. It's okay. It was just a bad dream. I've got ye."

CHAPTER

The next morning was a busy start as they readied themselves for their long ride. Robbie and Mary Ellen came
up to stay with Anna while Willie and their da met with Lord
Reay to finalize Willie's training agreement.

Anna packed the belongings she had in her da's room, but
a lot were still in Lizzy's. She knocked on Lizzy's door and
entered when she received no answer the second time. The
room was dark. Anna pulled back the curtains a bit to let in
some light. Lizzy gave out a groan.

"Lizzy, it's time to get up. We will be leaving soon," Anna
said.

"I'll get up when I'm good and ready!" Lizzy snapped.

Anna quietly packed her trunk and grabbed a servant to
carry it out, not caring that Lizzy was still in bed.

Anna's uncle came out of his room to request servants to
carry their trunks down to the cart. The servants were coming out of Lizzy's room with Anna's chest, and he saw Lizzy
still in the bed. As the servants went to close the door behind
them, he put his arm out to hold it open.

"Lizzy, get up now!" he ordered.

Her eyes opened wide as she turned toward him. "I was
just getting up, Papa."

Robbie, Mary Ellen, and Anna made their way down the
steps and out the main doors of the castle. The horses and
cart had been brought up to the castle so the servants could
load it up. She stood on the steps of the castle, looking out at
the grounds, now half empty.

A stream of people with their carts headed down the cobblestone road, out the portcullis. Beyond that, ye could see a trail of people on the path until they disappeared into the distant woods.

Anna walked down to her horse and pulled out an apple. "Here ye go, Butterfly. Did ye miss me, girl?"

"Does she ever answer back?" Alex asked as he walked out from around the cart.

Her heart skipped a beat at his voice. She turned around. His smile triggered her to smile back at him. "I think I can read her verra well." She turned back to her horse as she caressed its cheek, suddenly feeling warm all over despite the cool morning. "She's happy to see me. Aren't ye, girl?"

"Ye always think she's happy to see ye," Robbie said.

"And why wouldn't she be?" She cast a look at him that changed to a smile when she saw him smiling.

She went around the side of the horse to check the straps of the saddle.

"I had the tanner fix yer saddle," Robbie said. "I checked it already."

After she was satisfied with her inspection, she stood up just as Lizzy and her parents came out the door. They heard her before they saw her. She was ordering the servants around on which trunk should go in last for easy access. As soon as she saw Alex though, she stopped her ordering and walked down to them.

"Oh, Alex, ye did so good yesterday. I was so disappointed I wasna allowed to attend the banquet," she said before mumbling, "Only immediate family were allowed." She turned and gave Anna a glare before turning back to Alex.

"How is yer hand?" she asked. "I'm sure ye would have won both events had it not been for yer injury."

"It's fine, Ms. Duncan. Thank ye."

"Lizzy, please."

"Lizzy," he forced out of his mouth.

"I hope it heals soon," she continued.

"It's feeling much better. It was but a cut and will be completely healed within the week, no doubt."

"Oh, I'm so glad to hear that."

The rest of the group turned back to the castle as did Alex. Lizzy blabbed on and on as she tried to keep up with him, practically running to match his long-legged strides.

The servants finished loading their belongings into the cart and went inside. Robbie and Brodie went around the cart and horse to give one more final inspection.

"What in heavens are they doing?" Elizabeth asked her husband.

He looked out at Robbie and Brodie. "They're checking the horses and carts for the journey," he said matter-of-factly.

"I see that. Aren't they going overboard a bit? They just checked them," she babbled before adding, "I guess with all the ill luck she's been having," she said as she tipped her head toward Anna who was beside him, "everything must be double-checked."

Her uncle turned and gave Anna a casual look and shrugged his shoulders. He was never a man with verra many words, but with a wife and daughter like his, he most likely couldn't get a word in edgewise, Anna thought.

"It's that damn gemstone," Elizabeth continued, leaning into him as if it was something she dinna want anyone to hear, yet she raised her voice so Anna could. "I knew it was evil the minute she found it."

Anna put her hand on her waist where the necklace sat in a pouch under her outer skirt, suddenly uneasy about it. *Could that be why this is all happening? Is the stone bad luck?*

Her da and Willie came out of the castle. "Are we ready to go?" he asked.

"Aye," her uncle replied as he and his wife approached the horses.

"Oh, I wish we could have more time together," Lizzy blabbed on beside Alex as he walked with the group to their horses.

"Safe travels." He bowed to her and turned not even offering her help onto her horse. His eyes were opened as wide as he could open them when he turned around toward Anna and Robbie. Anna quickly turned and gave Robbie a hug to hide her laugh. She was not able to keep a straight face.

"I'll miss ye," she said.

"And I'll miss ye," he replied.

Then she turned to Mary Ellen and gave her a hug. "I'm so happy to have ye as part of the family," Anna said before turning to Willie. "And I'm sure going to miss ye, Willie," she said, holding back a tear.

"Next time I see ye, I'll be a soldier," he said.

"I hope it won't be that long before we see ye next," her da said as he pulled him in for a long hug.

Alex walked up to Anna, and as she looked into his dark piercing eyes, she immediately tingled all over.

"My lady," Alex said with a bow. "Safe journeying."

"Thank ye. And thank ye for"—she paused, not wanting to verbalize what had happened during the jester performance—"everything ye have done for me." She curtsied and quickly turned to mount her horse.

"I am indebted to ye," her da said and he pulled Alex in for a hug. "Thank ye," he whispered. Upon releasing him, he turned and mounted his horse and they started their long journey.

"I will see her home safely," Brodie said to Robbie as he mounted his horse and took up the rear.

As they started down the path, Anna could feel Alex watching her. Even if his looks dinna penetrate right through her soul, she'd have kenned he was looking because Lizzy kept turning around to wave at him. Anna was annoyed by her acts even though she kenned they were not returned. She fought the urge, herself, to turn and look at him one last time, but instead, she leaned closer to her horse's head and talked to it as she stroked its shoulder.

The connection with her horse always gave her a calmness, and she was able to put Lizzy's childish, lovesick ways from her mind…but the thought of Alex lingered. She could not help but smile when she thought of him.

*****

The first three days were long and made even longer with Lizzy asking Brodie questions about Alex until she started complaining about how uncomfortable she was. "When will we stop for the night?"

"Not yet," Anna's da called out from the front. "We have a couple of more hours of daylight left. Perhaps ye would prefer riding in the cart for a while."

"Yes, I believe that would be better," she replied. They paused long enough for her to make a theatrical slide off her horse and get in the wagon.

A couple of hours later, they stopped to break for camp.

"Can I go with ye to hunt?" Anna asked, not wanting to be left with her aunt and Lizzy any longer than need be.

Her da looked at Lizzy, then back to Anna with apologetic eyes, and said, "I ken, Anna, but we'll no have a fire to cook on or a tent to sleep in if ye and Brodie come along. Ye ken Brodie will not stay if ye go since he's been charged to bring ye home safely."

He turned and walked over to her uncle, grabbed his bow, and headed for the woods. Her uncle followed.

She spun around, frustrated. As she passed Brodie, who was unloading the canvas tent from the cart, she said, "Let's get the fire started before setting up the tent." She continued to walk away before he could say anything.

She dinna want to be around for the debate between Lizzy and her aunt on where and how to put the tent up, which was bound to happen just as it had the last two nights. She'd set up her tent on the rocky ground if it was far enough away from Lizzy's blabbering. This was the first time she'd spent this long in her presence in a verra long time, and it was wearing on her.

Anna and Brodie gathered some bigger pieces of wood from the edge of the woods and brought them back. They had the fire started before her aunt and Lizzy had their tent up, but at least she kenned where they were putting theirs up.

As Brodie gathered the canvas from the cart, Anna cleared a spot on the other side of the campfire from where Lizzy and her aunt's tent would be. They worked swiftly and with minimal conversation.

"Are ye okay, milady?" Brodie asked as they finished raising and securing the tent.

"Aye," she said as she let out a deep breath. She raised her hand to brush some stray wisps of hair from her forehead. "It has just been a long trip. Are ye going to set up a tent?" she asked.

"Nay, I'll sleep under the stars again tonight," he said as if it was his preference, but she kenned he would be sleeping in front of her and her da's tent.

Her da and uncle were not yet back. She looked around for a task to do to get out of helping her aunt and Lizzy.

"I heard water running when we were in the woods. There must be a stream nearby. Can we go and fetch some water?" she asked as she grabbed a bucket and headed toward the woods.

"Aye," he replied as he turned and caught up with her.

They made their way down a small deer path to the stream. She put her hand in the water and watched as the water flowed over it for a minute before putting her other hand in and washing them both. Grabbing the bucket, she filled it up and sat back.

Brodie quietly stood behind her as Anna sat for a few minutes in silence. She concentrated on listening to the water and watched as the sun began to set.

Finally, Brodie said it was time to go back. She took a deep breath and got up.

He grabbed the bucket and waited for her to proceed before him. She took a few steps back up the path toward the camp then paused. She could feel the falcon. She turned back toward the steam and looked around.

"What is it?" Brodie asked as he put the bucket down, turned, and drew his sword. He stood in front of her in a fighting stance and looked around.

Then she saw it and pointed. It followed the stream and landed a distance away from them. Brodie let down his guard and put his sword back.

"It's the same one," she said. "See the V on its chest?" she pointed again. "I saw it at the castle," she continued as she put her hand down. "I thought it lived there. Have ye ever seen it before?" she asked.

"I've seen a falcon or two before there, but I dinna ken if it was the same one," he replied.

"I wonder why it is here," she said.

"I dinna ken," he said, shrugging his shoulders as he picked up the bucket of water and flicked his head toward the camp for her to turn around. "They can travel a couple of hours in what it would take us a few days," he stated.

"Really?" she said still glancing at it.

"Milady," Brodie brought her back to their task.

"Aye," she said as she turned around and headed back to camp but in a better spirit than when she left.

Her da and uncle came back shortly with a couple of hares. She grabbed the game from them and started to prepare it as her uncle went to help his wife and daughter set up their tent, which was still not complete.

Anna would occasionally look up and around, though it was almost dark. Even after the food was cooked and eaten, she could still feel the presence of the falcon, though she could not see it.

As Anna was cleaning their plates with the water they had brought up, she looked up and saw it flying out of the woods through the clearing over them, as if it wanted them to see it.

Lizzy screamed and covered herself in the event it would swoop down and attack her. Anna chuckled to herself as she watched it fly away before she returned to cleaning up. She was definitely in better spirits now.

*****

In another day and a half, they came to her aunt's house, which was on the outskirts of the Duncan land.

Her da tossed a coin to a young lad that they passed and asked him to ride to the main house to announce their arrival and ask that food and a spare room be made ready.

"Aye!" the boy bowed, all smiles that his laird chose him for the honors. He ran to his house, calling to his mother before coming back out and mounting his horse.

By the time all their chests were unloaded and brought into their house, it was evening. From her aunt's house to hers, one could make it in a half hour easily if they were going fast on a well-rested horse without extra weight, but at the rate they were going it would take them close to two hours.

As they pulled away from her aunt's house, all three of them let out a deep breath. They dinna stop to eat but split the last loaf of bread they had while they were riding.

After two and a half hours, they broke out of the woods to reveal the huge stone mansion they called home. It was not as big as the MacKay's castle, but it was a grand sight. A large set of steps went from the front door down to the courtyard. The path curved around to the front steps and continued onto the stables in the distance, close to the edge of the woods. How she had missed home.

They only had the housekeeper Margret Duncan, who came into their employment five years ago after her husband died, and the stable master Donald Duncan, who was three years older than Robbie. Despite the age difference, they were inseparable until Robbie left for training some five years ago.

Donald came out, bowed to them, and grabbed the reins of the horses as they dismounted. Margaret came out the front door and ran down the steps, all smiles as she wiped her hands on her apron. Once in front of them, she made a quick curtsy.

"Welcome home! Welcome home!" she said. "I have some food for ye on the table and a spare room ready for Mister..." She paused, waiting for an introduction.

"May I present to ye, Mr. Brodie MacKay," the laird said. "This is Margaret, our housekeeper."

"It's a pleasure to meet ye, Margaret," Brodie said with a brief bow.

Margaret turned to Anna and said, "I have water heating up for a bath for ye."

"Oh, a bath sounds heavenly!" Anna declared.

"Go along then," her da said before turning to Margaret. "We will be in once the cart is unloaded."

Anna put some food on a plate and picked at it as she walked up the stairs and down the hallway to her room. Margaret was finishing filling the tub as Anna entered her room.

"Will there be anything else ye need?" she asked.

"No, Margaret. This is fine."

She put a piece of meat in her mouth as Margaret left and closed the door. Stepping toward the tub, she disrobed and slipped into the warm water.

"Aah," she said out loud. "This is divine."

She closed her eyes and took in the scent of roses. She smiled. Margaret had put rose oil into the water, just how she liked it.

She lingered a bit before washing off the dust of their journey and changed into a clean nightgown before crawling into bed. She fell asleep as soon as her head hit the pillow.

CHAPTER

*S*he was being held tightly from behind, a knife at her throat.
"Tell me where it is, or I'll kill her," the man holding her
said to another man who stopped struggling at his words.

*She continued to struggle to free herself from the man's grip.
She grabbed his arm, trying to pull the knife away from her.*

*A movement from the edge of the woods caught his attention.
At that moment, she kicked her heel into his shin, pulling the
knife away as the man being held broke free, throwing himself
at her attacker.*

"Run!" he yelled.

*She looked back for a second. She dinna want to leave him.
He was everything to her. He looked up at her, so full of love for
her and a plea for her to run as the two men forced him down.*

She turned and ran.

*****

Anna jerked out of her dream. Her breathing was heavy and
her heart was racing, but there was another feeling…a yearning for…for him. There was something about him, something familiar. Was it his eyes or perhaps the way he looked
at her? She had felt such fear leaving him as if it had sealed
his fate.

She pondered her dream for a bit more before pulling the
covers back and getting up to splash water on her face. It was
early yet, but she could hear the birds chirping. She quickly
dressed and went down to the kitchen to help Margaret.

"It is so nice to have ye back," Margaret said.

"It's nice to be back," she replied.

"How was the wedding?" she asked.

"The wedding was beautiful," she replied. "Robbie and Mary Ellen made a bonny couple," she said with a smile.

"And the games, did ye have fun?"

Anna paused, pulling some plates down, not sure how much detail to give. "Robbie took second in one event, and Willie took fourth," she replied. "Lord Reay was so impressed with Willie that he asked for him to train under him."

"Oh, how exciting."

"Aye," Anna replied somberly, "but I'm going to miss him."

"Aye," Margaret replied, "It'll sure be quiet around here without him."

Brodie came down shortly after. "I need to be on my way, milady," he said.

"Will ye not stay to break yer fast?" she asked him. "'Tis almost ready. I will wrap up some food for yer trip as well."

"Aye," he said. "Thank ye. I will go to the stable and ask Donald to prepare my steed."

They had a quick meal of oats and honey with biscuits. As promised, Anna had some cheese, bread, and smoked meat wrapped up for Brodie. She gave it to him as they bid him farewell.

*****

The days following were spent getting resettled. Anna helped Margaret wash all the clothes from the long journey. Her da was still nervous about Anna being alone, so either he or

Donald would escort her whenever she would go for a ride in the woods or down by the stream.

The lack of time alone, more so alone with her horse, was hard for her since Butterfly was her confidant. She hadn't been alone with her horse since before the games. When she rode Butterfly, she always felt that Butterfly was connected to her feelings; she wanted to tell her about all that had happened, how scared she had been over the attempts on her life, the feeling she had when she thought of Alex, and the intriguing falcon she had seen.

It was nearly a week since they returned when she took down a deer in the clearing while hunting with her da. "Nice one!" her da called out as he walked out to the clearing.

As Anna slid off her horse, she felt the peacefulness she did when the falcon was around. She had not seen it since that evening they had camped on the road with Brodie, but she kenned it was there.

Once on the ground, she paused as she looked up at the trees lining the edge of the woods. Then she saw it. She opened her mouth and started to point to tell her da but decided against it since it may also remind him of the other incidences of their trip. She smiled up at it before turning to her horse, stroking it, and smiled in a way one would to a best friend after a great secret was shared. Satisfied with her silent connection with her horse, she turned and walked toward her kill.

With the attacks behind them by about a month, she was slowly gaining bits of time outside alone, short as they may be. She would often go to the paddock when the horses were grazing while Donald cleaned the stalls or did other chores.

It allowed for her to be in the sight of others but far enough away that she could quietly talk to her Butterfly.

She still had occasional nightmares but dinna tell her da for fear she'd be escorted around for the rest of her days.

In the dreams, she always seemed to be running from someone, always waking up out of breath and her heart racing. But once, the one man…*him*, whoever *he* was…was running with her. Though he was familiar, she dinna ken him, yet in her dreams, she did. In the dream that they were running together, they were hiding, but she dinna feel as if they were being chased or threatened, per se. They were happy and carefree. Her heart fluttered as she realized they were hiding to steal a few kisses, away from prying eyes.

A crow screeched outside her window, waking her from that one.

Every few days, she would spot the falcon, usually in the evening. Her heart would flutter when she spotted it, but she never said anything. She wanted to just watch it for a while but dinna want to call attention to it.

One particular afternoon, her da went to tend to business with a drunken tenant. Anna offered to go help Donald clear a tree that had fallen at the edge of the woods. It was not unusual for her to be doing heavy work with her da, so he agreed.

The tree was big and would take several hours to clear. Donald cut the logs and carried the heavier ones over to the cart. He would split them later. Anna dragged the branches away and loaded up smaller logs onto the cart.

At midday, they stopped their work to eat some food that Anna had packed. While eating, she sensed the falcon again.

She would occasionally look up to locate it but did not find it.

Immediately after eating, Donald got back up to continue his work.

"I'll walk down to the stream to get some more water," she said.

"Aye," he said as she picked up the bucket. It wasna far. He'd be able to hear her if she called out for him.

She made her way down the path, enjoying the peacefulness of the woods. The path to the stream was steep but well-worn from her and her horse going down it so often. Tree roots ran across the path, making it easy to misstep if one was not careful, but Anna had walked down it so many times that avoiding the obstacles along it was instinctive.

The leaves had begun to change colors. The fiery red leaves mixed with the yellow and orange ones were a beautiful contrast against the evergreens.

Once at the stream, she filled the bucket and looked up as she straightened. She took a deep breath of the scent that only comes with autumn. Just then, she saw the falcon flying above the stream before perching across the water, not far from her. It was close enough that she could see the individual feathers on its wings.

"I was wondering if ye'd follow me," she said to it.

It blinked in response.

"Ye are a long way from home," she said. The falcon continued to stare at her. She placed the bucket down and sat on the ground.

"I dinna ken why, but I always ken when ye are near," she said to it as she studied it. It was majestic, perched there. The top of its chest was white while the lower part and its legs were almost striped, dark gray, and white, all except for the gray "V" mark upon its chest.

Its head and feathers on its back were dark gray with an almost bluish tint, as was the tip of its beak. The rest of the beak was yellow, which matched the outlines of its eyes and its massive talons.

"I feel ya, before I ever see ya." She smiled up at it. "It's...a peaceful feeling."

It tilted its head as if it understood her.

The ax stopped, and she heard a log being thrown into the cart, bringing her back to her task at hand. She immediately got up and said to the bird, "I best be going before Donald comes after me for taking too long. He'll never let me out of his sight again if not."

She picked up her bucket and left.

CHAPTER

A s the cold weather started to approach, there were a lot of preparations that needed to be done before winter. For the following month, her da hired tenants for harvesting the fields and stocking up on wood as he did every year.

There was a constant flow of workers, allowing her to sneak down to the stream with Butterfly more often. On one such early afternoon, she made her way down there, slid off her horse, and led it to the water. She took a deep breath, admiring the scenery around her as she stroked the horse.

The stream had partially frozen overnight but had mostly thawed. There were still some places that the ice had not yet completely melted. In a few more weeks, it would be completely frozen over until spring.

She picked up some stones and started skipping them across the water. She turned to Butterfly and said, "I wonder how Willie is doing." The horse merely looked up at her for a split second before turning back to eating some greenery.

She turned back to her stone throwing. "Ha. Seven skips, that one." The horse looked up once again and then continued on her patch of grass. She threw a couple of more and stopped mid throw. It was here. The falcon. She looked upstream and waited. It always came that way, and this time was no different.

It perched across the stream on the same branch it always did. She finished her toss with another seven skips.

"I see ye got away early today as well," she said as she smiled at it. "Butterfly and I sneaked away. We'd been planning it for days," she continued proudly. She finished tossing the two remaining stones in her hand and sat down.

"I had a bad dream last night," she said as she looked at the falcon and shook her head. It tipped its head as it looked at her. She took a deep breath and looked down at the water.

"I was sleeping and woke to smoke in my room. I couldna breathe and was coughing." She briefly looked up at the falcon.

"I could hear my parents' cries and yells in the room beside mine and ken they were trapped." She paused, picked up a stick, and started making marks in the bank.

She took a deep breath and continued talking as she drew with her stick, "I got up to make my way out to help, and then I heard a loud crash. The whole house shook. The cries immediately stopped, and I ken the roof had fallen on them."

She paused her talking and ceased her drawing to look back up at the falcon to see if it was still "listening." It was still looking directly at her with big eyes.

"I just lay back down on the bed." She paused as her shoulders slouched. "I dinna care to escape," she said to it, then quietly added, "I dinna want to live."

She shook her head as if to rid herself of the despair that ripped through her. She continued to draw with her stick for a bit longer as she pondered the meaning of her dream. Taking another deep breath, she looked back up at the falcon and said, "I ken it was more than just losing my parents." She paused. "There was already something missing. Someone, perhaps. Someone much more important to me."

She dropped the stick, erased her scribbles with her foot, and started looking for another good skipping stone. She felt better now that she told the falcon her dream. She really had no one to tell, and with all the nightmares she had been having, it felt good to tell without the fear of someone overreacting.

Picking up a couple more stones, she tossed one from a sitting position.

"Seven, again," she said with a smile. She could hear her da calling from the edge of the woods.

"Anna!"

"Aye. I'm coming," she called back immediately, dropping the remaining stones in her hand as she got up and grabbed Butterfly's reins. She looked back up to the falcon with a smile and said, "I guess I've been found." She mounted the horse and rode up the path to the clearing.

*****

"I need to go," he said. "Uncle Ian sent word that Douglas Gordon is drunk again. I should send him back to the Gordons."

"But then poor Sarah and her tot would be the outsider with no one to care what he does to her," she replied.

"I wouldna send her too," he quickly replied. "Margaret just got back from the village. Go see if she needs any help please."

"Aye."

*****

After a couple of weeks, most of the winter preparations were made, and the help was gone. Anna and her da walked back from gathering eggs one morning. It had been a cold night, and though the sun was shining and had melted the frost on the ground, the warmth of their breath could be seen as they talked.

They had ceased their talking as they heard a rider approaching at a fast speed. Her uncle raced in.

"It's Douglas again. He must have been out all night and came in drunker than hell this morning. I could hear him yelling and slamming things around, the bairn screaming."

"Aye." He turned to Anna handing her his basket of eggs. "Have Margaret prepare a room for Sarah and the bairn."

"Aye."

*****

Donald had seen Ian galloping in so he had the laird's horse saddled and ready to go for him when he got to the barn.

By the time they made it to Douglas's house, Sarah's cheek was bruised, and her lip was bleeding.

"Douglas." The laird slowly moved between the two of them, his arm out toward Sarah, and his other hand on the hilt of his sword ready to draw. Ian stood in the doorway as a backup.

"She's been cheating on me!" Douglas yelled, pointing to her. "She's a whore!"

"I swear." She looked to the laird then back to her husband. "I swear I've been with no one. He's drunk!"

"I saw him sneaking around the house when I came home."

"No one was here but me and the bairn."

"Who?" the laird asked him. "Who did ye see?"

"It was a MacDonald," he spat, not taking his eyes off her.

The laird slowly moved more in front of her. "Why would a MacDonald be way out here?"

"Because he's sleeping with her!" He pointed to his wife.

"I swear I wasna—" she was cut off by an explosion in the fireplace right behind where she was standing. The room was immediately engulfed in flames, and she went flying toward Douglas, knocking the laird off-balance as their shoulders collided as she flew by.

Douglas caught his wife and threw her against the wall where she slid down, lifeless.

The babe was screaming in the corner of the room.

The laird turned to his brother-in-law. "Ian, the bairn!" he called as he got up, drawing his sword.

Douglas's eyes grew big and looked in the direction of the crying. He edged his way to get to the bairn before Ian did, throwing anything he could grab at the laird.

Dodging the throws, the laird moved with him. Ian grabbed the bairn and ran for the door. As Douglas leaped to grab Ian, the laird lunged with his sword, driving it through the man's chest.

Ian handed the bairn to one of the bystanders watching and ran back into the house as the laird was pulling his sword out of Douglas's body lying on the floor. From out of the smoke, Ian could see someone coming up behind the laird with sword raised.

"No!" Ian yelled as the sword came down on the back shoulder of his brother-in-law. Ian caught the laird as he dropped, the attacker now yelling as his kilt caught on fire. Ian kicked the man back into the room where he was immediately engulfed in flames.

With his laird still in his embrace, he walked him out of the house. Both men coughing and gasping for air. Ian sat his laird down and started taking off his own shirt.

"Go around back and make sure no one comes out," he said to one of the men gathered outside.

Ian began to tie his shirt around his laird's shoulder and body, trying to stop the bleeding.

The crowd was speechless. Most stood with mouths opened, a couple of women had their hands to their cheeks, and a couple of more had tears streaming down their faces as they watched Ian tend to their laird. One man had taken off his shirt as well and handed it to Ian.

"Who was it?" the laird asked, barely able to speak.

"Dinna speak now," Ian said.

"Who?" he ordered, a little louder.

Ian took a deep breath and looked him straight in the eyes as he tightened his makeshift tourniquet and replied quietly, "A MacDonald,"

"Get me on my horse," the laird ordered.

"Ye canna ride," Ian started to say.

"Get me on!" he ordered. He wouldna be carried out in front of his subjects. Ian helped him up onto his horse before getting on his own steed.

"Get the physician to the main house," Ian ordered to someone in the crowd.

After they were out of sight, the laird started to slouch more and more. Ian moved his steed next to the laird's and jumped on behind him. He pulled his brother-in-law up against his chest to hold him up as well as apply more pressure to his wound.

*****

An hour had not yet gone by when Donald came running into the house. "Milady! Milady!" he called out.

An immediate sense of foreboding came over Anna as she heard him yelling for her. She ran out of the spare room she was preparing and ran down the hall to the top of the stairs.

"What is it, Donald?"

"There's a fire on the north side!"

She rushed down the stairs and out the front door to see black smoke pouring up in the distance. "That's the direction of Douglas Gordon's house," she declared. "Get our horses."

They ran to the stable. His horse was already saddled, so he quickly put hers on as she put the bridle on. They mounted their horses and raced toward the smoke. A sick feeling came from the pit of her stomach as they rode. They were only five minutes out when they saw her da and uncle coming toward them, her uncle's steed following behind.

"What happened?" she asked, looking at her da's slouched body. Her words were choppy from her tightened chest.

"He's hurt," he yelled. "I've sent for the physician."

"Douglas?" she asked, now riding beside him.

"Nay," he said.

"Then who?" she demanded as she looked at him with dread in her eyes.

"It was a MacDonald," he replied.

"A MacDonald?"

He nodded that she heard him correctly. The MacDonald's had a reputation of being a mean-spirited clan who had made enemies with several clans in the Highlands, but their land was nowhere near the Duncan land. *Why would they be here?* she thought.

"Where are they?" she asked.

"I only saw one," he replied. "He died in the fire. May he rot in hell!" He turned and spit.

"Donald, ride ahead and tell Margaret to prepare hot water and fresh bandages," she ordered.

Donald sped off to do her bidding. They rode in silence the rest of the way, a thousand questions going through her mind.

A MacDonald? Why? Is this somehow connected to the attempts on my life? She shook her head to rid herself of her thoughts. First things first, she had to tend to her da.

When they arrived at the house, Ian carried his laird up to his room. The makeshift bandages he put on were completely covered in blood.

"Donald, ye need to go to the MacKay castle and tell Robbie," she ordered. "Tell Lord Reay."

"Aye, milady."

"Do not stop for anything but to rest briefly." She turned to Margaret. "Get him some bread and smoked meat to eat for the journey."

"Right away, milady," she said, and they both left the room.

"Da, Da. Can ye hear me?" she said, cupping his cheek. He opened his eyes, barely, but enough. "Stay with me, Da," she cried as he closed his eyes again.

She turned to her uncle. "A MacDonald? Ye are sure? Ye saw him?"

"Aye," he said. "Douglas was yelling that he saw one snooping around when he came home all drunk. He accused Sarah of cheating on him," he paused. Anna stared at him, trying to comprehend it all.

"There was an explosion that knocked Sarah out. Yer dad ordered me to grab the bairn, so I did and took him outside. When I came back in, yer da was pulling his sword from Douglas." Her uncle ran his fingers through his hair before continuing.

"Behind him, I saw the MacDonald with his sword raised over yer father… I tried to warn him," he said, shaking his head.

Ian looked down at the laird. "He fell right into my arms," he said as he stretched out his arms, still shaking his head.

She stared at him, her eyes welling up. "And the MacDonald?"

"His clothes were already on fire. I kicked him into the flames," he said. "Damn him to hell!" he spat.

"Aye," she whispered her agreement.

They heard horses approaching, and they both looked at each other. Her heart stopped for a second. Ian went to the window. "It's the physician and his assistant," he said.

She let out her breath.

"I'm going back to investigate the fire and see if anyone else around there saw this MacDonald," her uncle said.

"Aye," she said. "Before ye do, Uncle, send me some men to stay here. One for the stable and one for the house. Perhaps a couple more who perhaps may have had some soldiering experience."

"Aye." He nodded. He took one more good look at his brother-in-law. As the physician came into the room, he turned and departed.

Her da's bleeding had stopped, thanks to her uncle's quick thinking, but when the bandages were pulled off to clean the wounds, it started again.

Outraged and helpless, all Anna could do was watch as the physician worked quickly cleaning and bandaging him up.

"Will he be all right?" she asked as she prayed.

"I dinna ken," he said. "I have done all I can for now. Yer uncle did a good job of stopping the bleeding. His quick thinking may have saved his life."

It wasna long before the men she had sent for came.

"Milady, the men are here," Margaret said. "What would ye have me do with them?"

"How many are there?"

"Four, milady."

"Put one of them in the stables to tend to the horses. I want two of them guarding the house at all times. They will rotate out, day and night."

"Aye, milady," she curtsied as she left the room.

*****

Her uncle returned later in the evening. "How is he?" he asked.

"The physician said he is alive because of yer quick action," she said, "but he is very weak."

"Has he woken at all?"

"Nay, not since we first brought him here." She patted her da's hand. "Did ye find out anything more?"

"Nay." He shook his head. "Nobody saw anything. I will be taking James and two others with me to see what I can find out about this MacDonald," her uncle said. "He had to have come through neighboring lands. Since our houses are close to the north border, he most likely came from the north. I will start there."

"Aye," she said as she turned back to her da.

CHAPTER

*S*he was being held tightly from behind, a knife at her throat.
"Tell me where it is, or I'll kill her." The man holding
her said to another man who stopped struggling to get free of his
captor at his words.

She continued to struggle to free herself from his grip. She
grabbed his arm, trying to pull the knife from her neck.

A movement from the edge of the woods caught his attention.
At that moment, she kicked her heel into his shin, pulling the
knife away as the man being held broke free, throwing himself
at her attacker.

"Run!" he yelled.

She looked back for a second. She dinna want to leave him.
He was everything to her. He looked up at her, so full of love for
her and a plea for her to run as the two men forced him down.

She turned and ran.

At one point, she looked back just as the man who had held
her pierced her beloved's heart with his sword.

He was a MacDonald.

*****

She jerked awake, her heart pounding as tears streamed down
her face. *A MacDonald!* The dream had been so real. *Could
my dream somehow be related to my da's attacks?*

She looked around. She had fallen asleep in the chair,
leaning over with her head on the edge of the bed and her
da's hand in hers.

She wiped her eyes and put her hand on her da's forehead. He was fevered. Pouring water into the basin, she placed a cloth in it and wrung it out before placing it on his forehead and then down his cheek.

"Da. Da, do ye hear me?" she asked as she worked at cooling him down. They'd never had any dealings with the MacDonalds, good or bad. She continued with the cool clothes as she tried to somehow relate her dreams to their present situation.

She heard horses and a cart pulling up midmorning. It stopped in front of the house, and she could hear her aunt barking out commands.

Margaret knocked and entered the room. "Yer aunt and Lizzy are here, milady," she announced.

"Aye," Anna replied with a bit of annoyance. "I heard them."

"She brought four chests of clothes," Margaret blurted. "She said she has come to help, but I think they're moving in!"

Anna put her elbow on the arm of the chair and her forehead in her hand. She just sat there for a minute without speaking.

"Milady," Margaret said. "What would ye have me do with them?"

"Put them in the east hall," she replied with a wave of her hand.

"Aye," Margaret said.

This is the last thing I need right now, she thought. The laird's quarters included a joining room for the lady of the house. A lot of her mother's things were still there; some were heirlooms passed down on her mother's side.

Anna got up and went to her mother's room. She looked around, taking note of the valuables. She had not been in this room for a long time. How she wished her mother was here now.

She went to the door that led to the hallway and barred it. Anna's mother was the oldest of them, so she had inherited her mother's pearls and wedding rings that were handed down two generations. Anna dinna trust her aunt not to be snooping around looking for them or anything else that may fancy her. She closed the door joining the two rooms as she went back to her da's room and sat back down on the chair.

Not long after, a knock came on the door, and Margaret entered with tea and food to break her fast.

"Milady," she said as she set the food on the table, "yer aunt would like to see yer father."

"He's not up for visitors!" she snapped.

"Aye, but she's almost at the top of the stairs. I tried to tell her."

"She's *not* to be in this room alone." Anna looked intently at her as she whispered to her.

"Aye, milady."

Margaret moved out into the hall as her aunt and Lizzy approached.

"Oh, look at him." Her aunt walked to the edge of the bed with both of her hands on her cheeks in a dramatic pose as if she had practiced it all morning. She turned to look at Anna. "It was awful. There was an explosion, then the fire—" her aunt started.

"I've been informed of that already," she cut her off in midsentence.

"Of course, ye have. Ye certainly don't want to be reminded of it again." She looked at Anna's father and asked, "How is he doing?"

"Feverish," she replied. "As to be expected," she added as an afterthought. "He comes in and out of consciousness."

"Well, we've come to help run things as ye are busy tending to yer father. It is such a big place and with all these men here coming and going."

"I've sent for Robbie," she replied. "He should be here in a week's time."

"Aye," she said. "Well, we'll get busy putting our things away before heading downstairs for some lunch." Her aunt looked at Margaret to make sure she understood she would be expecting her midday meal soon.

"Aye, milady," Margaret said as they left. She followed behind them.

*****

The physician stopped in shortly after Anna's aunt did. He and Anna rolled her da over on his side so he could check the wound and apply fresh bandages. He groaned as they gently rolled him back over.

"It looks better today than yesterday," the physician said.

"Da," Anna said to him, putting a cool rag on his forehead. He slowly opened his eyes a wee bit.

The physician pulled out a bottle of laudanum. "Drink this, me laird," he placed it on his lips and tipped it. "Just a bit… This will ease yer pain."

He handed the rest of the bottle to Anna. "Ye may give him some every few hours if he needs it."

"Aye," she said as she took the bottle from him.

"Continue with cool rags on his head until his fever comes down." Anna nodded. "And see if ye can get him to sip some broth, even if just a little bit. It will help keep his strength up."

He picked up his bag to leave before turning back around. "I'll be back in the morn."

"Thank ye," she said as he left.

*****

Anna spent the entire day caring for her da. It gave her much time to contemplate the situation.

Was his attack somehow related to mine? Why does someone want us dead? A MacDonald at that… My dream had a MacDonald in it. Was that the one that Uncle Ian killed? Her thoughts kept going over the same questions in her head, over and over.

Margaret stopped by before turning in for the night. "Milady, ye must eat something. Ye havna touched a bite of what I brought ye."

Anna looked at the untouched food and shrugged her shoulders. "I have not been hungry," Anna declared.

"Yer aunt and cousin have made themselves quite comfortable here. I had seen her looking like she was going to go down the west hall. I was able to distract her, but short of putting up a guard there, I do believe she will venture there sooner or later," she stated.

"Aye," Anna replied as she took a deep breath and sat back in her chair. "Perhaps I should get any valuable things out of my room," Anna said. "Would ye stay here a few minutes?"

"Aye, milady."

Anna went to her room and set her candlestick on her dresser, which was next to the window. She looked out to the stable. There was a small glow from the lantern the stable boy kept. *I don't think I have ever gone a whole day at home without visiting Butterfly*, she thought as she felt a tug of guilt over top of her concern for her da.

She looked out across the darkening sky in hopes of spotting the falcon. She kenned it was not there. She felt so alone.

Turning her attention to her task at hand, she opened the small wooden box that was beside her candlestick on the dresser. On top of all the items she had in it was the lapis lazuli gem necklace. She picked it up by the ribbon and let the stone spin in front of her eyes. She looked at it, remembering what Alex said about it. The brief thought of Alex gave warmth to her heart.

The stone of knowledge, he had called it. Knowledge of what? The future, the past? Would it be able to let me see who really did this to my father?

She put it in a sachet with a few other items and secured it under her outer skirt. She grabbed another dress and walked back to her da's room.

"Thank ye, Margaret," she said as she entered the room.

"Do ye need anything else milady?"

"No, Margaret. Have a good night."

Margaret looked at Anna. "Good night, milady."

CHAPTER

*S*he couldn't breathe. The room filled with smoke. There was screaming in the other room. She had to get to them. She opened the door, but the hallway was engulfed in flames. She closed the door. As she looked around, she could hear them screaming. She knew it was her parents.

Then she heard it, the crash. The house shook, and she knew the roof had collapsed. The screaming immediately stopped. The room was completely filled with smoke. She looked toward the window. She could get something and break the window and try to escape. But what for? She had nothing left. She kenned it was more than just losing her parents in the other room. There was something much more.

She coughed, gasping for air. She lay back down on the bed and looked toward the window. She should leave. But then it came to her. He was gone. The MacDonald had killed him; now with her parents gone too, there was nothing more left for her here. She closed her eyes as tears streamed down her face. This was it. She took in a deep breath, inhaling the thick smoke.

*****

She woke, gasping for air, tears streaming down her face. She ached…deep within her. The grief was so overwhelming. What was this dream about? It was so more real than a dream, more like a memory. It wasna the past. Could it be the future? She kenned it was her parents in the other room, but that could not be true if it was the future because her mother died in childbirth years ago.

And *him*…she kenned he was the same man in the other dream. She'd never seen him before other than in her dream, yet she kenned him. But that feeling…

Her da moaned, bringing her back to reality.

"Da," she said as she felt his head. He was still hot. "Da, can ye hear me?"

He slowly turned his head toward her and opened his eyes halfway.

"Can ye drink some water?" she asked as she propped his head up and held the cup to his mouth. He took a sip. She waited to give him more.

"How about some laudanum for the pain?" She set the cup of water down and picked up the bottle to give him a sip. "Just a wee bit."

*****

The next two days were much of the same as the first. She did not venture out of her da's room unless necessary. Most of the food that was brought up was taken away untouched. She could often hear her aunt ordering people around, which made her want to stay secluded even more.

Often, she would look out the window, hoping to see the falcon or perhaps Butterfly. Just a glimpse of one of them would ease her pain just a bit. She longed to talk to someone about her fears. Margaret was the only person she had had contact with. It had been instilled in her at a young age to not divulge her feeling with servants.

Her thoughts continued to recap the attacks on both her and her father. The same questions echoed in her head over and over. *Was my attack related to my da's? Why would the MacDonalds want them dead? Were her dreams related to the attacks?*

By the third day, his fever broke. He ate a half cup of broth but slept the whole day.

Feeling much better about his condition, Anna decided a bit of fresh air would do her good, so she ordered Margaret to watch over her da as she ventured out.

She left through the servant's quarters to avoid running into her aunt and went to the stables to see Butterfly early that morning. As she walked across the field, her heart felt lighter. Her da was on the mend. The closer she got to the barn, the better she felt. She was excited to take Butterfly for a run and release all the thoughts that had filled her head these past few days.

Reaching the stable, she noticed that the fill-in stable boy was not in the barn. She looked around, but as he was nowhere to be found, she put the bridle on Butterfly and led her out of the stall to saddle her up. As soon as the horse started to move, Anna could tell she was injured. She seemed to be favoring one side.

"What's the matter, girl?" Anna asked as she bent to look at her left leg that was warm and swollen. "What in the world!" She looked around. *Where the devil is the man who is supposed to be watching the stalls?*

She put Butterfly back in the stall, removed the bridle, and stormed out of the barn in search of him. As soon as she left the barn, she saw him walking to the stable with a bucket of oats.

"Galvin!" she called. "My horse's left leg is swollen!"

"Aye, milady. I came back from the privy yesterday afternoon and saw she was gone. I thought ye had taken her for a ride. An hour later, Lizzy came back with her. That's when I saw her limping."

"What!" she yelled. She could feel the heat rise to her face. Any bit of serenity she had begun to feel went right out of her.

"Milady, I swear to ye, I wouldna have allowed it had I been there."

She opened her mouth to speak then thought better of it and closed it again. She would speak with Lizzy herself. "Ye will put some cold water on her leg regularly," she said. She picked up a bucket and said, "I'll go down to the stream and get some fresh water. I'll be back in an hour." She turned and headed toward the path to the stream.

"Aye, milady. I truly am sorry," Galvin said.

She walked across the field at a fast pace to rid herself of her frustration before getting to the stream. She went down the path through the woods and sat down by the edge of the stream. She had been looking forward to coming out here to this peaceful place, and now she was as mad as a wild boar. She dinna want to be mad here. This was her sanctuary. She closed her eyes and took some deep breaths, listening to the sound of the flowing water. *That's better*, she thought. She took a couple of deeper breaths before opening her eyes.

She opened her eyes. There was a squirrel with a nut in his mouth running up a tree. She could hear the birds chirping to each other, and there were little fish swimming in the stream. That's more like it.

She sat there for a little bit longer, then grabbed the bucket and filled it. As she stood up, she sensed something downstream and felt a tug at her stomach. Setting the bucket down, she cautiously walked downstream.

She knew the woods like the back of her hand since she had played in it as a child and hunted as a young woman. She walked to where the stream dropped off considerably, creating a waterfall, perhaps the size of a grown man.

To get downstream without having to climb, she went deeper into the woods. Just as she cut back toward the stream, she saw something on the ground.

She went over and kicked it, loosening it from the ground. It was a leather bag, one that a man would carry. She picked it up, inspecting it before looking at the ground. It looked like there may have been a struggle there.

She walked a little farther into the woods, then she could smell it. Something was definitely dead.

She heard a couple of crows squawking as if warning each other of her presence. As she moved toward them, she could see them on something. Her hand instinctively grabbed the end of her shawl and brought it to her face, both to cover her silent exclamation and to hide the odor.

"Shoo, shoo!" she said, waving her other hand about. They flew off what appeared to be a body.

The body was facedown, and the flesh had been eaten where it was exposed. Using her foot, she turned him over and immediately jumped back. "Oh!" It was Donald. Looking at him, she slowly backed away, her heart pounding so hard that her chest hurt.

Robbie never got my message. I have to get back, she thought, but she could not move. She just stood there, frozen. A crow ventured back to the newly exposed flesh, then another.

Finally, she snapped out of it and started to turn and run, but she did not look where she was going. She misstepped, twisting her ankle on something, and rolled down the hill, hitting trees and rocks.

She immediately got up, but now she was dizzy and disoriented, partly from the shock and partly from rolling down the hill. Her head hurt where she had bumped it, and her arm was bleeding. A nice gash was taken out of her left forearm from a broken branch she had fallen into, and her right foot was throbbing.

Her shawl was now caught up in the brush. She grabbed it and started limping toward the stream, at least she hoped it was toward the stream.

She walked for a bit. She should have gotten to the stream by now. Her mind was so jumbled she couldn't think straight. *I need to calm down. Breathe, just breathe.*

Stopping, she closed her eyes and took a few deep breaths as she listened. *Okay, now I can hear the water.* Readjusting her direction, she continued walking until she found it. Once there, her panic had subsided, but her adrenaline persisted.

She sat down and untied the scarf around her neck and put it in the cold water to clean her arm off. She looked upstream. She really had gone a good distance downstream. She called out for help but kenned they would never hear her this far away, even if they were at the stream where she left the bucket.

Her ankle pained her. She took off her boot and dipped her right foot in the cold water. She sat like that until she couldn't take it anymore. She dried her foot with her shawl and put the boot back on.

Okay, I have to get back up, at least to where I am in yelling distance, she thought.

As she rose, she heard, "Well, well. Look at what we have here." She immediately turned around and started to back away. There were two men…in MacDonald tartans.

Her panic set in again. She yelled as she turned to run, but her ankle slowed her down. The one man with the dark hair grabbed her and threw her to the ground.

"No!" she yelled. He slapped her as he grabbed the front of her dress and yanked down tearing it. He grabbed her breast as she screamed. He slapped her again. "Ye bitch!"

"Kendrick! We dinna have time for this! He's expecting us," the other man said. "I'll no be getting a flogging because yer need to relieve yerself."

"Ack. Ye are always taking the fun out of everything." Kendrick stopped his attack, stood up, and grabbed Anna by the hair to get her up.

"Go get the horses," Kendrick said. "We'll take her with us a ways and leave her somewhere where we can come back and finish with her," he said. She yelled as she struggled. "Gag this bitch first!" he ordered as he grabbed her from behind, pulling her arms back.

Once gagged, she continued to struggle. He dragged her to his horse. "Give me some rope so I can bind her hands."

"I ain't got no rope. Ye used up the last of me rope, remember?" the other man spat.

"Ack!" he threw her on the ground and pulled out his knife. She struggled to get away. He grabbed the bottom of her skirt, putting his blade through the material before using his hands to rip the rest. She scrambled to get away, but he grabbed her leg and pulled her back.

He threw the strips of material he had cut to his partner. "Now bind her."

After he tied her arms and legs, Kendrick threw her upon the horse, belly down, and mounted behind her. The impact of being thrown onto the hard leather saddle felt like being hit in the stomach by someone swinging a log. She bit into the gag and clenched her hands into fists as tears welled up.

Her thoughts kept bouncing between her da and the body she found. *Robbie never received my message. What's going to happen to me? What's going to happen to my da?* Her mind kept reeling with all the scenarios she could come up with.

She tried to untie her bindings as her mind raced with thoughts of her da. The pulling on her bindings just made her wrists sore and red. Her head was throbbing from the pressure of it dangling, and it was getting hard to breathe.

They rode into the woods deeper and deeper for what seemed like an hour or two.

Finally, they stopped. "We'll leave her here and come back for her when we're done," Kendrick said to the other man. Without getting off his horse, he grabbed her by the back of her dress and shoved her toward the ground so she slid off the horse. Her tied feet hit the ground, and her knees buckled. She fell, hitting her head. A moan escaped but was muffled by the gag.

"We canna leave her like that," the second man said, waving a hand toward her. "What if she unties herself or scoots away?"

Kendrick looked down at her thoughtfully. "Aye," he said. "We would not want her running off before we have our fun," Kendrick dismounted his horse.

She frantically looked around. They were in somewhat of a clearing that had several large rocks. One could easily get a good view of the layout of the land if standing on one of them as they were already on high ground. Even if she could see where she was, she could not make a run for it; the most she could do was crawl by wiggling, like a caterpillar.

He cut some more strips of cloth from the bottom of her skirt and dragged her around a large bolder and toward the tree line. "Here's a good spot for ye, ma'am. Ye'll have a good view, and ye can see me coming back," Kendrick said. "Now ye'll have to wait a couple of hours as I have some verra important business to tend to first," he said as he slammed her against a tree. He raised her arms to a branch, tying them above her head before securing her legs to the trunk.

She squirmed and twisted her hips, trying to break free. He grinned at her attempt before ripping off another piece of material and putting it around her waist, preventing her from moving at all.

He continued smiling as he ripped her bodice the rest of the way, exposing her right breast completely. He grabbed it hard and bent down to suck on it. She thrashed her head and yanked at her arms, trying to break free. He pulled away, laughing, as he pushed against her ramming his body against her. The bark of the tree jabbed into her back through her clothing as he pushed against her. He watched her face as he did it again, smirking as he brought his head close to hers. She turned her face away, but he grabbed it and turned it back so she could see him. Just inches away from her face, she could smell his pungent breath.

"When we come back, I'll do things to ye that ye've only heard about." Then he let go of her face and turned around, mounted his horse, and started down the mountain.

She immediately tried moving her arms back and forth, trying to rip the rags on the bark while keeping an eye on where they were going. The cliff was rocky, and they moved at a very slow pace. Every so often, Kendrick would turn in his saddle and smile up at her.

I've got to get out of here, she thought.

She had an hour or two, he said. Certainly, she could break loose by then. Her head was throbbing still from hanging upside down for so long, and now she was dizzy. She dinna want to close her eyes until they were completely out of sight so she would ken which way not to go when she did escape.

She continued to move her arms as much as she could, but her arms were starting to hurt. She stopped and just watched them as they made their way down the hill, becoming smaller and smaller. When they got to the bottom, they went to the base of another cliff, going around it before disappearing.

She closed her eyes, and the tears that had been building up poured out of her. *How did this happen?* She felt angry as she thought that this had happened because Lizzy had injured Butterfly. She opened her eyes. *Certainly, someone must have realized I was missing by now.*

She looked over the valley to the mountains beyond. She could not identify where she was. At another time, she would've looked out at the same view in awe; now she was tied to a tree with her dress ripped open and one of her breasts hanging out. Though the sun was out, it was cold as the wind howled. She shivered as she closed her eyes again and cried some more.

She must have dozed off because when she opened her eyes, the sun had definitely shifted in the sky. She looked in the direction of where the two men had disappeared. No sign of them. That was good.

Her face and breast were wind-burned. She tried to move her arms again, but the pain was too much. She tried bending her legs to move her feet in order to break her feet free, but it was no use. She would not cry. She looked around, then she saw it. *Was that the falcon? Could it be?* It was far in the distance, circling around, looking below. It continued to circle for a few minutes getting closer each time it circled until it saw her and headed right for her.

At the sight of the falcon, the tears started to roll down her face again. As happy as she was to see it, she was humiliated at it seeing her that way, which was silly, she kenned. As it approached, she swore she could see sympathy in its eyes.

It landed on the branch that her hands were tied to and started pecking at the ties until it broke them. Her hands fell immediately, though they were still tied together by the original bindings. She moved her hands to her mouth and pulled the gag out of her mouth.

"They'll be coming back shortly," she said as she started to use her teeth to cut through the bindings on her wrist.

The falcon hopped to the ground and pecked at the ties at her feet. She anxiously looked in the direction where the men had disappeared. With as much as the sun had moved in the sky, they would have to be returning shortly.

The falcon broke the ties to the tree and the ones binding her legs together in the same amount of time it took her to cut through the ones on her wrists with her teeth.

She tried pulling on the one around her waist. She could not reach behind; the trunk was too big.

The falcon looked up from the ground, watching her struggle. She kenned it would take longer for her to break through the tie than it would for the falcon. She looked down at the falcon and their eyes locked before she looked down at its massive claws. Up close, they looked huge, each talon curved long and came to a sharp point. Realizing it was her only hope of escape, she looked back at the falcon's eyes and slowly lifted her uninjured arm for the falcon to land on, not breaking eye contact with it.

The falcon hopped up onto her arm and started pecking at the cloth. Its talons were digging in just enough to balance itself on her arm, but no more than that. The talons felt warm against her cold skin.

It broke through the binding quickly and immediately flew out of the way. She went running but stumbled on her hurt ankle. "Aah!" she cried out in pain as she fell to the ground, grabbing her ankle. She got up and wobbled toward the woods in the opposite direction from where the men would be coming.

The falcon circled in the sky several times then landed on a tree to the left of where she was walking. When she continued walking in the same direction she was already heading, it chirped. She looked at it as it tipped its head as if giving direction.

She stopped, turned to look at the woods where she was heading, then back toward where the falcon was perched on the edge of the cliff.

She changed course, picking up a stick to aid in her walking. The path stayed more on the ridge than into the woods. After a fairly short walk, she rounded a bend on the edge of the ridge where there was a small hollow, where the sides of two different ridges came together. It would definitely be a good place to rest for the night as it would be dark in a couple of hours.

If she had been wandering in the woods, she would definitely be easier to find, so long as they dinna go the path around the edge.

She walked into the hollow, which took her enough off the ridge that she could not be seen. She sat on a large boulder that most likely had fallen from the cliff above decades ago. She lifted her leg with the sore ankle up onto the bolder to get a better look at it. It was swollen but not too bad.

The falcon took off as she started to assess her injuries. She had a decent bump on her head that, for the most part, dinna hurt unless she pushed on it. Her wrists were raw from trying to break free from the restraints. Her arm had a gash in it, but it was hard to see how bad it was since the blood had dried down her arm.

She turned her attention next to her dress that was still flapping open, exposing her one breast that was bruised from him grabbing it so hard and had started to darken from the sun as well as her face and arms. Though the sun had been out all day, it had been a cold day, and she longed for her shawl that was no doubt at the edge of the stream. The night would be much colder.

Her mind turned back to her da. He had told her to not go out alone, and she did. *This is all my fault.*

She twirled the gag around so the knot was in the front and worked at it until she got it untied. She was trying to devise a way to use the neckerchief, which was used as the gag to close up the bodice of her dress.

Then she heard a shot and the falcon screeching. She got up and walked to the edge of the alcove. The falcon circled in the sky. "Ye missed," the one man yelled to Kendrick as he lifted his own gun to take a shot.

"No!" Anna yelled, sprinting toward him as she pushed the man off-balance. He was caught off guard and went over the edge. Kendrick grabbed his sword and turned toward her just as the falcon made a dive toward him from behind. It struck him in the back of his head with his talons.

The blow was so powerful that it knocked him to the ground. The falcon made another round in the air before making another dive, attacking him in the face.

"Aah!" Kendrick screamed as he cowered into the hill-side, covering his face. Anna looked at the horses just beyond him. She made her way toward them, cautiously looking at Kendrick. The falcon made another circle in the sky, screeching before making another pass, just missing him, but close enough that Kendrick continued to huddle with his arms covering his whole head, allowing her to pass by him on the path.

As she made it to the horses, she grabbed the horn of the saddle and used her arm strength to keep the weight off her hurt ankle as she put her other foot in the stirrup and pulled herself up. She turned the horse around and took off. The falcon made one more swoop but went toward the second horse, which instantly startled, leaving Kendrick alone, huddled, still holding his hand to his face.

She followed the path around the edge of the mountain until it opened up. She had no idea what direction she came from as she had been disoriented, but she kenned she needed to get as far away from Kendrick as possible. She headed for the woods.

She rode hard until it was dark, continuing at a slower pace for a while longer. She had lost sight of the falcon as she had gotten deeper into the thick woods. When she felt as if she would fall off the horse from exhaustion, she stopped to rest for the night.

She tied the horse to a tree and looked at what supplies the horse was carrying. There were a bedroll and blanket. She struggled to get them loose from the saddle, having a hard time seeing in the dark. Eventually, she yanked it out of the straps securing it, and immediately put the blanket around her shivering body.

There was a leather flask that she immediately opened and took a whiff. Whiskey. She took a swig, coughing as it went down, but it warmed her insides.

Opening the leather bag that hung on the side of the saddle, she reached inside and felt around until her fingers found something. She pulled out a strip of smoked meat and at once took a bite of it. There were no weapons and nothing to start a fire.

She took another bite off the meat as she unrolled the bed mat, laying it on the ground under a large tree that had fallen. Its branches made a small cover, and the trunk would provide shelter and warmth on at least her back. After one more bite and another gulp of the whiskey, she placed the items back in the saddlebag and lay down on her makeshift bed.

She gripped the blanket tighter around herself as she shivered, not only from the cold but from all the fears and vulnerability that finally hit her as she had no more tasks to take her mind off them.

She thought of her da. He was definitely on the mend, but she kenned that upon hearing of her gone missing, he would want to search for her. He would feel obligated to look.

This is all my fault. I'm so sorry, Da. I shouldn't have gone out alone, she thought. Then she remembered why she was on foot by herself. *I wouldna have been captured had Lizzy not injured Butterfly.* She had been so angry about Butterfly that she had forgotten to be on guard.

Her mind drifted to Kendrick and the other man. They were somehow responsible for her father's injuries. After all, what were the MacDonalds doing all the way on Duncan land?

Sleep finally came to her despite all the questions she had going through her head.

CHAPTER

*S*he was locked in a small cottage in the woods. No doubt there was a guard outside the door. She went to the window, tugging on it with no luck. She had to get out before they called the rest of the MacDonald gang.

How long would it take for them to come back for her? She kenned they were using her as bait. He would come, she kenned well enough, but if he came after the rest of them were here, he'd be outnumbered.

She heard a thump out front and a key in the door. She turned around to face the door as she backed away, grabbed a washing bowl and raised it above her head ready to swing. Her heart raced.

The door swung open. She dropped the bowl and ran to him. "They went to get him," she said. "We need to leave now."

He grabbed her hand and went to the door, looking around before leaving. He walked out the door, stepping over the guard's body, and moved to the edge of the cottage cautiously, pulling her with him. He peered around the corner once he got to the edge of the house. Nobody was there. "Let's go," he whispered as they ran to the edge of the woods, where his steed was tied.

A call went out just as they got there. He helped her up on the steed and mounted in front of her before kicking the horse into a run. She looked back. There must have been a second guard. He was chasing them.

"Hold on," he said.

She gripped tighter to him and lay her head against his back as the horse seemed to take flight as it jumped over a stream that was flooded from all the rain.

*****

She woke, her heart racing once more. She looked around quietly. It was a dream.

The sun just barely was out, and the birds were already chirping. There was a good bit of frost covering the ground. She dinna want to leave the warmth of her bedroll but kenned she needed to get going. *Kendrick could not have made it this far on foot in the dark, could he have?*

She quickly rolled up the bed mat and secured it to the horse before eating the rest of the smoked meat and taking another gulp of the whiskey.

She mounted the horse, placing the blanket in front of her and tying the corners at the back of her neck to keep herself covered and to break the wind as she rode.

*****

By early afternoon, she came to a small run of water. It was not big, but enough for her to get a drink. She dismounted and got her fill to drink as the horse grazed on some foliage.

She cleaned off the dried blood covering her arm still. It dinna look that bad. The swelling of her foot had gone down a bit but hurt badly to walk on it. The run, she hoped, would lead to a bigger stream, which hopefully fed into a village.

After the horse finished grazing and had a drink, they continued, following the run until the light started to fade.

She set up her bedroll under another large tree and closed her eyes.

*****

The next morn, she quickly packed up her bed. She grabbed a wild garlic plant and bulb she had found along the way and stashed in the saddlebag the day before, washing it down with some water before mounting the horse. She would follow the run until it came to a stream…and possibly civilization.

After a couple of hours, she spied a bilberry bush. Starving, she stopped to grab the last few on the bush. They tasted delicious. As the horse munched on some foliage, she scoured the bush thoroughly to make sure she dinna miss any before walking the horse back over to drink.

The run was wider now. She filled her flask and continued to follow it for quite some time. Finally, after several hours, she could see the edge of the woods. Pushing the horse faster, she broke out of the woods to find herself at the top of a mountain, looking out over a valley.

The run she had been following dropped off the edge of the cliff into a large stream below. She could see in the distance what could be part of a house of some sort. There was a stone chimney, but no smoke was pouring out of it, so she doubted it was in use.

Looking around for the best way to get down, she slowly started to make her way down the side of the mountain. Then she sensed it…the falcon. She looked up and was not disappointed. There it was, circling the sky in the distance. When it spotted her, it moved to circle closer as if watching her descend the mountain. Comforted by its presence, she smiled for the first time in days.

Once at the bottom, she walked the horse through the small clearing to the water's edge and dismounted. She knelt at the stream, drinking the cold water. The falcon landed on a treetop on the other side.

"So ye found me, aye?" she said as she turned to the falcon. It just stared. She stared back, taking in the beauty of the bird. "Ye saved my life."

They continued to stare at each other for a while. "What is it about ye that is so mesmerizing? It's…familiar" It chirped at her, and she smiled.

"Thank ye," she said as she got up. She mounted her horse, turning it toward a low spot in the stream so she could cross. The falcon flew upstream a bit closer to where the run fell into the stream, making a long narrow waterfall. It landed on a tree jutting out of the side of the cliff, squawking at her.

She turned her head to look in that direction. "I guess ye want me to go that way," she said out loud though it was not close enough to hear. She turned her horse in that direction. As she neared the cliff's edge, she had a sudden feeling that she had been there before.

Slowly, she made her way there, then she spotted it. The square hole in the side of the cliff. Looking down, she saw a rock that would fit perfectly into the hole. She kenned it would.

She could almost feel the gemstone in the sack beneath her clothes as she remembered what Alex had said about it. *The stone of knowledge.*

She had dug out that rock and found the gemstone as a wee lass. No…she had dug the crevice out and hid it. How can that be? She looked from the hole to the falcon. Slowly, she put her hand in the hole.

"I've been in the sun too long and have had little nourishment," she said as she yanked her hand out and turned to look for a place to cross the stream.

The light was fading fast, and she'd like to find that cottage before dark. She found a shallow place in the stream to cross and made her way through the small woods. By the time she found the cottage, it was almost dark. The house had been damaged and unkept for quite some time. The roof and one of the exterior walls had collapsed in the main part of the house, but a couple of rooms were still intact, except for holes in the roof. "Well, it'd be warmer in here," she said to the horse that she had ridden into the house.

The falcon landed on the roof at the edge of the hole. It watched her as she readied herself for bed.

By the time she had gotten out her bedroll and ate the last of the garlic she had found, the sun was completely down. She lay on her mat and looked up at the falcon, then the sky through the large hole in the roof. The stars splashed across the heavens. Perhaps her da was looking out his window at the same stars. She prayed that her father was okay. She thought of Butterfly. She had enough to worry about with her da, but Butterfly crept into her thoughts as well. Thinking about Butterfly made her angry with Lizzy.

Her body was shivering so much from the cold that she had to concentrate on relaxing her body just to stop the shivering. Once her shivering was under control, she looked back up at the falcon. "Thank ye," she whispered to it. Its presence gave her comfort as if she was not alone. Finally, sleep overtook her.

CHAPTER

It was dark, and she was out of breath, but she had to keep running. She had to hide it. If they found the stone, it would be lost to her for eternity. It was the key to her destiny...to finding him.

She made it to the base of the cliff. Taking out her knife, she used it to pry the rock out of the side of the mountain that she had done so many times before and placed the stone inside with care as tears ran down her face. It was her link to him, the only link left. She placed the rock back into the hole, using another rock to pound it in place so it was lodged securely in order to last a long time without falling out, a very long time.

She made her way back before anyone kenned she was gone.

*****

She woke to the sound of an owl in the night. She was breathing hard, and her heart was heavy. The feeling she had in her dream was so real. Moving her hand down to where the pouch laid under her dress, she fingered the stone through the layers of material just to make sure it was still there before wiping her eyes. She kenned with every bone in her body that she was meant to find it. But why? What was so important about it? And what connection did it have with *him*? She dinna ken, but she kenned that she needed to protect it no matter what.

She lay there for a while, watching the sky. *I hope Da is okay. I have to get back to him. What do the MacDonalds want with us? I have to get word to Robbie.* Her mind drifted from one thing to the next.

I have to get some sleep, she thought.

She could hear the leaves rustling in the wind as the cold air blew through the holes in the roof, blanketing her body. The falcon was no longer on the roof. She felt so alone. She concentrated on watching the small snowflakes drifting down slowly through the hole in the roof. She had been warm from the adrenaline her dream had created but coldness slowly consumed her. Eventually, she drifted back to sleep.

*****

She could not breathe as the smoke filled the room. Everyone was gone now, her parents…him. She dinna want to live anymore. She coughed and gagged. She felt the ring on her finger. She could barely see the red of the ruby through the thick smoke. She went to the front of the hearth and got down on her knees. Using her dagger, she pried one of the stones in the floor up. Slowly, she slid the ring he had given her off her finger and took the brooch out of her pocket. Wrapping them in a cloth, she lay them in the void below, placing the stone back in its place. As she wept, the tears rolled off her face, falling on the stone.

She was getting dizzy now. She looked over toward the window, human instinct telling her to escape, to save herself, but with her parents gone too, there was nothing left for her here. It was better this way. Since he was gone, the void inside her was too much for her to bear. It left a sharp lasting pain that made breathing a chore. Nay, it was better this way. Crawling on the ground beneath the thick smoke, she made her way back to the bed, coughing and gagging. She climbed up on the bed and lay down.

"Until next time, my love," she thought. "I will see ye again."

*****

A crow squawked. She sat up, gasping for air. The sun was beaming through the hole in the roof. She looked around the room. A bed and dresser had once adorned the room but now lay in piles of weathered and rotted wood. A chill went through her that had nothing to do with the coldness of the air. This was it, the room in her dream. She just sat there for several minutes with her thoughts racing as she caught her breath. Tears welled up at the emptiness she felt of losing these people whom she did not remember but kenned had been real.

Looking around, she spotted the stone by the hearth she had seen in her dream. Her heart skipped a beat. She crawled over to the hearth where she had in her dream and brushed the years of dirt and leaves from the ground to expose the stone floor. Reaching into her pocket, she pulled out a piece of flint she had picked up along the way and began to use it to clean out the debris between the stones.

Her heart raced as she cleared the stone, freeing it from the adjoining stones. She had nothing to use to pry it out. She looked around to find something to aid her. The dresser wood was too thick and rotted. She got up to go outside, but as soon as she put weight on her foot, pain shot through her ankle.

"Aah!" she called out. She'd been so distracted she'd forgotten about her injured ankle.

She carefully made her way outside. The ground was covered with a small layer of snow. She found a small but sturdy stick and brought it inside. Working the stick between the two stones, she tried to pry the one out, but the stick snapped, lodging itself between the two stones.

"No!" she called out as she let out a sigh. She sat there on the floor, just thinking.

The crows outside started squawking, and she heard them wrestle through the leaves before she saw them fly off as she looked out the hole in the roof. *Someone's coming!* She quickly used her hand to push the dirt and leaves back over the stone. *If they find me, they're not getting the ring hidden below. I ken it's there.* She made to get up as the falcon landed on the roof, looking into the room through the hole.

She breathed a sigh of relief smiling as she looked up to it. "Ye startled me," she said.

It hopped down into the room, carrying something in its talons, and landed on the floor just long enough to release the object, then flew back through the hole. It landed on the roof at the edge of the hole and watched her.

She looked down at the object curiously then back to the falcon that looked from her to the object then back to her, as if saying it was for her. She looked back down at the object. It was wrapped in a cream-colored cloth and tied with a ribbon.

"What do ye have here?" she asked as she crawled over to it. She picked it up and slowly unwrapped it to find a dagger in a leather scabbard. The hilt of the dagger had a falcon which was encircled by a belt with the words "Vraye Foi" on the belt above the falcon. "True Faith," she translated it out loud.

The crest was familiar. *Where have I seen it before?* she thought, studying the emblem. *Alex wore a brooch like that.* Just the thought of him made her heart race. *He wore a MacKay tartan, but he is a Boswell. This must be the Boswell crest.* She brushed her thumb over the crest before pulling the dagger out of the scabbard. She looked at it for a few seconds as the realization hit her. Turning back to the falcon, she said, "Ye are Alex's falcon. Thank ye."

As she flipped over the blade, she caught sight of the flint she'd been using to free the stone. She looked around for something more to build a fire. Years of leaves and branches had fallen through the hole and lay on the ground, but frost currently covered them. She looked at her bed mat.

Crawling over to it, she lifted it, suddenly very grateful that she had hastily laid the mat down without clearing the floor. She pushed the debris out from under the mat to the middle of the floor, picking out the small twigs that would be drier kindling than what was outside.

She went outside and grabbed some pine needles from under the pine tree and several other sticks. Putting the kindling in a pile below the hole in the roof, she used the flint and blade to create sparks.

As she worked at building the fire, she thought of her father and felt a wave of gratitude for the lessons her da had taught her with her brothers, the outdoor skills of hunting and making camp. Her vision blurred with tears she refused to cry. *God, please let him be okay. I have to get back to him.*

After a few sparks, her dry kindling caught fire. She blew on it gently to get the fire going as she placed the pine needles on it slowly. As the fire grew, she placed the twigs, then smaller sticks, a little at a time. Soon she had a nice little fire going. Placing a few more sticks on the fire, she made her way outside to gather larger sticks, which she set down beside the fire.

She warmed her hands by the fire, which started to tingle. She dinna realize just how cold she had been until the feeling came back into her hands. The tingling started to be hurtful, and she fought back the tears. She looked up at the flacon and nodded her thanks to it.

She sat close to the fire, warming her hands for quite some time. It felt so good. Looking around, she spotted the stone by the hearth she was trying to pull out. Her heart leaped as she recalled the dream. She grabbed the dagger and scooted over to the hearth. *It's under the stone, I ken it*, she thought.

She used the dagger to pry it out from between the others. After a couple of minutes, she had forced it out just enough that she could grab it. Her hands still stung a bit from thawing out, but she bit her lower lip as she fought the pain until, finally, she was able to pull the stone out of the floor.

She reached into the void, feeling loose stones and pebbles. Her hand weaved through the pebbles as she dug around until grabbing something wrapped in a cloth.

She pulled it up. It was wrapped in a piece of tartan, MacLeod. *He wore a MacLeod tartan, the man in my dreams.* She looked at it in her hands then to the falcon. It was watching her intently as if anxious to see what she had dug up. She smiled up at it before turning back to the object in her hand.

Her heart pounded. Very slowly, she unfolded the piece of tartan to reveal a beautiful ruby ring and brooch, both lined with tiny diamonds.

She moved her fingers over the small diamonds of the brooch and sat there, just staring at it for several minutes.

Stunned, not only by the beauty of it but the realization that she has dreamed of it and found it. She tried to comprehend what it all meant. This was hers, she kenned it from the deepest part of her soul. The reality of it baffled her. *How can this be?*

She had not realized that the falcon had taken flight until it had come back in with something else in its talons. He flew in the hole of the roof and released the contents of his talons onto the floor. A grouse. Her stomach seemed to growl at the sight of it.

She immediately placed the brooch and ring in her pocket and moved over to the kill. She picked up the grouse, letting the strands of flowerless heather that had hidden it from land prey fall to the floor.

She reached for the dagger. Normally, she would pluck it, but she was so hungry that she skinned it and cut it into small pieces so it would cook faster. Skewering two pieces on a stick she propped it up with the stone she had taken out of the floor so it would cook over the fire. She cut two more pieces, putting them on another stick, and did the same with them.

The pieces were small enough that they did not take long to cook. She pulled the first skewer off the fire and blew on it until it was cool enough to eat. Once eaten, she put two more pieces on the stick and placed it on the fire.

After she got a few bites in her belly, she skewered the other half of the bird whole and put it over the fire.

She smiled up at the bird. "Thank ye," she said to the falcon. It just watched her.

While waiting for the rest of the meat to cook, she picked up one of the sticks she had used to cook the smaller pieces of meat and started drawing in the debris of the stone floor as she thought of the events of the past few days. *We've never had a quarrel with the MacDonalds before this. And what of my dreams? Were they really of me or someone else? I've heard of seers before, but certainly their visions were detached from the intense feelings I had in my dreams.*

As she was drawing with the stick, she noticed a black mark the charred end of the stick made on her shift. Immediately, she got an idea. She looked up at the falcon and asked, "Will ye bring a message back to yer master to give to Robbie?"

Sending a note to Robbie would allow her to go straight back home to take care of her da.

She grabbed the cloth that the dagger was wrapped in and smoothed it out on the ground with her hand before grabbing a feather from the grouse. She checked on the meat cooking, turning it over to cook the other side. Grabbing the dagger, she used it to cut the tip of the feather to use to write a note.

Checking the meat once more, she sighed before placing it back on the fire and started her note. Using the blood on the floor from the grouse, she wrote a rough message to her brother, briefly explaining her da's injury and her slim escape. After blowing on it to dry it, she quickly rolled the cloth up, taking care not to smudge any of the blood that may still be wet. She laid the scroll on the ground and held the end of it, looking up at the falcon with pleading eyes.

"Will ye deliver this?" she asked.

The falcon hopped down, grabbed the note with his talons, and flew off. As soon as it flew out of the hole in the roof, she grabbed the meat, waving it on the stick to cool it faster as she contemplated her situation and her next move.

Realizing that they had stayed near the stream on the other side when she had first found the stone, she made the decision to make her way back to find the road they traveled when going to the MacKays.

She took a bite out of the meat. This was the best she'd felt in a couple of days. Her foot still hurt a bit, but she was warm, had food in her belly, and was hopeful. She at least kenned somewhat where she was. Over the past couple of days, she seemed to be traveling with no idea where she was going. She now had a plan.

She leaned back on her arms once finishing her food and looked around. Her eye caught on the void in the floor. She reached into her pocket and pulled out the ring and brooch, trying to piece together her dreams and reality.

The horse snorted as if to bring attention to her that he was still there. She looked at it and said, "Aye, let's get ye to the stream."

She put the ring and brooch into the sack with her necklace. Finally warm after two days, she dreaded leaving the warmth of the fire. She put two more pieces of wood on the fire to keep it going before mounting the horse.

The coldness hit her as soon as the horse walked out of the room. She kicked the horse to move it faster and guided it toward the stream. Once at the stream, she dismounted and sat at the edge, taking off her boot to look at her ankle. It was still swollen but verra little.

She stuck it in the chilling water, closing her eyes as if not seeing her foot in the icy water would make it less cold. She pulled it out after only a few seconds. *My foot doesn't hurt that much to justify that cold of water. Besides, I'll be riding all day, not walking.*

She filled her flask, drank it, and filled it again.

The stream was larger than the one at her home. It was large enough one might call it a river. Both sides had large banks, unlike hers that only had a small bank on the one side and wooded on the other. There was a field behind her, which separated the stream and what remained of the house.

She dried her foot off and put her tattered stocking back on, then her boot. Mounting the horse, she turned it back around. She took a good look at the house and land. It was so familiar. A tug at her stomach made her steer the horse in the direction of an overgrown clearing on the side of the house. There was a lone tree in the middle of the clearing. As she neared it, she saw grave markers.

Realizing she had tugged the reins and had brought the horse to stop, she nudged it on despite the uneasy feeling she had. She kenned who was buried there. She dismounted the horse, letting it graze close to the tree as she slowly walked over to the nameless grave markers.

"I dinna understand," she said out loud as she fell to her knees. *And I'm not sure I want to understand*, she thought.

She pulled the overgrown heather from around the stones and lingered there for just a bit before getting up and turning.

Taking in the view of the house and land once more, she had a vision of her as a wee lass playing while her father cut wood and her mother hung clothes to dry. They were not the parents she has now, nor did the girl look like her as a lass. This girl had straight dark hair unlike the golden curls she had as a child, yet she had all her memories.

There had been a garden that the cook maintained for vegetables and a small fenced-in area where they kept the pig and goat. A couple of sections of the fence still remained upright yet crooked from years of wind blowing across the field of heather.

Taking a deep breath, she exhaled slowly, trying to clear her mind. Somberly, she walked toward the horse, but before she got to it, a wild cat pounced out of the overgrown grass, hissing as it caught a field mouse.

The horse spooked and made a startled jump before taking off running, leaving Anna in the middle of the field. The cat had taken off with its meal in the other direction.

"No!" she called out, her hands flying to the sides of her head. *This can't be happening.*

Perhaps the horse is on the other side of the house. She made her way slowly, being careful how she stepped so as not to injure her ankle anymore. When she got to the house, she went around the other side, looking for the horse, but it was nowhere to be found.

So much for leaving today, she thought. As the realization hit her that she would not, she hastily grabbed some more wood from outside before limping back inside.

Once back in the room where her bedroll still was, she plopped the wood on the floor and grabbed some smaller sticks, placing them on the hot coals. She blew on it until fire flared before adding more sticks.

She turned to grab the flask for some water before realizing that it was in the saddle pouch. *Great,* she thought. *Well, at least I'll be warm.* She grabbed a long stick and the dagger and started whittling the end to make a point, trying to burn some of her anger off. At one point, she stopped whittling, frustrated with her situation, and looked around. Her anger gave way to sadness. This had been her room, her home.

She slowly got up and walked to the next door in the hallway. It had been her parents' room. The roof had collapsed, taking down with it the outside wall.

The dream came back vividly with all the emotions. *It was more than a dream, more than a seer's vision.* The emotions were so intense it made her nauseous.

She turned around and moved down the hallway, letting her fingertips brush against the blackened stone wall. The hallway gave way to what was once their great room, not as fine as hers now but a simpler one. It was where they had played, entertained, and ate. The outside wall had caved in here as well leaving it completely exposed to the elements. The inside wall had once been adorned with one long tapestry that had been handed down for generations. It had been burned to ashes like the entire family. The whole generation was gone.

She moved on to the kitchen that had fared better than the other two rooms. All the walls remained, but the roof had completely fallen in. A giant table had once been in the middle of the room. She remembered rolling dough to make bread with her mother or the cook. She could almost smell the bread.

She sadly turned around and headed back to her room. Sitting down near the fire, she picked up the dagger and piece of wood and continued to whittle it to a point.

CHAPTER

Robbie and Brodie were just walking back from the barracks after being on duty since early that morning. They both looked up as a bird screeched, carrying a roll in its talons.

"What the devil!" Robbie exclaimed as it landed on the ground in front of them, stepping off the rolled-up cloth.

Robbie and Brodie glanced at each other. Robbie shrugged his shoulders before turning back to the bird, cautiously bending down to grab the roll, never taking his eyes off the falcon. He unrolled the cloth to reveal a rough note appearing to be written in what he believed to be blood. He stared at it for a minute. He clenched his teeth, and his shoulders went tense.

"Well, what is it?" Brodie asked.

Robbie looked up. "It appears to be from Anna. She claims that my da has been attacked, and she was taken. She made an escape but was injured... She's alone, in the woods! She sent word with Donald, our stable master, but found him dead." He paused, massaging his forehead as he reread the harshly written note. He dropped his hand from his head and said, "I need to go."

He quickly turned back toward the road, his long strides moving in double time.

"I thought that all this turmoil was over once they had gotten home. I should have gone with them," he spat.

Brodie caught up to him, placing a hand on Robbie's shoulder from behind to grab his attention. Robbie stopped and turned impatiently.

"I'll go with ye," Brodie said. "I'll go to the stables to have them ready the horses." He looked at the falcon then back to Robbie. "Are ye going to write her back?"

"Write her back?" Robbie said, not really expecting an answer, looking to the falcon and back to Brodie, who replied with raised eyebrows and shrugged shoulders.

Robbie looked at the falcon, trying to wrap his head around the fact that this bird had the ability to deliver a message. The falcon just stared back at him, waiting. "Aye. I cannot believe she got a falcon to deliver this to me!"

"We saw that exact falcon on our way to yer family home. She pointed out the mark on its breast. It landed not far from us. She said she thought it lived here as she'd seen it by the river."

"Go to the stables. I'll go write my message and meet ye at the castle," he said. "I will need to get Willie too…and some rations," he mumbled out loud more as a mental note than anything.

Brodie went toward the stables and Robbie to the soldiers' quarters. He often stayed with Brodie, Alex, and a couple of other soldiers, especially when he got off duty in the dark. Willie stayed with the youth trainees in the barracks.

The falcon flew off in the direction that Robbie went and perched itself on the roof across the way from his quarters. Robbie watched him as he walked in and got some stationery to write a note.

Robbie sat at the table and started his message. As he wrote, he occasionally looked out the window to make sure the falcon was still there as he quickly scratched a note to Anna with his intent to leave immediately.

He rolled it up, sealed it, and went outside. The falcon had not moved from its position. Not sure how to give it to him, he held his arm out while holding the edge of the scroll. The falcon sprung off the roof and swooped down, grabbing the scroll with his talons, and disappeared to the back of the house.

Robbie turned around to go inside the house, fighting the urge to go around back and watch it disappear.

He sat down to write a message to Mary Ellen, explaining his sudden departure. He would have to have it delivered to save time. It would be a half of a day out of the way if he would go to tell her himself.

As he rolled the message up and sealed it, Alex walked down the stairs. Robbie looked up. "Ye just getting up?" he asked, seeing him all disheveled, not that he would have blamed him for sleeping so late since Robbie relieved him of guard duty early in the morn.

"Aye," Alex said as he combed his fingers through his long ruffled hair as if it would help.

Robbie quickly explained what had happened, showing Alex the note Anna had scratched on a scrap of cloth.

"A falcon ye say?" Alex questioned, looking at Robbie with raised brows.

"Aye," he said. "I've seen it on occasion here. It has a distinct arrow mark on its breast." He paused. "Ye've seen it before?"

"Nay." Alex shook his head. "I've never seen one like ye described," Alex replied as he looked down at the note on the table. "It seems that there will be trouble. I'll go with ye, though I have a couple of things I need to take care of first. I will catch up with ye tonight. I'll be a couple of hours behind ya."

Robbie's lips curved slightly, contradicting the other features written all over his face, concern, anger, helplessness. "I was hoping ye would. Ye have a good sense of danger, and I could use yer help. Ye are a true friend," Robbie placed his hand on Alex's arm. "Let us go to Lord Reay now to gain his permission to leave. Brodie will meet us up there."

On the way to the castle, they discussed their journey. Robbie kenned Alex was familiar with the way for the first half of the journey. They had traveled home together for holidays, departing only toward the last day of their journey once they were in the lowlands. It made for good company on a journey that would be otherwise monotonous.

As they got to the castle, Brodie was tying up their horses and Willie's. "I suspected ye'd be coming, so I told the stable master to make sure yer horse was well-fed and watered just in case," Brodie said.

"Aye, thanks," Alex said. "I wouldna leave Robbie to face this alone as ye ken." He slapped Robbie on the back. "I ken ye'd both do the same for me. I have a couple of things I need to tend to first though, so I'll be a couple of hours behind ye."

They walked up the steps of the castle and requested an audience with Lord Reay. While waiting, Robbie summoned a servant and requested food for their journey and his message to be delivered to his wife.

Their request for leave was granted. Robbie and Brodie went to get ready while Alex rode Willie's horse to the youth barracks to deliver the MacKay's message releasing Willie for a leave to go home.

After handing Lord Reay's message to the commanding officer, Alex waited for Willie to explain to him the reason for leaving.

"Robbie received word that yer father and sister were injured. Pack lightly as ye will be traveling at a fast pace," Alex said.

"Aye," Willie replied, clearly worried. *There is no time to console the lad*, Alex thought. *Robbie will have to do that while they traveled.*

"Once ye are packed, meet us at our quarters," Alex ordered.

"Aye," Willie quickly turned to go inside.

Alex walked back to the barracks while Willie packed and secured his supplies to his horse. He broke off the end of the loaf of bread he had stuffed in his sash at the castle and ate it. He needed his strength. He could not get his mind off Anna, alone in the woods. *We're coming. Just keep safe until we get there.*

They heard Willie approach as he galloped at full speed down the path, kicking up dust from the dirt road. He stopped in front of the soldiers' quarters. Robbie and Brodie were just finishing securing their supplies.

"I'll catch up with ye tonight," Alex said as he bid them Godspeed.

*****

Alex went inside after they left. Reaching in his pocket, he grabbed a piece of cheese he had brought from the castle, shoving it in his mouth as he took the steps two at a time to his room. He was hungry, but it would have to wait. Closing the door, he slid the wooden bar into place so no one could enter. He pulled the rest of the loaf of bread he had tucked under his sash and laid it on the bed before placing the cheese from his pocket there as well. He reached into his boot and pulled out a sealed scroll and laid it on the bed in a separate pile than the food.

I need to hurry. Opening the curtains and the window, he moved to the corner of the room out of view from anyone who may be able to see inside. Undressing, he neatly folded his clothes, placing them in another pile on his bed.

Closing his eyes, he concentrated on his breathing, in and out, in and out. The feeling started slowly. It brewed from within his chest until he could feel it go down his arms and legs. It flowed to his fingers and his toes, strengthening with every breath he took.

A heat came over him, and he gave in to the sensation, felt himself change, his feet and toes cramped for a few seconds before spreading out into talons. He flexed his muscles in his arms, anticipating the brief intense pain the transformation would bring. As he felt himself changing, his arms stretched out as if by instinct, and he felt the cool air through his feathers. A burst of energy gave him the need to fly immediately. Before heading out the window, he grabbed the scroll on the bed with his mighty talons.

He soared higher and higher, feeling the wind on his face. The trees grew smaller as he ascended, the people became miniature. He could cross a distance in this form so much faster, not only due to his speed, but he dinna need to deal with the rivers to cross and the mountains to climb or go around. It was a straight shot from one point to the other.

This was the first time he had transformed twice in one day. Heck, he had transformed more these last few months than he had since the first time he discovered he could. The need to be close to her was constantly there, she was all he ever thought about.

Before he had met Anna, he would transform just to feel the wind blowing hard on his face as he soared through the clear blue sky. The adrenaline, driving him from the empty feeling he felt inside, which he couldna tell anyone. How would anyone understand? Hell, it took him years to understand himself.

CHAPTER

18

She had planned to be well on her way back home by now, but she had thought she'd have a horse. Her ankle still pained her, so she figured she would not make it far being on it all day. Also, she had comfort knowing that Robbie would get the message and she would meet him on the road.

She didna ken how far she was from her home and the MacKays, but she prayed the delay would not make her miss crossing paths with Robbie. Staying one more night would not only allow her to rest her ankle a bit but allow her to get some provisions for her journey. She'd stay warm for the night and fill her belly.

Using the ribbon that had tied the cloth wrapped around the dagger, she sewed her bodice together by making holes with the dagger on the torn edges of each side and secured it closed. It did not look good, but it would keep her warmer and modest, even if she was alone.

Eventually, she would need to walk back to the stream to get some water, but she'd wait until later in the afternoon. She had whittled a spear and wanted to get some meat to smoke for her journey. Perhaps she could spear a fish at the stream to eat tonight.

First, she gathered wood and brought it in, stacking it by her small fire to dry, making sure she'd have enough to make it through the night. The wood was damp from the snow, but it would dry out a bit by the fire.

She went outside with her spear and found a spot to wait. There was definitely plenty of game available, but not all practical to kill, given her circumstance. Her mind kept going back to her da and Kendrick. Every time she thought of Kendrick, anger raged inside her that changed into fear that he may be close. She would find herself looking around, on guard. *I'll be prepared if he shows up here*, she thought as she held her spear tighter with one hand and checked that her dagger was in her pocket with the other.

Close to an hour, she waited until, finally, her chance came when a hare stopped a little bit in front of her. She very slowly lifted her spear. She would have to be swift with her throw before it saw her. As she thrust the spear, it turned her way and made to run, but the spear hit good and true.

Anna immediately went over to gather her reward proudly. It was the first time she had ever hunted with a spear. Actually, she had never even considered spear hunting. She carried her kill back to her fire to prepare it and warm back up. Halfway through skinning it, the falcon reappeared.

"Ah, ye are back," she said.

He placed the scroll on the stone floor and flew up to perch on the edge of the hole in the roof. "I had planned on being well gone by now, but my horse got spooked and ran off," she said in frustration. "I figured I'd prepare some food for my trip back and give my ankle another day to rest," she babbled on to the falcon, not caring that it could not understand her.

Putting the dagger down, she grabbed the scroll. "Well, that was a fast response!" she said as she broke the seal and read the message.

She flipped the parchment over and used the rabbit's blood to scratch a note, stating she'd lost her horse and would be leaving in the morn with the hope to meet him on the road. She kenned a road was close by since they had camped on the other side of the stream where she had found the gemstone as a child. They would not have camped too far from the road with a load of people and a cart.

Since he was older, she had thought that he might remember the spot where she had found the stone. She took off the broken seal and reheated it at the end of a stick before resealing the scroll.

As she went to place it on the ground, the falcon flew in and landed on the stone floor with another rabbit.

"Oh, thank ye! I dinna hear ye leave," she said to it. "I wrote to tell Robbie I'd meet him on the road. We've stayed by the stream as children," she rambled.

He grabbed the scroll and flew off.

Anna made racks by propping up some sticks near the fire. She prepared the meat into strips and hung them on racks to smoke before placing more wood on the fire. She sat there for a bit, debating whether or not to fish, but thirst finally got the best of her. She left the warmth of her fire and went to the stream to get some water and perhaps a fish to eat tonight.

Cautiously, she walked to the stream, being careful not to stress her ankle. She would be on it all day on the morrow. The small bit of snow that was there in the morning had melted, giving way to the fallen leaves on the ground that was now wet and slippery.

Once at the stream, she got her fill to drink. The stream was not deep where she was, so she looked around to find a better spot. She found a deeper pool where she could see a decent-sized fish swimming around. It had taken several tries, but she finally stabbed a fish, almost giving up in frustration.

By the time she got back, the sun was halfway set. She put more wood on the fire and cooked the fish. A full belly, a good night's sleep by a cozy fire, and food for her trip would do her well.

She lay down, keeping her hand on her dagger and looked up at the sky, hoping the falcon would come back. *Could Kendrick have tracked her here? Did he find his horse and was now lingering outside right now? I wish the falcon would come back.* She felt so alone.

*****

Robbie stopped as he saw the falcon flying toward them as it followed the wagon path. The falcon swooped down, releasing the scroll right above him. Robbie caught the scroll as it dropped.

"Whoa!" Willie called out. "That was so awesome!"

The falcon flew off, not waiting for Robbie to read it. He wasna going to be a messenger all night long.

Robbie read the message before relaying it to Brodie and Willie. "I ken where she is," he said. "We camped there as children."

As an afterthought, he said, "Alex and I camped there once on our way home from a holiday as well."

The falcon flew through the opened window and landed in the corner of the room. Alex stretched his head, looking down, and let his wings rest at his side as the transformation back into human form began. He felt himself growing as his wings slowly warped into arms and his talons to feet. Crouched on the ground, he balanced himself with his deformed arms as they took proper shape so the weight of his head did not topple him over.

Though he had to concentrate on not throwing himself off-balance while gaining all his weight at once, it always took less focus to change back. He figured it was because it was his true form.

He closed the window and curtains. The water in the basin was cold, but he did not want to waste time, so he washed up with it before getting dressed.

He really was only about two hours behind them. Perhaps he could catch up with them when they stopped to make camp.

He would have loved to close his eyes for a wee bit but dinna dare. The thought of Anna alone armed with only his dagger kept going through his mind.

I'm starving, he thought. The transformation always left him hungry, sweaty, and tired. He could eat half a cow after one transformation, let alone two.

He grabbed the loaf of bread and cheese he'd brought down earlier from the castle and ate it on his way to the stable as he thought of the attack on the cliff. The men wore

MacDonald colors. He had suspected that the MacDonalds were responsible for the attacks on Anna at the castle, but he had tried to push the thought out of his head...until he saw the stone. At that point, he kenned it in his heart. The attack on the cliff confirmed his suspicions.

The more he thought about it, the quicker he walked. He arrived at the stables irritated. The stable boy had already fed and watered his horse. At the sight of Alex coming at such a fast pace, the boy began to ready his horse.

"I'm almost done, sir," the boy said as he finished strapping the saddle. Standing up, the boy continued, "He has been fed and watered, and I double-checked everything."

Alex mumbled his thanks as he glowered at the boy, his thoughts still on the attack. He mounted his horse and took off.

*****

Alex ran the horse hard for a couple of hours until the light started to fade. The stream ran the same direction as the road, sometimes a good distance away but sometimes fairly close. Most folk traveling dinna ken it, but he'd seen it from above. Other than the cliffs, the stream and wagon path were the only thing separating the endless trees as far as the eyes could see, and he had an awesome view when transformed...with exceptional eyesight.

His night vision was good too. Had he not already transformed, he would have again just to see how close he was. Had they stopped for the night or continued? If they had stopped for the night, no doubt it was close to the water. They would have had to water the horses so they'd be refreshed in the morn.

He'd find them either way when he got close enough. His instincts were better than most. He had trained himself to be aware of everything around him, it just took a bit of concentration. He laughed to himself. Robbie always teased him that he had animal instincts. Perhaps though, it was animal instinct carried over from the falcon side of himself.

There had always been rumors in his family about a great-uncle who was a shape-shifter. Like all children, Alex was fascinated with all mystical stories. He enjoyed listening to traveling minstrels and storytellers tell their folklores of sea monsters, shape-shifters, selkies, and fairies, but to have an ancestor be one, now that was something special.

It was even said that was how the falcon made its way into the Boswell crest.

He chuckled to himself as he thought about it. Once he had gotten out of his little corner of the world, he had pushed all those childish fantasies aside. Little had he kenned.

*****

He rode for another hour until he felt the urge to turn off the path. The forest was dark, and he kenned there was probably a small path further ahead that would have led him back to their campsite, but he preferred the cover of the trees. Soon, he smelled the smoke, confirming his intuition was right. It wasna long before he saw the tiny twinkle of the campfire through a break in the trees.

As he approached the campsite, Robbie and Brodie reached for their swords.

"It is I," Alex called out.

"I ken ye'd find us," Robbie said.

He dismounted his horse and went over to grab whatever they'd cooked. "I'm starving," Alex said as he helped himself.

Robbie handed him a flask of ale, and he gratefully took a swallow.

"I'm glad ye could make it," Robbie said.

After tending to his horse, they sat around, and Robbie filled him in with the details of the second note.

"I ken where this place is that she mentioned," Robbie said. "It's about halfway from the MacKay's castle to my home. Ye've actually camped there once with me on one of our holidays a couple of years ago. It usually took us four days' travel total, but we always had a big load on the wagon…and my aunt and Lizzy."

They all chuckled.

"We traveled much faster today, so we should get to that spot before nightfall tomorrow if we keep the same pace."

"Ye said she'd leave her spot in the morn?" Alex asked.

"Aye, but she's on foot. She will not get far," Robbie replied.

As they lay down to sleep, Alex looked up at the stars, knowing she was looking at the same ones. He woke up in the night several times, fighting the urge to fly off and check on her, but he kenned he needed to rest to keep up his strength. He sensed that she was safe. He had to trust in that.

CHAPTER

Anna woke as the sun peeked through the hole in the roof. She rolled up her mat and tied it with strips she had made the night before from the bottom of her shift. Putting her arms through the straps allowed her to carry it on her back.

Since it was cold, she kept the blanket wrapped around her and put her food and dagger in her pockets before starting.

The frost had once again covered the ground. She debated on going back and building a bigger fire, but the days were just going to keep getting colder and shorter. She had to go now. She may be cold, but at least her foot barely hurt.

The stream had a thin sheet of ice over it that broke easily with a tap of her walking stick. The thought of the icy water in her hand made her shiver, but she kenned she needed to drink before starting her journey.

After she got her fill to drink, she found a spot that was low enough to cross by stepping on the rocks, except for one longer stretch. She picked up a large stone and tossed it into the stream. The water splashed up around it as it broke the ice, leaving most of it jutted out of the water, allowing her to cross without getting her feet wet.

By the time she got to the road, she estimated that a good three hours had gone by from the time she had gotten up. *What I would give to have a horse?* she thought. Suddenly all the fears began to fill her mind. *Did I miss my chance of meeting Robbie? Is Kendrick close by? Is my da out looking for me while injured?* The list went on.

She walked in the direction of home on the road, attentively listening for someone coming in the event she would need to find cover before finding out who it was.

*****

They broke camp early and headed back to the road despite the fog, which hovered on the ground until the sun came completely out, allowing them to finally move at a much faster speed. By midafternoon, they had gotten to the campsite where Anna had found the stone.

Alex crossed the stream and headed toward the abandoned house. Robbie followed.

"Look!" Robbie pointed and sped up as the house came into view. He dismounted and walked into the partial house.

"This is where she had been staying," he said as he inspected the ashes left by her campfire. "It looks like she left this morn. She could not have gotten far on foot, though." Robbie quickly mounted his horse and turned back.

On their way back to the stream, they came across the tree with the graves under it and the unmarked stones. Robbie casually looked at them before moving on with the others in tow, but Alex lingered for a bit, his heart heavy. He caught up with them at the stream as they were filling their flasks with water.

They picked back up where they left the road but at a quicker speed. By early eve, they would normally be setting up camp, but they continued, determined to find her that day.

The sun was low in the sky when Alex felt a sense of urgency. She was in trouble and close. He kicked his horse into a run. The others followed immediately.

After several minutes, he came upon her, wielding her dagger as a wolf snarled at her. She had backed herself into a tree. The rest of the pack hovered inside the edge of the woods as three of them ventured out, closing in on her.

"Yah!" he yelled as he kicked his heels into the side of his horse to urge him faster. Alex ran his horse right between her and the wolf closest to her as he leaned over with arms stretched out. Without a second thought, she jumped into them. He lifted her and sat her on the horse sideways as a shot rang out from Robbie's pistol. A loud whine escaped from one of the wolves as proof that he hit his mark. The other wolves scattered.

He held her firmly against his body as they came to a halt. He could feel how cold she was with her body against his chest with just her dress and a thin blanket to shield her from the brisk Highland air.

"Are ye all right?" Robbie asked as he rode up to them.

"Aye. I thought this was it," she said with a shaky voice. "Ye came just in time."

Robbie pointed to the wolf that he shot and turned to Brodie. "Drag that out of the middle of the path."

As Brodie dismounted to do his bidding, Robbie offered his flask of water to Anna. She took a long drink.

Alex helped her remove her bedroll from her back before securing it to the back of his horse. Once removed, she was able to swing her leg over the horse and sit properly. He immediately pulled her back against him in hopes that his body heat would warm her. He kenned it was not all from the cold but partly from the fear of being eaten by the wolf. Holding her, he could feel her tension ooze out of her and into him as if it were penetrating his heart.

"Let's make our way to the stream to water the horses and make camp for the night," Robbie said.

They turned their horses toward the stream and entered the woods.

Alex wanted to lay his cheek against the top of her head and tell her that he wouldn't let anything happen to her, but instead, he kept quiet and just held her with one arm as he steered the horse with the other.

Anna was trying to keep her composure, but Alex could tell she was crying. A couple of her tears fell on his arm. She took a few deep breaths. He could feel the minute her tension started leaving her as she started to relax little by little against him. He kept a firm grip on her.

It was dark by the time they made it to the stream. They all dismounted, and Robbie went to Anna and gave her a big hug. "Ye are freezing!" he said, but before he let her go, Alex had put his blanket on her.

Robbie turned to Willie. "Get a fire started," he ordered.

Brodie went off to secure a meal while Willie went to get some firewood.

Anna turned to Alex. "Where is yer falcon?" she asked. "I was very grateful for him."

Robbie looked at Alex with raised eyebrows.

Alex's heart skipped a beat. He had been so worried over her that he did not think of what he would say when approached about it. He already kenned she suspected it was his falcon. Had she not said as much? He hadn't thought of the consequences of what being found out might bring. Death perhaps, if the wrong person kenned the truth.

It doesn't matter, he thought. *I'd do it all over again to keep her safe, even if it means being burned at the stake for sorcery.*

"I have no falcon, milady," he replied.

Her expression saddened.

She pulled out the dagger the falcon had brought to her. "The falcon brought me this." She showed him. "I saw yer brooch at the banquet with the same crest. Is it not yer crest?"

He took the dagger and appeared to study it, even in the dark. "Aye, it is," he said.

"Is it yer dagger?"

"Aye," there was no denying it in front of Robbie. Once he saw it in the light, he would ken it was his. He'd seen it several times before.

Alex stole a look at Robbie whose eyebrows went down and his expression was thoughtful.

Alex handed it back to Anna. "Ye can keep it." Out of the corner of his eye, Alex saw Robbie nod as the left side of his mouth curved just a little as if he had just figured it out.

"It came to my rescue," she said to them and proceeded to tell all that had transpired at home until then…leaving out the part about remembering the cottage. By the time she finished, Willie had a nice fire going.

Alex took Anna's bedroll out and placed it on the ground so she'd not be sitting on a cold ground, and she sat down beside Willie and gave him a hug. Brodie came back with the meal and started to prepare it for cooking.

Alex grabbed the reins of the horses, two in each hand, and turned toward the stream. Robbie grabbed two of them from him and followed. Alex kenned he had some questions to answer. They walked to the steam in silence as the guilt of not telling Robbie washed over him.

Robbie was his best friend. Hell, he was closer to Robbie than his own brother, and he had never once whispered a word of any of this to him. He kenned Robbie would never hold it against him, never tell a soul. Had the roles been reversed, he'd do the same.

He had come close to telling him once a couple of years ago. They had been sent out with the MacKay factor to collect taxes. One night, he couldna sleep and started getting a feeling in his gut. He left the camp and transformed in the woods to check it out.

There was a raiding party almost upon their camp. He had often wondered if they had seen him transform. He smirked to himself… They'll never tell.

Alex had swooped down at Robbie in his sleep who woke in a startle just as the first man stepped out of the woods. Robbie raised the alarm. The factor slaughtered the entire party as they ransacked the cart.

Robbie questioned him about where he had disappeared to after he came strolling out of the woods all disheveled. He just shrugged his shoulders as he helped get rid of the bodies.

Robbie kenned he had missed the skirmish. The struggle was loud enough to be heard from the woods, but once Alex had transformed back and clothed himself, it was over.

Robbie commented that he had "flown off like a startled bird." Alex immediately looked up at Robbie, and their eyes met. He couldna tell from his expression if it was in jest or as a question. Someone called out an order, grabbing their attention.

Alex learned to trust his instincts better that day, and he never sporadically transformed again.

Once at the stream, the silence continued a bit as the horses drank.

"I wish ye would've told me," Robbie said as they watched the horses. Alex did not reply.

"I'd heard the rumors of sorcery in yer family and had suspected…that night with the factor…when we were attacked…" Robbie broke off, searching Alex's features for confirmation in what little light the moon let off. Robbie continued when Alex dinna respond, "And I ken the penalty, but that would never change my loyalty to ye. I wish ye would have trusted me."

Alex kenned that had he told Robbie earlier, Anna would have been rescued earlier. "I dinna ken about yer father's attack," Alex said, still keeping his eyes on the horses.

They fell silent for several minutes. Robbie turned to look at him then at the sky. "What's it like?" he asked, smiling.

Alex looked up to the sky. "It's…invigorating." He took a deep breath and raked his fingers through his hair before becoming serious once more and turned to look at Robbie. "I'm sorry. I should've told ye, considering the circumstances, but…I just couldna," he said. "I did what I could to keep her safe."

He stole a look across the water before turning back. "I couldna very well have flown off to save her…just disappeared for days to rescue her with no word. For one, I would have had no weapon. No way to protect her." *Let alone clothing to change into*, he thought.

"I would have been flogged for disappearing and released from my duties. Or more likely hung or burned at the stake if

I had said why. I couldna chance saying what I kenned without incriminating myself. If ye would have left on my word, ye would have been taken for conspiring with a sorcerer."

Looking up to the sky, he took another deep breath and combed his fingers through his hair again. He turned back to Robbie, clearly torn. "I ken what people say about my family, I'm no sorcerer," he said before whispering. "I couldna chance it."

Robbie patted him on the back. "Yer secret is safe with me, friend." Robbie turned so he stood directly in front of him. "I give ye my word," he said. He grabbed the reins of two of the horses. "I am indebted to ye for what ye have done for my sister."

Alex just stared at Robbie, watching him walk back to camp before he finally grabbed the other two horses and followed. They walked back to the camp in silence. Alex felt lighter as if by telling Robbie his secret, some weight was lifted off his shoulders. But with that shared secret came a touch of fear.

"We were going to start eating without ye," Brodie said. "How long does it take to water the horses?"

*****

As they ate, Robbie asked about the MacDonalds Anna had mentioned.

"I dinna ken about the one in the fire. Uncle Ian said he kicked him into the fire. I pushed one over the cliff, and the falcon attacked the one called Kendrick before scaring off the other horse," she replied, not really wanting to recount the incident, yet realizing it was necessary.

Robbie looked at Alex from across the fire, their eyes briefly locked.

"I hope the falcon is okay," Anna said. "I've not seen him all day…since I gave it the message to give to ye." She paused before saying, "They were trying to shoot it. I had to save it. I dinna mean to kill the man," she said, clearly distraught over the fact that she had.

Robbie put his arm around her shoulder and pulled her closer. "I'm sure the falcon is fine. He delivered the message," he said, looking once again at Alex then back to her. "I promise ye."

"He saved my life," she whispered to him.

"Ye are safe now, Anna. No harm will come to ye now."

They were quiet for a little while, and Robbie felt Anna relax against him. "Why don't ye go in the tent we set up? The rest of us will take turns staying up on guard duty." He looked at Willie and said, "Ye too. I want ye to stay with Anna." Willie gave Robbie a displeased look but got up and helped Anna up before picking up her bedroll to bring it into the tent.

Once in the tent, the others talked about how much longer the journey would take and discussed their plans for leaving until they were sure Anna had fallen asleep.

"What grievances do the MacDonalds have with the Duncans?" Brodie asked quietly.

"None," Robbie replied. "We dinna have any relations with them, good or bad."

After a bit of silence, Alex shook his head and whispered, "That's not it."

After saying nothing more about it, Robbie prodded him on, "Would ye care to enlighten us?"

"Anna said that yer father gave her the stone on yer wedding day. Yer family had had no trouble before that," he explained. "That is a valuable stone known for its magical powers. The first incident was a couple of days after the wedding, was it not?"

Robbie nodded.

"It had to be someone at the wedding," Alex said.

"My aunt was there when my da pulled it out," Robbie said as he thought back to his wedding day. "I heard her gasp and whisper something about the devil. I just ignored her. There is something she doesn't like about Anna." He paused as he thought for a bit. "It wasna always like that."

"She said she found the stone. Perhaps that's what changed if yer aunt was there when she found it."

"Perhaps," Robbie replied. "Perhaps the stone is cursed."

"No," Alex said. "Yer da has had it all this time, no?" Robbie nodded. "Who was at yer wedding with MacDonald connections?"

"I dinna ken anyone," Robbie said.

"Jacob," Brodie said. They both turned to him. He continued, "I lived next to him growing up. Jacob's mother is a MacDonald. Jacob's father died when he was young. His mother remarried a mean old drunk. She would send Jacob to her brother's for weeks at a time to keep him away from her abusive husband."

"What is his uncle's name?" Alex asked as his body tensed in anticipation.

Brodie thought for a moment. "Gregory," he said. "Gregory MacDonald."

Alex let out a deep breath and turned his head to look the other way.

"Ye ken him?" Robbie asked.

"I ken *of* him," Alex replied. "I've no met him personally."

"I would never have thought Jacob was capable of such an act," Robbie spat as he put his hand to his forehead to rub it. "He sabotaged my sister's saddle!" the anger coming out in his tone.

"I do not think this is Jacob's doing, but if he ken his uncle wanted a lapis lazuli stone or even just mentioned it casually, Gregory MacDonald may have taken it upon himself to get the stone," Alex explained.

Robbie put another log on the fire, and they decided on who would take the first shift staying awake.

CHAPTER

Anna could hear them saddling up the horses before the sun came out. She got up and ate the bread that was offered to her while the others took down her tent and loaded up their horses. Alex brought his horse over to her. She kenned she'd be riding with someone as they were short one horse. Her heart skipped, reminding her of how his presence made her feel. Last night, she did not have time to think when he swooped her up from being devoured by wolves, but now she wasna sure how she felt about having her back up against his chest all day long. A heat came over her body just thinking about it.

She looked around as she petted his horse. Everyone was busy with finishing securing their packs onto their horses. She mounted the horse. Alex immediately mounted behind her.

She tried to keep some distance between them, sitting up stiffly, as awkward as it was. She could feel his arms brushing up against her as he held the reins. After ten minutes of riding, Alex pulled her back to rest against his chest. It took a while for her to finally relax against him.

Alex was all she could think of. The way it felt to be up against his broad chest. She could feel it lift as he breathed. Her whole body seemed to tingle. She tried to think of something else, but then her thoughts wandered to her da and his attack, her injured horse and Lizzy, or worse, Kendrick. *I guess thinking about Alex is better than thinking about the past days' events*, she thought as she could feel the heat rising to her face and throughout her body. Suddenly she was thankful he could not see her.

They rode once again with minimal stops, at a decent pace. By early afternoon, Anna could feel Alex getting tenser as they went on. His arms, which earlier were just resting around her waist, were now stiff, pulling her securely against him. She could feel he had stiffened in his seat, which made her all the more apprehensive. She looked around, but nobody else seemed overly anxious. They had all been aware of their surroundings all day, looking ahead and in the outlying woods.

Perhaps she was just getting to be a burden to him. *Well, I dinna ask to ride with ye*, she thought, suddenly feeling rejected. She was starting to tense up herself. After a while, he moved his horse beside Robbie's and practically plopped her onto Robbie's horse and moved ahead. She felt embarrassed but refused to show it to anyone. She sat straight in the saddle, ignoring his rudeness.

Without a word, Robbie moved closer to Willie while Brodie slowed down to take up the rear. Everyone's alertness went up. Nobody said anything, but Robbie's grip tightened on her waist, pulling her against him.

Fifteen minutes went by, and still, the tension was high. Then all at once, four MacDonalds came out of the surrounding shrubs, encircled them, swords drawn. Kendrick was among them, his eye glazed over, and a scratch that was not yet healed went from his eye all the way to his ear. It was clear his eye was useless.

Robbie blew out a breath at the sight of him, knowing it was Alex's doing.

"Remember me, pretty lady?" Kendrick said to her with an evil grin. She squinted her eyes in anger. She would not let him see her fear. "We've got some business to finish."

Out of the woods came a man on a horse, clearly their leader. "Not before my business is done."

Anna felt her heart thump. It was the MacDonald from her dream…but older. She was paralyzed with terror. As she grew rigid, Robbie tightened his grip on her.

Alex instinctively drew his sword and moved his horse between the MacDonald and her. As their eyes locked, the MacDonald slowly grinned in recognition. "Ye," he said to Alex. "Ye ken what I want, and *she* has it!" He pointed his sword toward Anna.

In that instance, Anna realized that Alex was the "him" in her dreams. Her heart was beating so fast she thought she would die. She kenned how her dream ended.

Alex swung his sword, meeting the MacDonald's sword halfway as Robbie jumped down off his horse, tossing the reins to Willie, yelling, "Get her out of here!" as he attacked Kendrick.

She dinna want to go, but Willie tugged her reins, pulling her out of range, where they watched from a safe distance. Willie drew his sword and stood guard over Anna should one of the men approach.

Robbie's sword sliced through Kendrick's side before he turned on another one, killing him. Brodie took down the other two.

Anna watched the fight in slow motion, not taking her eyes off Alex and the MacDonald. She was so scared for Alex that she could not move.

Alex's opponent was much more skilled than his companions. Their swords clashed with every swing. At one point, the MacDonald predicted Alex's attack and leaned back on his horse, deflecting the blow before countering the attack, cutting Alex's arm.

Anna sucked in her breath as terror overtook her. She did not want to watch, but she could not pull her eyes away from the fight.

After a couple of thrusts, Alex's sword finally hit flesh, giving the MacDonald a matching gash on his arm.

The MacDonald looked around to find himself outnumbered and injured. He kicked his horse into a run.

Brodie turned his horse to follow. "No!" Alex yelled. "We must stick together."

Brodie immediately reined in his horse as Anna and Willie raced out to them. Anna's eyes locked on Alex's, and for a moment, time stood still. It was as if it was just the two of them. There was something between them that was beyond the here and now. Her fate was somehow tied to him.

"Alex. Do ye hear me, man! Ye are bleeding!" Robbie yelled, breaking the spell they were in. Alex looked down at his arm which was bleeding heavily. He sheathed his sword and put his hand over the cut to apply pressure.

The shock of her realization made Anna unmovable. Sitting there on Robbie's horse, she barely noticed the commotion going on around her.

Alex is the man in my dream. He will die by the hand of the MacDonald. She kenned it to be true, just as much as she kenned it would be defending her as in her dream. *It will be my fault.*

Brodie untied his neckerchief while moving his horse beside Alex's. Alex held his arm out to Brodie, but his eyes were on Anna as she tried to figure it all out in her head. Brodie wrapped Alex's arm with his neckerchief and pulled it tight before tying it. By the time he was done, Robbie had dragged the bodies off the path and a bit into the woods.

"Only three bodies were there. The one with the cut on his face got away," Robbie said to Brodie and Alex.

"Kendrick," Anna whispered. Robbie turned to her with apologetic eyes.

He got back on his horse behind her. "Let's go home," he said to her as they took off at a fast pace to put some distance between them and the men. After a while, they slowed to a more normal pace, but nobody talked at all.

Finally, Anna asked, "Do ye think we'll make it home today?"

"We're on Duncan land right now," Robbie answered.

She looked around, noticing familiar landmarks as they crested the hill, giving a full view below. She was having a hard time thinking with all that had transpired, her dreams colliding with reality. She must be crazy.

They dinna have much daylight left since the days were now shorter, but they would arrive home at a decent time if they dinna stop to eat. Normally, when they'd come this route, they would be dropping off her aunt, but they were making a much straighter shot.

"How's yer arm doing?" Robbie asked Alex. Anna had been wondering the whole time but couldna get up the nerve to speak to him, let alone look at him. Being in his presence was unnerving enough. She had purposefully not looked at him at all, but she looked at him now since Robbie posed the question.

"Fine," he replied, looking at Robbie then to Anna.

She immediately faced forward again.

*****

After a half hour past the sun setting, they rode into the courtyard. She saw a face peek out of the window in the foyer, and then the door opened.

"Milady!" Margaret called, quickly curtsying before coming down the stairs to her. "I've been so worried about ya." Then she noticed Robbie. "Sir, it is so good to have ye home." She curtsied to him as well.

"My da?" Anna asked.

"Aye, he's doing much better," she replied. "He wanted to search for ye when ye went missing, but he was not even able to sit up in his bed for more than an hour, much less ride a horse. He has gotten better in the last two days, though. There would have been no stopping him in the morn from going out looking for ye."

As she slid down from the horse, her blanket fell off her. She grabbed it quickly and wrapped it around her but not before Margaret saw the state of her dress.

"Oh dear," she said, "perhaps ye should change before visiting him."

"Aye," she said as she started up the steps toward the house.

"Milady," Margaret called out, "yer aunt has made a run of the house. She'll no doubt be greeting ye in the hall."

"Aye," she said despairingly. The last person she wanted to see was her, especially looking like this.

Robbie moved in front of her and pulled Willie beside him. They entered the house, blocking the view of Anna with Alex and Brodie on each of her sides and Margaret following behind her.

Sure enough, Elizabeth and Lizzy were both there, blocking the stairs.

"Robbie, ye are home," her aunt said in disbelief, looking a bit displeased. She made no attempt to curtsy.

"Prepare guest rooms and some food," he said.

Her aunt looked at Margaret, making no indication that she had any intention of doing his bidding.

"Now!" he snapped at her.

She scrambled out of the way of the stairs, ordering Lizzy to go up to prepare the rooms.

"Margaret," Robbie called, "Alex has been injured. Please get some warm water and fresh bandages for him so Brodie can tend to his wounds."

"Aye, my lord." She curtsied and turned toward the kitchen. As the three of them went up the stairs, Alex and Brodie went into the parlor and sat by the fire to wait for Margaret to bring in the supplies.

Anna went to her room. It was clear that someone had been through her things as some items were slightly out of place, and some of the drawers were not shut all the way. The thought of Lizzy and her aunt helping themselves to her belongings irritated her. She put on a different dress but left her hair in disarray.

They all went to their da's room together. He was sleeping but stirred when he heard the door close behind them.

"Da," Anna said as she ran to his side.

"Aah, my Anna! I've been so worried!" he cried. "They said ye'd disappeared, and they found Donald's body. Ohh, I'm so happy ye are safe!"

Robbie and Willie walked up to the bed behind her. He sat up in bed, spreading his arms to give Willie and Robbie a hug.

"How's yer back?" Anna asked.

"Much better," he replied.

"Can I take the bandages off to look?"

He nodded. She slowly took them off, revealing a scab that went from his shoulder all the way down to his waist.

"It is healing nicely," she said as she covered it back up.

"Ye are lucky to be alive," Robbie said.

A knock came on the door, and Margaret entered with some food.

"Thank ye, Margaret," Robbie said.

"I have two tubs being brought up and will have warm water in a bit," she explained.

"Bring one of them to Anna's room and the other in mine," he ordered. He turned to Willie. "Ye can grab some clean clothes and bathe in my room. Then come back here. Ye will sleep here."

He turned to Anna. "Ye'll sleep in Ma's bed. Keep the outside door bolted."

Willie and Anna both grabbed a plate of food and took it with them as they prepared for their baths. Robbie briefly filled in the details of their journey and asked about the fire and what Uncle Ian had found out.

"He dinna find out any information. He went back out with a search party to find Anna," he explained. "I have not heard anything else from him."

By the time Willie came back, his da was looking fatigued. Anna came back shortly after, and Robbie left.

"It's so nice to have ye home," Da whispered as he drifted off to sleep.

CHAPTER

They had finished eating under a tree by her house. There wasn't a cloud in the sky. While she had lain back with her eyes closed and face taking in the warmth of the sun on her cheeks, he picked a heather blossom from the ground and pulled the petals out, letting them fall in her hair. Once done, he pulled out an object wrapped in a cloth and put it in her lap.

Opening her eyes, she raised to a sitting position as the petals fell onto her lap. She looked at the object before raising her eyes to him. "What is it?" she asked as his eyes twinkled and his smile beamed.

"Open it," he replied.

She took the object in her hand and slowly unwrapped the cloth to reveal the beautiful blue stone cut in the shape of a diamond with two sides of it shorter than the other two. She looked up at him. "Ye cut yer stone," she said as she searched his eyes, seeing only pure love for her in them. "But it is an heirloom."

"Aye," he replied, pulling out the other piece as he showed her how they pieced together on the smaller sides to form a very large-shaped diamond.

He looked at her and said, "This way, if fate separates us again, we will find each other easier. I think because they are from one stone, perhaps its power will lead us together quicker."

"We'll always find each other," she said with a smile as she cupped his cheek and whispered. "We always do."

"Aye." He slowly leaned down in for a kiss, his eyes locked on hers.

She stopped breathing, and her heart sped up as his lips drew closer ever so slowly. She was sure her heart would explode with the anticipation of the kiss. Finally, their lips touched for a brief second, and he pulled away slowly, leaving her wanting for more. His eyes never looked away from hers. His smile was so sincere, so loving.

She'd never tire of his kisses.

*****

Anna woke up, her heart pounding. She'd slept all night. A strip of sun shone in her eyes from where the edge of the curtains came together. She got up and threw a couple of logs on the hot coals and opened the curtains a bit before quickly crawling back inside her cozy blankets.

She looked at her pouch on the bedside table and reached for it, loosening the drawstrings and emptying the contents of it onto her lap.

She picked up the blue stone. It was such a vibrant color blue. She studied it for a bit. So there was another piece. The other piece from her dream had seemed familiar…or at least the shape was familiar, but she could not remember where she had seen it before. She put down the stone and picked up the ruby ring and brooch. Looking at it, she kenned it was another heirloom of his that he had given her.

*****

Alex came down to relieve Brodie of his shift in the morning and found Robbie already down, breaking his fast. He pushed a plate of food toward Alex. "How's yer arm?"

Alex shrugged and grabbed a biscuit.

"I want to scout the perimeter of the land around my house after ye break yer fast," Robbie said.

"Okay," Alex said as he grabbed some more food and sat down. They ate in silence, and Alex kenned that Robbie had a lot more questions that he would be asking once they got out of hearing range from the house.

After they got their fill to eat, they made their way to the stable in silence. Galvin was up tending to the horses when they walked in. "Sir." He bowed. "Are ye leaving already? Ye just got here."

"We're just going for a ride," Robbie replied. Galvin went for his saddle. "We can get it. Carry on."

"Thank ye, sir." He bowed again. "Yer aunt said she will be leaving today. I have to hook the cart up to the horses…"

"Cart?" Robbie asked.

"Aye. She brought four trunks with her when she arrived."

"We'll be back by midmorning," Robbie replied. "We'll help ye then. She doesna leave with anything before I get back. Is that understood?"

"Aye, sir."

They saddled their horses and were on their way.

"Ye dinna trust yer aunt?" It was more of a statement than a question.

"My mother was the oldest daughter. They had no other siblings, so my mother acquired most of her parents' valuables. My aunt is a very materialistic woman. I wouldna put it past her to help herself to what she feels should be hers since my mother has passed away."

Alex just nodded, knowing all too well the dilemma.

The large open fields around the house were enclosed by woods in the distance. They took their time walking the perimeter of the field. At one point, Alex paused, looking around before venturing off into the woods. Robbie followed.

Remnants of a small campfire a short distance into the woods was situated in a way that one would have a good view of the house and the people coming and going.

It wasna warm, but it dinna have frost on it like everything else. By the look of the area around the fire remains, the person had sat between the fire and the house, blocking the light of the fire from anyone at the house seeing it. No doubt he had his back to the fire, keeping a constant eye on the house.

Someone was in these woods right now, somewhere. They couldna have gone too far.

Turning back toward the field, Robbie took the lead over to a grove where his mother was laid, away from the woods where someone may be hiding and could possibly overhear.

At first, he did not say anything. He just looked at his mother's tombstone for quite some time. Alex let him collect his thoughts. Finally, he turned to Alex.

"What the hell is going on?" Robbie quietly spat out. "Ye said ye dinna ken the MacDonald, yet he clearly recognized ye…and Anna recognized him too. She gasped and tensed up when he came out of the woods. I felt her whole body go stiff."

He gestured with one hand toward the house. "She dinna even tense up that much when that…Kendrick threatened her."

Alex was quiet for a moment. He looked up to the sky as he chose his words carefully. "Neither I nor Anna have met the MacDonald," he began, pausing to look Robbie in the eye, "in this lifetime."

"What!" he countered in disbelief.

Another minute of silence went by as Robbie just stared at him, waiting for his explanation.

"Yer sister and I are soul mates," he started. "A curse was put on us once because she had chosen me over another whom she had been promised to. He'd sworn that we would forever love each other but never find happiness together. The MacDonald is the one who holds the curse over us."

"Are ye for real?" Robbie blurted. "Anna has never said anything before about this to me."

"Ye are not born with the knowledge. It comes to ye at different times. Sometimes in a dream or perhaps when ye visit a place ye've been to in another life." He dragged his fingers through his hair in frustration as he took a deep breath before continuing.

"There's this emptiness inside ye, like a piece of ye is missing, but ye don't ken what, or if ye did remember, ye don't ken who until ye cross paths. At that moment…ye ken."

He looked toward the house briefly before turning back. "Sometimes ye don't cross paths until the other one is married and has a life together with someone else and a family. But once we see each other, it's as if nothing else completes the other, but ye can do nothing, and we both suffer in silence."

Robbie just looked at him, not sure what to think.

"Sometimes one dies well before the other, and when we meet again, one is old, and the other is young." He looked back up at the sky to collect his thoughts again.

"In our last life, my mother was a MacDonald and my father a MacLeod. I had inherited jewels from my mother's side of the family, one of them being the stone that Anna has. My mother had inherited it at the death of my grandmother, but my mother's brother wanted them." He paused a minute for Robbie to take it all in. "My uncle's son, Gregory, the one who attacked us had sworn to his father that he would get it back."

Alex studied Robbie for an indication of what was going through his head, but he could not read him. Alex continued slowly, his loathing of the man coming out in the deepness of his voice. "Gregory MacDonald is the one who holds the curse over Anna and I."

Robbie turned and looked at his mother's grave for a bit as he took it all in. He looked at the sky and out to the woods. Alex just watched him.

Robbie finally turned back to him, shaking his head, and asked, "How long has this been going on?"

"Centuries," Alex replied. "The last time, we had been captured by Gregory. He had threatened to kill her, but she was able to escape as I held them off, but they killed me." He gave a scornful snort before saying through clenched jaw. "This is the first time I've encountered the same man in two lifetimes holding the curse over us." Alex raised his head to the sky and took a deep breath before continuing. "Prior to being captured, I had taken the lapis lazuli that was much bigger and had it cut into two pieces in a way that they could be pieced together and made whole. The stone is known to give the one who holds it greater awareness. I had thought perhaps if she came into possession of the stone that she would remember about us before starting a life with someone else." He paused and ran his fingers through his dark hair, discouraged with how his plan had been self-defeating.

"I now see just how selfish that was of me. I dinna think what would happen if she wore it."

"Can ye not just kill the bastard and be done with the curse?" Robbie asked.

"I have always believed so. I have killed him several times, but it is either after he has killed her, or I have died in the process." He let out a quick breath. "It's not like I am born a soldier every time, ye ken." Alex continued, "I dinna want Brodie to go after him yesterday and do the deed himself. I think I have to do it, but perhaps that would have been enough and we could have been together, then that alone would have broken the curse. But more likely, Brodie would now be dead, and I would have his life on my hands. I dinna ken. I am sorry, Robbie."

"How did ye ken Anna was taken?"

"I had flown down to possibly get a glimpse of her." Alex watched Robbie's face to see some kind of sign as to what Robbie felt about that, but again, his expression held no clues. He continued, "I had seen evidence of a struggle downriver from where she likes to sit. Her cloak was there, and I saw blood on it."

Another moment of silence weighed between them as Alex let Robbie think more about it.

"How does the falcon come into the curse?" Robbie asked.

"It doesn't," Alex smiled as he replied. "I found out five years ago that I could change. It scared the hell out of me at first."

"Five years ago," Robbie said. "I've kenned ye for longer."

"Aye," he said softly. He had always been torn between telling Robbie or not. He could clearly see now how it would have benefited him. "The penalty for sorcery is death." He couldna look Robbie in the eye. He looked out across the field. He tried to change the subject. "I'm sure Jacob dinna mean harm to Anna when he mentioned the stone he'd seen her wearing, but it happened."

"Aye." Robbie ken that Alex purposely changed the topic. He laid his hand on Alex's shoulder. "Alex, I swear on my life that I will never breathe a word of that, or any of this, to anyone."

Alex locked eyes with Robbie and saw his sincerity. He acknowledged him with a nod. It was all he could do.

They turned and slowly made their way back to the edge of the woods. "How did she die if she got away?"

"Gregory MacDonald burned her house down, killing her and her parents. It was the abandoned house where she had set up camp in. It must have been shortly after I died."

"How do ye ken that if ye were dead?" Robbie asked.

Alex turned and grinned at Robbie, "Because yer sister talks to animals."

Robbie tipped his head to the sky and let out a hearty laugh.

"She had a dream," Alex explained. "She dinna ken the meaning when she had had it."

"But if she died right after ye did, how do ye explain the age difference? Ye are five or six years older than she."

"I dinna ken," shrugging his shoulders as he replied. "I dinna have all the answers, Robbie. Perhaps she died again as a child."

The rest of their ride was in silence as they finished their inspection of the area. They had found a couple of more spots where someone had camped, making the house watched from every angle.

They went back to the stable and helped hitch the wagon up to his aunt's horses and brought it up to the steps of the house. Her chests were already sitting out there, and Robbie just opened them and pulled out his grandmother's set of silver candlesticks in one and a small tapestry with his mother's family crest from another. In a third chest, he pulled out a porcelain tea set with a matching tray.

They loaded the chests onto the cart before carrying the items in and handing them to Margaret to put someplace safe.

"Aye, sir." Margaret curtsied as she took them. "The midday meal will be ready in a wee bit," she added.

At the site of Elizabeth at the top of the stairs, Alex walked back outside, sure that Lizzy was not far behind her.

As Elizabeth walked down the stairs with Lizzy in tow, her attention went to Margaret walking away with the candlesticks. Though she said nothing in reference to them, her expression gave away her displeasure.

"We will be leaving now that yer father is well on the mend. And it seems that ye have plenty of help now."

Robbie stepped out of the way of the door. "I'm sure we can handle everything from here on." He bowed but dinna escort them to the cart but watched from there until they rode out.

He turned to enter the dining hall as Alex walked in from the kitchen. Robbie let out a laugh at Alex for his youth-like way of avoiding Lizzy.

Alex lifted his eyebrows and shrugged with a smile.

Margaret came with a tray she'd made up for his father. "I'll take it up to him," Robbie said as he grabbed the plate.

He knocked before entering. Willie and Anna were talking to their da who was looking very tired.

"I brought ye some food," Robbie said as he placed the tray on the bedside table. He turned to the others. "The midday meal will be served shortly. Go ready yerselves, and I will be down shortly."

The two of them scrambled out to ready themselves.

"I'm so glad ye found Anna and that ye all are here. I was so worried and couldna even get up, let alone go out looking for her."

"Everything will be fine."

"It was the stone," his da said. "The MacDonald wanted the stone, didn't he? I never should have given it to her. I dinna ken." He shook his head.

"How would ye have known?" Robbie asked. "We'll get him. I'll no rest 'til he's dead."

Robbie moved the tray closer to his da. "Ye look tired."

"Aye," he said. "We've been talking for quite some time. I felt good when I woke up. Perhaps after I eat and sleep some more, I will be down for dinner. It will be nice to have us all around the dinner table together."

"Aye," Robbie said. "I will make sure everyone gives ye some time to sleep."

*****

Brodie had come down, so the five of them sat around the table for the meal.

"How many men did Uncle Ian bring up to watch the house?" Robbie asked Anna.

"Just Galvin, to take care of the horses, Hamish, Colin, and Andrew. Andrew, though, works his shift and goes back to his wife. She is far along in pregnancy, and they lost their previous bairn at birth."

"Do any of them have soldiering skills?" Alex asked.

"Only Colin," Robbie replied. "Most of our tenants are farmers and tradesmen. We will go to gather some more men today and see if we can find anything more out."

"Aye," Brodie and Alex agreed.

"He cannot go," Anna said, looking at Robbie, clearly disturbed by his comment as she extending her opened hand toward Alex. "He's not well."

"He just helped me load up six trunks into a cart. He's fine."

"Look at him!" She looked from Robbie to Alex and back to Robbie. "Can ye not see he's not well?"

Robbie looked at Alex, who looked back at him with raised eyebrows. He turned back to Anna. "He looks a bit tired is all," Robbie replied, turning back to Alex with a half smirk on his face. "How do ye feel?"

"Oh, for heaven's sake, take off his bandages!" she snapped, very out of character.

Robbie went to take off the bandages that Brodie had put on the night before. As Robbie's fingers touched his skin, he could feel the heat from Alex. The smile was immediately replaced with a frown.

"Christ man, ye are burning up!" he said as he took the bandage off, revealing a cut where the edges were red, swollen, and oozing pus.

"It's infected," Robbie said.

"Margaret," Anna called.

As Margaret entered the room, Anna ordered, "Heat up some water and get me some clean bandages for Mr. Boswell's wounds."

"Right away, milady."

"I guess ye are staying," Robbie declared.

They turned their attention back to eating, and Robbie continued to talk, "We found evidence of lookout spots around the parameters of the woods, three different ones." Robbie turned to Anna. "Ye are not to go out without one of us three with ye."

She nodded.

"I mean it, not with Galvin or any other person we may bring here. Only Alex, Brodie, or me," he replied, exasperated.

She nodded again, but he continued to stare at her, waiting for her verbal confirmation. "I understand."

"Good," he said.

Immediately after eating, Robbie looked at Brodie and flicked his head toward the door, indicating that he was ready to leave before turning to Alex. "Get some rest once yer wound is cleaned and bandaged."

Alex grumbled a response as they left.

*****

With her mind still spinning from her dreams clashing with reality, she focused on her task of placing warm compresses on the cut to drain some of the infection out. She did not want to talk about any of her thoughts until she had it sorted out in her mind.

"How did ye ken it was infected?" Alex asked.

"I think ye ken the answer to that yerself," she replied, not answering the question or looking him in the eye.

"Aye, I do, but I want to know if ye ken."

She exchanged the cloth for another warm one, looking around to see if anyone was around, clearly not wishing this conversation to be overheard.

"I ken…a bit." She replied.

She put on a clean bandage quickly, trying her best not to touch him in the process. The feeling she had just being in his presence was nothing compared to the touch of his skin.

She finished up and turned to leave, but he gently grabbed her hand, turning her to face him again.

He opened his mouth to say something, then closed it before reopening it, and said, "Thank ye, milady."

Heat rose from her hand where he had touched her all the way up her arm and spread through her entire body, and she kenned it had nothing to do with his fever.

"Ye need some rest," she replied, pulling her hand out of his before turning and walking away.

I canna believe that is all I said. Not a thank ye for protecting me…or dying defending me from the same person decades earlier. Just, "Ye need some rest." What is the matter with me?

*****

Robbie and Brodie dinna come back until sunset. Anna had wanted so badly to visit Butterfly but dinna dare. She had hoped that they would have come home sooner.

They arrived back with three men and another five to arrive on the morrow with one woman to help Margaret. The men would stay in the great hall.

Alex did not come down for the evening meal, but their father did.

"It is so nice to have my three children here at the table together," her da said as he raised his glass to them all.

"So ye are feeling better?" Robbie asked.

"Aye," he replied. "Every day I feel better than the day before."

Robbie told his da about the scout sites they had found and the tenants that he had hired to keep watch.

"Well, Colin and Bernard fought over in France, so ye have some experience there," his da replied.

They discussed their strategy for finding Gregory MacDonald.

Bored with the conversation, or at least that's what she told herself, Anna grabbed a small plate of food and a bit of wine and excused herself. She went up to peek in on Alex. The room was cold. She placed the food on the bedside table before walking over to the fireplace and adding more wood to the fire.

His covers were tightly wrapped around him. No doubt he was cold from the fever. She got another blanket and laid it over him.

She sat in the chair beside the bed watching him, trying to understand everything. Her dreams, she kenned had been real and not just a dream. It was him and her in another life. *We were meant to be together, how else could one explain it?* she thought. *We'll always find each other.* Those were her words from her dream.

They had been killed over a stone in her dream. Perhaps she should have just given the stone to the MacDonald in the first place. Was the value of the stone that important that it justified his life? Giving it to him, they would have lived happily ever after then and would have prevented what had happened in this lifetime as well…but then she wouldn't be here now, with her current family, the people she loved.

What if Alex dies from his wounds? A pain jabbed her heart. She was scared for his life, yet she barely kenned him. Something inside her told her that if he dies, she would be lost without him.

"I just dinna understand," she whispered as she put her head in her hands and cried.

He quietly rolled to his side and laid his hand on her knee. She dropped her hands and quickly got up. "I…I'm sorry for waking ye."

She left the room, his hand still reaching for her.

CHAPTER

*S*he stood at the top of the stairs with her cream-colored gown of satin and her crown of fresh heather. In front of her stood the two of them and the assembly below, facing her; on the right, the one she was sworn to, which would be a great union between the conflicting kingdoms, and on the left, the one she loved.

She had fallen in love with another and had been found out by her betrothed. It was well-known that her betrothed had a number of mistresses that he kept.

Her lover would be sent to the dungeon for his stolen kisses, or worse, hung.

Everyone was quiet, waiting for her decision. As she descended the three steps toward the one she loved, she could hear the intakes of breath.

The moment her hand touched his, the one she was sworn to unsheathed his sword. "If I cannot have ye, no one will! I curse ye, both! For eternity, ye shall long for each other, but yer union will forever be unattainable!" he yelled as he drove his sword completely through her from behind. The sword came out of her front, almost piercing her lover. As her betrothed pulled out the sword, her lifeless body fell into the arms of the one she loved, and her crown of heather fell to the marble floor in a pool of blood.

*****

She jolted to a sitting position from a deep sleep. Her hands instinctively went to where the tip of the sword had exited her chest, but she kenned there would be no blood. A birthmark branded her where the exit wound was, signifying the truth of the curse.

It had happened a long time ago, and now it all came flooding back, the first time, and all the times in between, from then until now. The secret had been buried within her. A secret she could not tell. No one would understand. No one…but one soul.

Shaking, she wiped the tears from her eyes and wrapped her blanket around her as she got up. Quietly, she slid the wooden slat bolting the door, and pushed open the door of her mother's room to the hallway. The fire in her room cast a small bit of light into the darkened corridor, but once she turned down the other hallway, all was dark. She counted the doorways until she got to his. Slowly, she pushed on the door, peeking in to see him asleep on his bed.

She silently crept in, curling up in the chair beside his bed…close to the one she loved.

She studied him as he slept. The connection was there from the moment she first saw him. She did not understand at first, but now she kenned the truth of it. But it would never be. All of a sudden, it all fell into place, the attacks, the MacDonald. It wouldna have mattered if she would have given him the stone or not. He wouldna have stopped until one of them was dead, and neither would he stop now. She closed her eyes, letting the tears flow until she finally drifted off to sleep.

*****

He had heard her walk in but did not let on to it. He opened his eyes but for a split second to see who it was before closing them again, feigning sleep. He heard her crying, but he did not want her to run off again, so he kept his eyes closed. Once her breathing became rhythmic and he was sure she fell asleep, he opened his eyes and watched her silhouette in the chair cast from the small flames in the fireplace. He yearned to touch her, to carry her over to the bed and hold her in his arms. He'd have more than just Gregory MacDonald after him if he did that.

Perhaps this time, he could succeed in ending the curse now that Robbie ken. He now had an ally. Maybe he could convince Laird Duncan of a quick wedding with Anna if Robbie agreed. That would not likely happen in the middle of all this chaos, though. Gregory MacDonald would not stop until he had the stone and either one or both of them were dead.

No, his best bet was to kill the MacDonald himself. With Robbie and Brodie's help, he had a better chance than ever before.

He felt better with the resolution, but watching her sleeping in the chair, the empty feeling of never being able to have her was still in the pit of his stomach. It was their destiny.

He could feel his injuries wearing him down even though he just lay there. He fought the need to sleep for as long as he could before finally drifting back to sleep.

CHAPTER

She had made her way back to her room before anyone upstairs had gotten up, though she could hear sounds in the kitchen below.

Her mind was going so fast with all the memories, trying to understand all of what was going on as she readied herself for the day. She wanted to see Butterfly, if just to talk to her, to get her thoughts all out of her mind.

Thinking back on the stone, it would not have mattered if she had given it to Gregory MacDonald. They were doomed anyway.

She grabbed her cloak and headed downstairs.

"Milady, are ye going somewhere?" Brodie asked.

"Not without an escort," Robbie declared from the top of the stairs.

"I want to see Butterfly," she stated as she turned to look up at him.

"I'll take ye," Robbie said as he descended the stairs.

Robbie turned to exchange a few words with Brodie before dismissing him from his shift, but she was not listening. There was something about what she had just said that had struck her. She thought for a minute. Butterfly... then she remembered. It was what he would call her. She named her horse the same name as her pet name. A smile came across her face as she remembered. Every name she had thought of to name the horse just did not seem right. It had to be Butterfly. It was there all along, in the back of her mind. Everything was.

"Well, do ye want to go or not?" Robbie asked her, snapping her out of her trance.

"Aye," she said as she pulled her cloak closed.

As they walked to the stables, she glanced up to the sky and the edge of the trees. "I hope it's okay," she said. "It would occasionally visit me here, the falcon, that is."

"I'm sure it'll be back," Robbie replied as he put his arm around her shoulder and pulled her closer as he chuckled.

"What's so funny?"

"Ye," he replied. "Leave it to ye to befriend a falcon that later becomes yer rescuer. Ye have always had a thing for animals."

She was so happy to see Butterfly. Robbie talked to Galvin as she coddled the horse and checked out her leg that had been injured.

"Can we take her for a ride?" she asked Robbie as he was coming over to her.

"Later," he said. "I want to be here when the other men arrive."

*****

They broke their fast in the main dining room as usual while the others ate in the great hall so Robbie and Brodie could prepare the day for the others. Uninterested, Anna grabbed some food to bring Alex.

He was still sleeping when she got to his room. She placed the food on the bedside table and walked over to the hearth, adding a log to the fire.

If she concentrated, she could feel that he was sick without even touching him. She dinna ken how it worked, but there was definitely a connection between the two of them.

The sick feeling did not seem as intense today as it did yesterday, so she hoped he was getting better.

She put another log on the fire and sat down on the chair beside his bed. She took out the stone and studied it, feeling it with her fingers. It was so smooth. There were no imperfections, at least to the visible eye.

She remembered the dream. A warm feeling came over her as she remembered opening the gift. The stone had been much larger before he split it. She wondered if he still had the other piece.

She was studying the stone so intensely that she did not realize that he had woken. He lay there just watching her caress the jewel he had given her decades ago.

At one point, she looked up and saw him looking at her. She could feel the heat rise to her face. She immediately got up, putting the jewel in her pocket, and moved the tray of food closer to him.

"I brought some food for ye in case ye were hungry," she said nervously.

He pulled himself up to a sitting position and grabbed the tray.

"Thank ye," he said.

"I'd like to check yer arm when ye are done eating." She wished she had checked it before he started eating so she dinna have to sit there and watch him eat. She had so many things going through her mind but dinna trust herself to speak. She heard someone zoom down the hall, reminding her that this was no place to talk of those thoughts anyhow.

Shortly after, the footsteps were heard going the other direction before a distinct sound of steel hitting the stone ground and an "Aw" as the steps stopped for a couple of seconds before continuing.

"It appears Willie was invited to sword practice," Alex said with the most beautiful smile she'd ever seen.

She chuckled. "Aye, it appears so."

God, he is so handsome, she thought and quickly got up to put another log on the fire for fear that her thoughts were written all over her face.

He took a sip of his tea and a spoonful of porridge.

"How are ye feeling today?" she asked.

He opened his mouth to say something and clearly decided better of it. He turned and took a sip of tea. She looked down at her hands, sure her face was red. After swallowing, he replied, "A little better than yesterday."

"That's good. Had ye not rested yesterday, ye would for sure have felt worse today instead of better."

He smiled and said, "I've gotten more sleep between yesterday and last night than I have had total in two weeks."

They could hear activities going on outside, and she walked over to the window to take a look.

"Sword practicing?" he asked, just to keep the conversation going. It was obvious to both of them, but he could sense her discomfort being in his presence.

"Aye," she replied and just watched for a while, occasionally looking up to the sky and tree lines in hopes of spotting the falcon. She let out a sigh after the third time she searched the sky and turned around. Once again, he had just been watching her. She felt her heart race, and the heat rush to her face again as she walked over to him.

"Let me change yer bandages," she said, thinking it was best to get it over with so she could leave. She removed the tray and took off the bandages. "It's looking much better today than yesterday," she said, sounding pleased. "Yer fever is down from yesterday a lot, but ye still have one. Ye need to rest today," she ordered as she bandaged him back up. "Can I get ye anything else for now?" she asked him.

"Not now," he replied, "but perhaps later I can redeem myself in a game of chess."

She raised her eyebrows, and a smile came on her face. "Ye can try," she said as she turned and left.

She went about her day with the anticipation of spending more time with Alex doing something that would distract her from the awkwardness she felt when she was with him.

She visited her da who was in his parlor, trying to catch up on his affairs. After, she went to the kitchen to help with the plans for feeding the extra mouths.

Following lunch, Robbie and Brodie escorted Anna on a ride of the perimeter of the property, not getting too close to the edge in case someone lie in waiting. They discussed their plans on how to secure the home best as she searched the tree line and sky for the falcon.

The fact that she had not seen the falcon in a while disturbed her. *Perhaps Kendrick found it, killing it out of revenge.* Her heart was saddened at the thought. Why else wouldn't it have come after all it had done for her? That was the only thing that made sense.

The evening meal was served in the great hall on the opposite side from where the men's makeshift beds were. She sat at the head table with her family and Brodie. Only on special occasions did they eat this way.

Anna's attention kept drifting to Alex no matter who she was talking to. Her heart would instantly start beating faster, and she could not concentrate on anything. She just wanted to be with him. When Margaret came by to fill her glass, Anna asked her to prepare a tray for Alex.

"Aye, milady, straight away."

Everyone sat there, enjoying the company even after they were done eating. Anna excused herself from the table.

"Ye don't want to stay for a bit?" Robbie asked.

She kenned that he wanted to keep an eye on her. "Someone needs to bring Alex some food," she replied. "And he challenged me to a game of chess."

Robbie smiled. "Well, I ken that is not something ye take lightly," he teased and made to get up.

"I can take her up if ye wish," Brodie said.

"Aye," Robbie agreed as he sat back down. He turned to Anna. "But ye stay there until either I, Brodie, or Da comes back for ye. Do ye understand? Nobody else. I'll not have ye wandering the dark halls."

"Aye," she mumbled and turned toward the kitchen.

She grabbed the tray while Brodie grabbed a torch.

At the top of the stairs, Brodie lit the torch that sat in the sconce. With the sun down, there was no light spilling from the windows at either end of the hallway.

The flames of the torch cast eerie shadows as they passed doorways. Anna had always walked these halls in the dark and never concerned herself with how easy it would be for someone to hide in a doorway. The thought of it now sent a cold chill up her spine.

Once at Alex's room, Brodie opened the door and entered first, looking around before letting Anna in.

"How are ye doing?" she asked as she set the tray of food down.

"I'll be better once I redeem myself in that game of chess," he replied.

"I'll get the chess set," she turned to leave the room, but Brodie put his hand out to stop her.

"Let me go first." He turned and went out into the hall with her behind him. She directed Brodie to her room, and he entered first with the torch in one hand and sword in the other.

"All right," he said, clearing her to enter. She quickly went to a box that kept her chess pieces and grabbed the wooden board as well. Brodie escorted her back to Alex's room.

Alex had moved the tray to his lap to give room for the chess game. She placed the board on the table and started setting up the pieces.

Brodie added a few logs to the fire and turned to Alex. "Robbie ordered her to stay here until one of us or her father come to pick her up." Anna frowned as she continued setting up the pieces.

Alex nodded before Brodie took his leave.

Alex turned to look at her, noticing her frown, he said, "Everyone's just concerned for yer safety."

"I ken that," she replied sadly. "I just feel like I'm a prisoner in my own home."

He watched her set up the chess pieces as he ate. He smiled as she carefully placed each piece in its proper place, making sure they were all facing the correct way.

After he finished eating, she removed his tray, and he began the game by moving one of his pawns. She countered with one of her own pawns.

The conversation came easier for Anna with something else to do other than just stare at each other, though they kept the conversation to pleasantries.

Robbie came in after half of an hour. "How are ye doing?" he asked Alex.

"Well, physically, I am feeling a lot better, but my pride on the other hand…" He dinna finish but just motioned to the board with his hand. His queen was already gone, along with one of his bishops, both castles, and half of his pawns. She still had most of her higher-ranked pieces.

"Playing chess with her is never an ego booster." Robbie laughed.

"How goes it down there?" Alex asked.

Robbie filled him in on the plans he had for the men he brought. He would wait a couple of days to give Alex time to recuperate before making plans to hunt down the MacDonald.

After Anna finally got his king in checkmate, Robbie declared it was time for all to retire. She put all the pieces in her box and picked up the board.

"Perhaps, my game will be better on the morrow," Alex said to her with a smile.

Anna turned back to him and answered with just a smile.

"Not likely," Robbie blurted out as he escorted her out the door.

CHAPTER

Halfway through the morning meal, Alex came down to join them. Anna's heart skipped a beat as she watched him take a seat next to Robbie. His color looked better, and she could sense the fever was down.

After the meal, Anna took him to the parlor to check his arm. "It is healing nicely," she said. "And yer fever seems to be gone."

"Is he clear for guard duty then?" Robbie said as he walked through the door.

"No heavy lifting or sword fighting," she stated, turning to Robbie to make sure he understood.

"Guard duty does not require sword fighting unless necessary." Robbie smiled as he nudged her.

Anna gave him a look of dissatisfaction before saying, "I'd like to go riding."

"I figured as much," Robbie said. He leaned into her and said, "I saw ye sneak an apple into yer pocket while we were eating."

"I dinna sneak anything," she replied, clearly appalled by his choice of words. "I merely put it in my pocket!"

Robbie smiled, clearly pleased he had gotten her all worked up.

Winking, he said, "Later, we will ride. For now, ye may go to the stable to coddle yer dear horse for a while. Alex can accompany ye." He turned and left the room.

Her heart leaped at the mention of Alex escorting her. "I need to grab my cloak," she said to Alex.

"Aye," he said. He got up and followed her up the stairs.

She tried to ignore the annoyance that he was following her, but the closer she got to the top of the stairs, the more irritated she became. Once at the top, she spun around and snapped, "Am I not allowed to roam the house during the daytime either without someone by my side?" Only after blurting it out did she realize that he had turned down the other direction at the top of the stairs.

He turned to her. "I merely mean to grab my cloak and sword," he said, then put both hands up and added, "Just in case. I promise not to use the sword unless absolutely necessary."

She could feel her cheeks getting red with embarrassment as she quickly turned back toward her room. She sat down on her bed for a little bit to give herself time for her cheeks to return to normal color before going back down the stairs.

By the time she had made it to the front door, he was already outside waiting at the top of the steps, watching the men doing their drills.

She looked at the barn in the distance and took a deep breath, preparing herself for the conversation she kenned they would have.

They walked slowly in silence until they were way out of hearing distance. "I am so sorry," he said to her.

"Sorry?" she replied. "For what?" she asked, briefly looking at him but continuing to walk.

"I gave the stone to ye to help ye remember. I dinna think what would happen if ye had worn it." He paused. "I dinna want ye to forget me 'til we found each other."

He stopped and turned to look into her eyes. "This is all my fault. It was so selfish of me." He fought the urge to take her in his arms and hold her.

She looked into his eyes and saw more love than she could ever have imagined and more heartbreak than one human should ever have known. Her love for him matched what she saw in his eyes. No word could ever explain the love she bore him.

"It was not yer fault," she said as she turned again toward the stable and continued walking. She wanted to hold his hand as they used to in their previous life. It was unusual, they kenned each other more than any one person could in a lifetime, yet they dinna ken what each had gone through in this lifetime, like they were just on a long trip away from each other.

"How much do ye remember?" he asked.

"I remember the curse. I ken the MacDonald who attacked us on the road," she replied. "That is when I realized that ye were the same person in my dreams."

They made it to the stable, and she took the apple out of her pocket and fed it to her horse. "There's my Butterfly," she said.

She turned her head toward Alex and smiled with a twinkle in her eye, confirming that she remembered his nickname for her.

Alex leaned back against a wooden post with one knee bent as he studied her while she talked to her horse. He didn't say anything but was content to watch for however long it took. She talked to the horse much like she did to him in falcon form. She would confide in her animal friends as one would with a best friend or a lover. He could watch her all day. Once done, she turned back to him.

"Are ye all done?" He smiled as he asked with the most affectionate look on his face.

"Aye." She smiled.

He pushed himself off the post, and they left the barn to walk back to the main house.

After a while, she asked, "Do ye still have it?" she looked at him. "The other half of the stone?"

"Nay," he replied. "I had it on me when Gregory MacDonald killed me."

She grew quiet again for a while. "He killed my whole family," she whispered. "He burned our house down in the middle of the night."

"Aye," he replied. "I visited the house after I remembered about us."

"I could have escaped," she confessed, "but I heard the roof collapse on my parents." She looked up to the sky, trying to hold back her tears. "I could not deal with losing them after I had already lost ye… I hid the brooch and ring beneath a stone in my room before laying back down and letting the smoke take me. I was not about to let him take that too."

He was quiet as she confided in him. *God, it feels good to have her trust me again.*

She continued, "I took refuge in the house after I was attacked and dug it out." She looked at him all proud of herself.

He smiled back at her, enjoying her boastful look.

He nodded as they made their way to the stairs. They climbed the stairs, and he opened the door for her. "Have a good day, Anna." He bowed before turning and walking back down the stairs.

*****

The morning seemed to drag, but at least she could get a glimpse of him from the window as he stood in front of the kitchen entrance that was below her room.

Now that she remembered, she couldna imagine life without him. She welcomed the feeling that came from being in his presence. Before she understood their connection, she avoided him, but now she just wanted to be near him.

Her mind kept going back to the curse as she looked at him. Her heart broke for what she kenned would happen. It always did.

As if he kenned she was looking at him, he turned and looked up at her window. She immediately moved to the side, embarrassed. The heat rushed to her face, but she laughed to herself despite her childish gawking.

At the midday meal, she was disappointed to see that Alex was not there. The meal seemed to drag. She moved her food around her plate between bites as her mind drifted to thoughts of him.

After eating, Robbie got up and said, "I'll be right back in a bit to take ye on yer ride."

"I'll be ready." She got up and went upstairs to ready herself. She grabbed her cloak before going to the kitchen to snatch a carrot for her horse.

Alex was waiting at the front door eating some bread and cheese. "Are ye ready?" he asked.

"Is that all yer eating?" she asked.

"Unless that carrot is for me," he replied with a smile.

She looked down at the carrot and put it in her pocket. "Ye should eat something more to get yer strength back. Ye should not be overdoing it."

He smiled and opened the door for her. "I'll be fine."

Robbie was giving orders to the men, so Alex and Anna walked to the stables.

"So when did ye realize that *I* was Robbie's sister?" Anna asked.

"Not 'til we met at the games a few months ago," he replied. "But I ken who ye were the second I saw ye at the games talking to the other women. Robbie saw me staring at ye and brought me over to introduce us."

As they got to the stable, Anna said to Galvin, "We're going for a ride, Galvin."

"Aye, milady. I'll get yer horses ready."

"And Robbie's too, please."

He saddled up Alex's horse, giving Anna time to coddle and feed the carrot to Butterfly. After their horses were ready, they mounted and went outside. Robbie was just reaching the stables. He had two bows slung over his shoulder, and as they exited the stable, he tossed one bow to her, then a quiver with arrows in it.

"Are we hunting?" she asked excitedly.

"Not exactly," he said, "but if we see a stag or two, I thought we could use the meat. I dare say with this many people to feed, our livestock will be gone before winter comes."

"I would have changed into my hunting clothes if I'd have known," she replied.

"Are ye daft, lass? Ye are not going to be running around in trousers in front of all these men, tenants of ours at that, may I add!" he snapped.

"I dinna think of that," she replied, sneaking a look at Alex who raised his eyebrows with a smirk on his face, clearly proving Robbie's point. She secured the bow and quiver to the saddle.

They took the same path they had with Brodie. Halfway around the perimeter, they turned toward the grove where her ma was buried to wait out a deer and discussed the best strategy to finish the MacDonald.

She half listened. She had a great view of the edge of the woods and all around her. She focused on looking for deer for a bit, then she would turn to the sky and the treetops at the edge of the woods before giving a sigh and turning back to look for deer.

She continued the routine of searching for deer, then the sky before sighing when no falcon appeared. After the fourth sigh, Robbie gave her shoulder a little shove. "Will ye stop that sighing already?"

She snapped her head toward him and glared. "I dinna ken I was sighing," she said quietly. "I was hoping to get a glimpse of the falcon when I was out here."

"I ken that, but the sigh after every time ye look is a bit much." She bit her tongue but continued to squint at him before turning to look for deer. Her heart wept for the falcon that she was convinced was killed by Kendrick.

Displeased, Alex gave Robbie a look of unspoken disapproval. Robbie just shrugged his shoulder.

Close to an hour went by when a nice stag stepped out of the woods. She made ready her bow. It was not yet close enough. She waited. The talking ceased, so she kenned they had seen it as well. They waited a bit longer, and it moved closer. Slowly, she raised the bow but continued to wait a few minutes more until it moved into position. She released the arrow.

She humphed with pride as it hit its target. Her eyes gleamed when Robbie gave her a brotherly shove. "Good shot!"

She turned to look at Alex who was just watching her, studying her. *God, his smile is so beautiful.* He nodded at her.

"Let's go get your prize," Robbie said as they trotted off. They dismounted as Robbie made sure it was dead and loaded it on his horse.

They continued their path a distance away from the perimeter, Robbie and Alex deep in conversation. Anna was starting to get uncomfortable the farther they went, looking around. Her heart raced as she unconsciously started to slow down. "Can we cut through the meadow?" she quietly asked.

Robbie and Alex turned and saw the look of fear on her face.

"Aye," Robbie said as they turned. Robbie looked at Alex who always was the first person to sense danger. Robbie raised his eyebrows questioningly.

Alex shrugged his shoulders as he moved over so she could ride between them instead of Robbie's other side. He concentrated on his awareness. His guard had been down with his interest in her, no doubt. He could feel it then. It wasna strong, maybe just one scout or perhaps remnants left by a scout. When he first had these senses, he could not distinguish between a strong threat and a minor one. A threat was a threat.

This threat was not strong enough that he would think that an attack would occur, but that could change overnight.

They went to the house where Robbie let Anna off at the front entrance. "Go inside, and I will take Butterfly back to the stables," he ordered.

He dropped off their kill, ordering a couple of the men to tend to it.

Robbie and Alex turned the horses toward the barn. "Was there someone out there?" Robbie asked.

"I dinna feel any strong danger," he replied. "That was the same spot where the one camp was. Perhaps there was a scout, but it was not Gregory."

Robbie did not look convinced, so Alex continued, "When I first had these intuitions, I couldna distinguish a strong threat from an unimportant one. A threat was a threat."

They dropped the horses off at the barn and walked back.

"I will explore it more tonight in the cover of darkness," Alex said. He looked at Robbie to make sure he understood his intent without verbalizing it.

Robbie nodded.

"I'll need to get some food and rest first, though," Alex said.

On returning to the house, Alex searched Anna out to make good his promise of a rematch in chess before the evening meal. They played in the parlor, and though he lost, he had definitely given her more of a challenge.

Uncle Ian arrived while they were playing chess. He had made it back to his house earlier in the day and found out from his wife that Anna had come back. Robbie and his da talked with him in the drawing room for quite some time.

"Well, did ye find anything out?" Robbie asked.

"Just some deserted campsites on Duncan land that I'd never seen before."

Filling him in on the events that had taken place, he stayed only for a bit, wanting to leave for home before sunset.

Roasted venison was served for the evening meal in the hall. Alex got his fill to eat and excused himself to retire early.

The meal was a feast for most of these men. They were cheerful and loud, but Anna's joy left when Alex went upstairs.

CHAPTER

It was a warm day, and she was sitting by the stream with her feet in the water. She looked up to see the falcon flying in low, following the river downstream. It landed on the other side of the stream.

She smiled at it as it stared at her. Her focus briefly set on the mark on his chest. She'd seen that mark before, but where?

Then she remembered.

*****

She woke up and pondered the dream. She pulled out the stone. The other piece was shaped like the arrow on the falcon's chest. Could he be the falcon? Her heart sped up, and she was exhilarated by the realization that her falcon was not dead.

She had heard of shape-shifters. If she could believe that she is eternally bound on this earth and to Alex, why not believe in shape-shifters?

She sat up. Had she ever been with him when she'd seen the falcon? She'd been with her family and Brodie but never him.

That would explain the dagger. And his family crest even has a falcon on it. Perhaps it is something that runs in the Boswell lineage. That would definitely explain the sense of peace she got with the falcon since she was bound to him.

All of a sudden, she remembered how she talked to the falcon. What things had she told it? Her dreams. Things that she would not tell anyone else. Though he would have understood her dreams.

He had saved her. She would not be here today if it was not for him, and they would not have met for another couple of decades perhaps if he had not.

She got up and walked over to the window, looking out over the grounds below. She looked up to the sky smiling, happy that she had figured it all out. There were a million stars out and a moon, three quarters of the way full.

Then she saw something in the distance. She watched it as it flew toward the house as if it was going around to the other wing of the house. It was the falcon. It saw her in the window and changed directions.

She quietly opened the window so as not to wake her father in the other room. The cold night air hit her, and with it came the falcon, which landed on the windowsill. She looked at it...him. Slowly, she raised her hand and pet his head with two of her fingers, letting them go down his back. She leaned down and whispered, "Ye should have waited until that wing of yers healed completely."

He was very still as she moved her fingers down to his breast where the marking was. A breeze came, making her shiver all over, and suddenly, she became aware of how her gown formed around her body. Her hardened nipples protruding through the thin material of her chemise.

She could feel the heat rise to her face. Quickly, she pulled her hand away, crossing her arms while rubbing her hands along them as if to warm them, but it was more to cover herself up.

She tossed a look toward her da's room and turned back to the falcon. "Ye'd better go," she whispered.

He turned around and flew around to the other wing.

She quietly closed the window and put a couple of more logs on the fire before crawling back into bed. As cold as it had gotten from the window being opened, she was not cold at all. The heat she felt inside was nothing she had ever experience before. A need…an ache, deep inside. Oh, how she wanted him.

*****

His room was freezing from the window being opened for so long. He threw some more wood on the hot coals and quickly got dressed.

So she kenned. He was sure she dinna ken when they were out in the field yesterday the way she was looking for the falcon.

She dinna look too upset by it, though he couldna concentrate on much with the way her gown clung to her every curve in the wind. And her hand stroking his chest, all he wanted to do was change back into his human form and take her into his arms, kiss her, and—

No, I have to stop and focus, he thought as he put his boots on. He quietly left the room and made a stop at the kitchen to grab anything edible before meeting Robbie in the parlor.

"What the heck took ye so long? I saw ye come out of the woods a half hour ago."

Alex shrugged. "I'm hungry," he said as he held up his hands full of jerky and a biscuit. "It happens."

"Well, what did ye find out?" Robbie asked.

"There are two scouts patrolling the area right now. One on the north end and the other on the south. The third scout camp is empty. There is another camp about a two or three days walking distance, I'd guess with perhaps five men," Alex replied.

"We could take out the scouts tonight," Robbie said.

"Aye, we could," he replied. "We'd have to go through the woods as they would see us from the moonlight out in the field. There's not a cloud in the sky." He thought for a bit. "No, they have a good angle no matter where ye enter from the woods."

"We could leave under cover tomorrow in the cart going to the village and attack the other camp at night," Robbie suggested.

"And leave Anna protected by some tradesmen," Alex said as he shook his head. "What if Gregory MacDonald is one of the scouts here?"

"Ye dinna ken?" Robbie asked.

"I wasna going to get close enough to get an arrow through me," he stated. "It would have been different if it was daylight. I would have been able to tell."

"The barn is fairly close to the woods," Robbie indicated. "Tomorrow we will have a distraction and get ourselves to the barn before nightfall. We will attack the two scouts watching the house."

"We canna leave any sign of a struggle. We'll need to rid the bodies," Alex said.

"Aye, I'll take care of that,"

"What kind of distraction will ye have?"

"My da's been wanting a banquet while the family is here all together. I've not been here in almost a year, other than to quickly gather my belonging before the wedding. And Willie hasn't been here for a few months. The planning of it will have people coming and going. Perhaps we can have someone pick up some whiskey on the morrow. After it gets loaded, we will get to the barn under the cover of the cart.

"Aye," Alex said. "That sounds like a plan."

CHAPTER

27

Anna woke up early and sat by the window, watching the sunrise. She'd never get bored of it, how the colors spread across the sky. It was definitely her favorite time of day.

The realization of her discovery last night hit her. How does she act now that he knows that she does? Does she say something about it or just ignore that she kens?

Then the thought of how she must have looked in her thin chemise with the wind blowing her gown, outlining every bit of her. She suddenly felt embarrassed but at the same time amused at her lack of modesty. Once again, she felt a yearning for him, a heat building up deep inside her.

She got dressed quickly, hoping that perhaps she could eat quickly before Alex came down. Her face would give her thoughts away if she made eye contact with him. She would just have to ignore him if he was there.

She went downstairs and peeked into the dining room, no Alex.

"Where's da?" she asked Robbie as she sat down.

"He's in the drawing room, planning a banquet," Willie said.

"A banquet?" she asked. "Is this the best time for a banquet?"

"In five days' time," Robbie replied, "and aye, it fits in with our plan."

She looked at him, not too pleased with his answer as she grabbed the porridge and poured it into her bowl. Robbie handed her a bowl of fruit, which she added to the porridge.

"Can we go riding again?" she asked.

"Aye, we can go after we eat. It's really cold out there, so dress warmly," he replied. As an afterthought, he said, "And bring yer bow. With a banquet coming, I hope to get one this morning than to have one of the men miss their drills in order to hunt later."

"Can I go hunting too?" Willie asked.

"Nay," Robbie replied, "ye have drills too." He ruffled his hair as Willie jerked his head away, looking around to see if anyone outside of them had seen.

Not wanting to be at the table when Alex arrived, she gulped down her food and went upstairs to grab her cloak and bow. Robbie was already outside waiting when she got back. As they headed toward the stable, she glanced at the men who were already training as they passed them, but there was no sign of Alex. Even though she did not want to talk to him, she was disappointed that she did not get a glimpse of him.

Robbie snickered as she looked around. "Ye are smitten with him," he said.

"With whom?" she snapped as she moved her attention to straightening her knitted arm warmers.

"Alex," he replied as he swayed to the side, bumping shoulders with her.

She jerked her head up to glare at him. She could feel the heat rising to her face as she shoved him and moved faster, but that just made him laugh some more. Ignoring his snickering, she sped up.

Reaching the barn, she went in and turned toward Butterfly's stall as a hand went over her mouth. She was yanked into a stall, arms thrashing as she tried to break free so she could call out a warning, but it was no use.

Robbie walked in, and as he turned, he was clobbered over the head with a piece of wood and knocked out. They dragged him into a stall across from where she was and propped him beside Galvin's passed out body.

"Somebody wants to see ye, lovey," a man whispered in her ear from behind.

Her heart raced as the panic set in. Without setting eyes on him, she kenned who it was. It was Kendrick. He licked the back of her neck. Immediately disgusted, she tried to jerk out of his grip, but it only made him laugh.

*****

Alex threw his cloak on and grabbed a bit to eat. He put a couple of biscuits in his pocket and popped a piece of cheese in his mouth before grabbing a couple pieces of smoked meat. He was starving, but he purposefully didn't come down to break his fast with Anna at the table.

Hoping the cold air and the walk would clear his mind of the image of her last night, he headed to the stable. Ugh, he couldna get his mind off last night, her in her chemise caressing him. He could feel himself hardening just thinking about it. He shook his head in an attempt to get the thoughts out of his head.

He was still some ways away from the stable, but he would have expected them to be saddled up by now, waiting for him. His heart started beating faster in his chest, and he kenned it was not because of his thoughts from last night.

He sped up. As he got closer, the sense of dread made him move even faster. He unsheathed his sword as he entered the stable.

There was a man at the end of the row holding Anna from behind with a pistol pointed to her head. He looked at her. Her hands were tied and her mouth gagged, her eyes full of remorse. He looked back at her captor, Kendrick.

"Drop the sword!" he ordered.

He hesitated. "Drop it, or I'll kill her." He cocked the pistol.

Alex slowly laid the sword down on the ground with his other hand held up and opened. Something hit him in the head, and everything went black.

*****

The men dragged them out the man door in the back of the barn where their horses waited. They tied Alex's hands and feet and plopped him over a horse. Doing the same with her, Kendrick mounted behind her and the other man behind Alex. The stable blocked the view of the men doing their drills in the courtyard, which enabled them to make it to the woods unnoticed.

It didn't take her long to get dizzy from her head dangling. Closing her eyes, she could feel them building up with tears that were just making her headache that much worse.

"Here we are again, lovey," Kendrick said. "It appears we are meant to be together." He pinched her behind, making her jerk. She bit into her gag in an attempt to keep from crying.

He used his foot to pry her head up before grabbing her hair to pull her head up as far as it would go and leaned down as close as he could to her ear. "We'll have plenty of time to finish what we started," he said before letting go of her hair. Her head just plopped down, and she let the tears roll.

This is it. We've barely gotten to ken each other this time, and now it's over. When's it going to end, God? Have I not yet paid for my crimes? I just dinna think I can take this anymore.

It was hard for her to judge which way they were headed from her view, especially since they were in the woods. At one point, she heard Kendrick take a drink of something.

"Give me some of that, Kendrick," the other man said. "It's freezing out here. At least my insides can be warm."

"Ye drank all yers, now ye want mine. No way!" he snapped. "If ye are cold, take his cloak," Kendrick pointed to Alex.

"Aah," the other man said. "That's a nice cloak."

The other horse stopped, and the man hopped down. Kendrick stopped and turned the horse a bit to watch. Anna turned her head to see what was going on.

"I never had a cloak as fine as this before," he said as he leaned down, reaching under Alex's chin to undo the button.

Alex jerked his head up, hitting him in the nose. "Aah!" the man yelled, moving his hands to his nose. "I think he broke my nose!"

Kendrick laughed.

"Aah!" He pulled his hands away from his nose and looked at the blood. "Ye bastard!" He brought his knee up and smashed it into Alex's face. Then he grabbed his hair, pulling his face up, and reached under his chin to unbutton the cloak before dropping his head down.

Alex turned his head to look at Anna, tears streaming down her face.

The man swung the cloak on over his own. "Aah, this is nice, man." He rubbed his hands up and down the heavy wool.

"The hell with the cloak," Kendrick said as he dismounted his horse. "Get a look at those boots."

"Aye," the other man replied. "Let's see how easy it is taking those off."

Kendrick bent and picked up a log. He brought it down over Alex's head. His body went limp again.

She tried to scream, but it was muffled by the gag in her mouth. Kendrick walked over to her and leaned down, wiping her hair away from her eyes. She glared at him, though she trembled inside with fear.

"Keep it up, and I'll give ye a good wallop too."

He walked around, cut the binding that were tying his feet together, and started taking off Alex's boots. Once off, he replaced the binding at his ankles.

"Haha!" he called out, holding them up for the other man to see. He put them on his feet before securing his boots to the back of his saddle. Both men mounted their horses.

"Let's go. We've wasted enough time," Kendrick said as he kicked his horse into motion.

*****

About an hour later, the man with the cloak pulled out one of the biscuits Alex had stashed in his cloak pocket.

"What are ye eating?" Kendrick asked.

"A biscuit I found in the cloak pocket," the man replied.

"Are there any more?"

"Aye, but none for the likes of ye," he replied, "unless, of course, ye care to trade me for a swig of yer whisky."

There was a pause, then Kendrick handed over his flask. "Just a wee bit, man," he said.

The other man took a gulp and handed the flask back before tossing him a biscuit.

There was perhaps an hour of sunlight left when they came to a small house in the woods. Kendrick grabbed her by the back of the cloak and shoved her off the horse down to the ground. She'd landed on her feet, but since they were tied and she was so dizzy, she fell back into a sitting position.

Kendrick dismounted.

"Untie his feet. I'll not be carrying him inside," Kendrick ordered.

"I'll do no such thing. He already broke my nose!"

Kendrick picked up Alex's head by his hair and looked him in the eye. "Ye kick him, and I'll have my way with her here and now." He glared at him with his good eye.

The man took a dagger and cut his legs loose before yanking him down off the horse.

Kendrick grabbed Anna's arm and yanked her up off the ground. "Get up, ye bitch!" he yelled. Opening the door, he shoved her in, then Alex.

She stumbled in, landing on the floor. It was cold and dark inside. The only furniture was a table and two chairs. One window allowed the evening sunlight in.

"Sit down," he ordered Alex as he dragged a chair over to the middle of the floor with its back to the door. Alex sat down and glared at him as the other man tied him down.

"Go bring the horses to the stream," Kendrick ordered the other man.

The man let out a humph before leaving and closed the door.

Kendrick turned to look at Anna. He grabbed her arm and yanked her up off the floor, dragging her up against the wall. His face had deep groves from where the falcon's talons had carved him. Her eyes bounced between his good eye and the one glossed over.

Backing her up to a wall, she tried to dart away on the side with his bad eye. He grabbed her neck squeezing it, only lightening his grip once she stood in place.

With his other hand, he grabbed her breast and squeezed it hard. She could hear Alex struggling in the chair to get loose.

"Oh, calm down!" he yelled as he pulled back his arm and punched her in the stomach. She buckled over. Grabbing her by her hair, he dragged her to a chair, facing Alex, and tied her there.

Gripping her hair again, he yanked on it until she tipped her head to face him. He took his finger and touched her chin, sliding it across her face and down her neck.

"Perhaps we can finish before he gets here," he said. She jerked her head to the side. Laughing, he walked behind her, putting his face against hers so they both faced Alex, cheek to cheek. Smiling, he moved his hand between her legs and slowly started to pull the layers of her skirt up.

"Perhaps he'd like to watch."

She yanked her head away from his and squeezed her legs together as Alex yelled and struggled in his chair. The chair bounced off the floor as he struggled.

Kendrick laughed as he let her go and walked out the door.

She held back her tears. When the door closed behind him, she tipped her head back to face the ceiling in an attempt to keep them under control, but a couple of tears escaped. She took a deep breath to calm herself.

"Anna," Alex said.

She could not look at him. She felt so humiliated.

"Anna. Do ye have the dagger on ye?"

She nodded but continued to face the ceiling with her eyes closed.

"Anna, I promise ye," he said as he started to used his chin to push his plaid off his shoulder, "this will not end here."

He brought his hands up as much as he could and leaned down to unbutton as much of his shirt as he could reach. "Anna," he said. A couple of more tears escaped, but she didna move.

"Anna, look at me…please," he pleaded. His anger gave way to the need to comfort her. She took another deep breath and brought her head down and opened her eyes. Her eyes gave away the guilt she felt.

"It's not yer fault," he said.

She looked down at where he had unbuttoned his shirt, his chest partly showing. "Look at me," he said again. She raised her eyes back to his.

"Do ye trust me, Anna?" he asked. Her tears started to roll down her face, which he could see in the last of the sunlight.

He closed his eyes as he took a deep breath, opening them once more to lock on hers. This was the first time he'd ever done this in front of someone. He dinna ken what it would look like, but he wanted her to watch him. It was the most intimate thing he had to give her, and though he dinna ken her long in this lifetime, their souls kenned each other.

He focused on his breathing until he felt the change starting to come, the heat spreading through him until he gave into it. He felt himself shrinking, forming into the falcon. He kept his eyes open, never taking them off her. She just watched him, with no emotion, numb to everything.

It does not matter. None of this does. Either one of us or both will be dead soon, she thought.

The urge to fly came over him like an explosion. He shook the rest of his shirt off himself and hopped out of the ropes that had bound him to the chair, landing on the floor where she followed him with her eyes.

He turned his back toward her and let the sensation take him over again as he turned back into human form. He immediately grabbed his shirt and put it on to cover his naked body before turning to her. Her face was expressionless, rigid, like a statue.

He gently removed her gag as their eyes met. "Where's the dagger?" he asked.

"In my right boot," she whispered, still expressionless.

He knelt and reached under her dress until he found the dagger and carefully pulled it out. He quickly cut her loose, handing her the dagger before turning to finish putting on the rest of his clothes.

When he turned around to face her again, she was looking at the ground but slowly raised her head to meet his. His right cheekbone had a big bruise where the man had kneed him, and his eye was swollen half shut.

Her hands were down by her side, but she gripped the dagger so hard her knuckles were white. She was shaking.

He opened his arms to take her in, but she dinna move.

"It'll be all right. I'll get ye out of here," he promised.

She shook her head. "So we can do this again some other time," she said. "Any time we're together, it'll be the same thing," she spat. "It would have been better if we never found each other."

"Don't give up on me now, Anna," he pleaded, "please."

She slowly lifted the dagger as she shook her head.

Swiftly, he grabbed her wrist. "We're getting out of here," he said. "It's the jewels he's after. I'll take ye home, to the safety of yer family, and I'll take the stone to him."

She shook her head. He gently took the dagger from her and pulled her up for a hug. He could feel her despair. He just held her tight for a couple of minutes as she cried.

He slowly moved her to the chair again and sat her down. He knelt in front of her. He placed the dagger on the floor and took her cold and shaking hands into his. "This is my fault," he said, his eyes locked on hers. "I'll make this right. I swear to ye." He bowed his head, kissing her hands to seal his promise before resting his head on them.

He sensed someone coming. He grabbed the dagger and went to the door. When the door flung opened, he stabbed, grabbing his victim, and flung him inside to the ground. It was Kendrick.

He looked around outside before closing the door and turned. Kendrick was lying on his stomach, moaning but clearly trying to maneuver a way to grab his pistol that lay in his belt.

Alex wanted to flip him over and run him through, looking at him face-to-face but dinna want to chance the pistol going off and killing Anna or him, leaving Anna all alone to defend herself. He raised the dagger high and finished him off before turning him over and grabbing the pistol.

He turned to make sure Anna was still where he put her. She just stared at Kendrick's body with a blank face.

Kneeling, Alex quickly took his boots off Kendrick and put them back on his own feet.

He went to the door and quietly opened it to survey the outside. The other man was gone, perhaps to get Gregory.

He placed the pistol in his belt and went over to Anna. "Come on. We've got to get out of here," he said as he grabbed her hand, but she made no attempt to move.

He placed the dagger in his boot and picked her up gently, carrying her to the horse. He sat her on the horse and mounted behind her, holding her close as they went into the woods.

The moonlight did not offer much light since they traveled through the woods. Their pace was slow, and Anna fell asleep as he held her against his body.

He couldna get the words she had said to him out of his mind. *It would have been better if we never found each other.* It kept going through his head. His body ached at the truth in her words. Up until they had met, she had lived a happy and carefree life. Had he never given her the stone, she'd not have been in this position. He could have avoided her to save her from the inevitable pain that was fated to them.

After several hours, he stopped the horse and slowly slid down, cradling her body. Taking her over to a big rock, he backed up against it and slowly lowered himself down to a sitting position.

She moaned a bit from the change in position, but he cradled her on his lap with her head on his chest curled under his chin. He closed his eyes to catch a bit of sleep as he held her tight.

CHAPTER

S he heard a couple of birds and opened her eyes. The sun had not yet come out, but it would soon. It was that time when the birds would wake in anticipation of the sun appearing and warming up everything that it touched.

Normally, she would have enjoyed just listening to the birds, but right now, it reminded her that they needed to get going, to continue their run from being hunted.

It was definitely cold. She was chilled to the bone where she was exposed to the air despite her cloak wrapped around her, but the side that lay against Alex's body was warm. She wished she could just stay this way forever, safe in his arms, but she kenned that would never be allowed to happen.

She lay there as still as possible so as not to wake him and to avoid continuing their journey home. She wanted to be close to him. She needed his touch, but kenned it was limited, either one or both would not make it. It was their destiny, their curse.

She thought of her family and how upset they would be if she died. She thought of Butterfly then Alex. *I love him so much.*

The sun finally showed its first light. A layer of frost covered everything, but the birds dinna care. They sang their songs louder and louder as the sun shone more and more.

The horse snorted at them. Alex stirred beneath her. She slowly got up. She kenned they needed to put more distance between themselves and their captors. She walked over to pet the horse in order to avoid looking at Alex.

The coldness hit him immediately. He'd already been awake for a while but kenned this would be the last time he would hold her. She was mad at him and rightfully so.

He had gifted her with the stone in hopes that she'd remember him and wait. There were times when their lives had finally crossed paths, but life together was unattainable for one reason or another. He would spend the rest of his days in agony, wanting her, for a lifetime. She was the only thing that would make him whole.

She had every right to be angry. He got up off the ground and looked around to orient himself. He kenned the direction they needed to go. He had noted last night from where the sun set.

"We need to get started," he said to her.

"Aye," she said as she mounted the horse.

He pulled the dagger out of his boot and handed it to her. "Take this in case we get separated."

She looked down at the dagger, noticing his emblem on the hilt. She eyed it for a minute as if she looked right through it, not really seeing it. Finally, she grabbed it, placing it back in its scabbard inside her boot as he mounted behind her.

*****

They traveled in the direction of her family home. He was sure the search party would be spread out far enough that each person could only keep the two people beside them visible. They'd have a better chance of finding someone, given they wanted to be found.

By late morning, a call came out as Robbie trotted over to them. An echo of "over here" was heard farther away each time.

Her da made it to them the same time Robbie did, and he dismounted as she did and ran into his outstretched arm. He held her tight. She fought back the tears that longed to be shed.

"Are ye all right, Anna?" he asked as he pulled her away long enough to see her. She nodded, and he pulled her back in.

Robbie looked from her to Alex. Alex kenned he looked bad. His vision was obscured by the bump on his cheekbone and swollen eye, which he was sure was black and blue.

He dismounted, and Robbie pulled a flask of whiskey out and offered it to him, but neither exchanged any words.

Alex looked at Anna, who was now drinking down a bit of whiskey herself.

"How many are there?" Robbie asked quietly. By now, Brodie had joined the two of them.

"I dinna ken," Alex replied. "They took us to a cottage in the middle of the woods. We'd got there as the sun just started to go down."

He stole a look at Anna then looked back. "Two of them tied us up and left. We got loose before the one called Kendrick came back in. I killed him."

He took another swig of the whiskey. "The other one was gone by then. I presume to get the others. We took the horse and rode most of the night, but our pace was slow. We stopped only for a couple of hours."

He combed his fingers through his hair. "I need to go back."

"I'll go with ye," Robbie said.

"No," Alex snapped. "Ye need to keep Anna safe."

Robbie looked at him for a minute before nodding.

Alex handed the flask back as he took a deep breath and walked over to Anna and her da. She turned to face him as he stopped beside her.

He held his hand out, his palm facing up. "The gemstone," he said. "Give it to me. That's what he wants. I'll bring it to him. He will have no need to come back for ye."

She looked at him as if he was daft. "He'll kill ye!" she snapped.

He didn't flinch. His hand stayed out, waiting. "It's the only way," he said. They stood there for what seemed like forever, but he kenned it was only a few seconds.

Robbie walked over and put his hand on Anna's shoulder. "Anna," he said quietly, "give him the stone."

She turned her glare at him. She wanted to say that Gregory MacDonald would kill him no matter what, because it was his destiny, a curse, on them, because she loved Alex instead of Gregory, but instead, she dug into her pocket, which had an opening to access her pouch beneath. She felt around for the stone and pulled it out by the ribbon, letting it dangle above his hand before releasing it.

His fingers slowly closed, as if in slow motion, until she could see it no more, and she looked into his eyes, glaring at him. His heart broke, but he would not show her. He gave her a bow with as much sincerity as he could, for he kenned it would be the last memory of him she would have.

Robbie handed Alex his sword that he had picked up from the stable.

Alex turned and walked toward his horse as he sheathed his sword. Robbie followed him as he took the cloak off his back. When Alex mounted the horse, Robbie held his cloak out to Alex. Alex just looked at him. When he dinna take it immediately, Robbie pushed it closer. "Take it."

Alex accepted it and swung it over his back, buttoning it beneath his chin. Robbie grabbed some smoked meat from his pouch that was wrapped up and his flask of whiskey, handing both of them to Alex as well.

Alex took them both and tipped his head to Robbie. He took one more look at Anna before turning the horse around and proceeded back the way he came.

*****

They mounted their horses and headed back home. Robbie and her da discussed their options of keeping her safe. With no one focused on her, she finally let the tears roll down her cheek, trying to be as still as possible so as to not alert her da who sat behind her that she was crying.

She dinna say anything to him, no goodbye, be safe…I love ye. She understood now that she had loved him from the first time she had laid eyes on him. She had pushed the feeling away because it just didn't make sense to her why she had such strong feelings for someone without even knowing him. The feeling of love for him was stronger than any feeling she had ever known, and now she will never be able to tell him.

He'd saved her life, not once but several times. She kenned he loved her…and now he went to give the ultimate sacrifice for her so she could live in peace…but peace without him was a lonely place to be…for a lifetime.

CHAPTER

They arrived back at the house by early evening. It was decided that first thing in the morning they would all head out to the estate of Robbie's in-law. They would stay in a small cottage a bit away from the main house so they could have some freedom but safe on MacKay land, under MacKay protection.

Margaret heated some water and had a tub brought up for Anna. Once alone, Anna got into the tub. She could smell the rose scent of the water, just how she liked it, but no amount of pleasure could ease the feeling she had inside her. She sat in the water, numb. As the water started to cool down, she dunked her head to wash her hair. She went through the motions of washing up, emotionless. Once clean, she changed into a clean dress before going down to the evening meal. She was distant and did not say much. Everyone was making plans for the trip and their long absence from their home.

She just picked at her food, not really eating anything, so she went to her room and packed a bag. It didn't take her long. They may be there for a while, but they would not be taking a cart, so everyone had to pack lightly.

She sat on the bed and pulled out the ruby brooch and ring. She studied them before sliding the ring on her finger. She could remember now when he had first put it on her.

"Let's get married as soon as we can," he said. "I think if we are joined, it would break the spell."

But her parents wanted time to plan the perfect wedding for their only daughter. They couldna give a reason good enough for the quickness of a wedding. They certainly could not have told them that they were cursed. Who would believe that?

She heard someone coming and quickly pulled the ring off and put both pieces back in her sack.

"Milady," Margaret said as she came in. "I made some chamomile tea for ye. I put it in yer mother's room and have a nice toasty fire in there for ye."

She kenned Margaret was sent to make sure she was securely in the room adjacent from her da's with the hallway door locked.

"Thank ye, Margaret," she said as she got up off the bed and moved to the door. Anna pointed to the sack on the floor. "I've finished packing."

"Aye," Margaret said as she followed her down the hall and into her da's room. "I'll be sure to have someone bring it down. I'll pack some food for ye as well. Will ye be needing anything else, milady?" she asked once Anna was safely in her mother's room.

"Nay, Margaret. Good night."

The room was warm just like Margaret had said. She took her clothes off down to her chemise, remembering the last night she was here at the window in her gown as she stoked the falcon's breast. A solitary tear rolled down her cheek.

It was Alex the whole time. He'd been there for her at her lowest point, and she dinna even ken it was him. She pulled the cover's back and sat down, slipping her legs under the covers. She took a sip of tea in an attempt to keep the rest of the tears from coming. She concentrated on her breathing to clear her head as she finished her tea.

She had thought that she had the tears under control, but as her head hit the pillow, she could not hold them back any longer. Burying her face in her pillow, they poured out until sleep finally overtook her, ceasing the tears from rolling.

*****

They broke their fast quickly and were off before the crack of dawn. Nobody talked about Alex in front of Anna.

She was grateful to have Butterfly with her. It gave her comfort, but how she wished she could gallop away from everyone for a time. She would tell her how sad she was and pour her heart out. Anna kenned that she would not be let out of everyone's sight for that to happen.

Their trip was hard riding as they were all anxious to get to MacKay land. At one point, on the second day, they stopped to water the horses and eat their midday provisions. She started getting apprehensive, but nobody else appeared to be alarmed.

When readying to leave after their break, Anna went to mount her horse. She felt a sharp pain in her chest to the point that she took her foot out of the stirrup, held her chest, and leaned up against the horse. She kenned something had happened to Alex. Their connection to each other was so strong that she seemed to feel the pain that he physically bore.

"Are ye okay?" Robbie asked.

Knowing she could not explain it to him, she nodded before taking a deep breath and proceeded to mount the horse despite the pain. "Aye," she forced out. How could she expect someone to understand the bond she had with this man she barely kenned?

As she rode the rest of the day, she could feel her insides trembling. She was nauseous from the realization that Alex was seriously wounded. The fact that she kenned it would happen dinna make the outcome any easier.

*****

On the third day, Brodie and Willie parted. They would proceed back to the castle, and by midafternoon, the rest of them arrived at Robbie's in-laws, which gave them plenty of time to settle into their cottage and clean themselves up before the evening meal. The cottage was small and not far from the main house, but it offered more freedom than if they were in a guest room in the main house.

The evening meal conversation was pleasant, and no one mentioned the circumstances as to why they were there, which Anna was grateful for.

Anna and her da excused themselves shortly after finishing their meal due to the tiredness of their long journey.

*****

Early the next morn, Robbie requested an audience with the laird, but he dinna get the appearance until after the midday meal.

He explained the past events and requested further leave to aid Alex. There was a minute of silence as the laird contemplated. "Aye, ye may take yer leave, but ye will be giving up yer Christmas leave to make up for yer lost time."

"Aye, my lord," Robbie replied.

"I'll give ye ten days," the laird granted him, "and ye are acting on yer own accord. In no way do ye represent this land of yer mother's. I have no fondness for the MacDonalds, but any conflict between ye and the MacDonald will fall on the Duncan family and not mine."

"I understand," Robbie bowed, "Thank ye, my lord."

*****

Robbie left in search of Brodie, whom he found on duty at the portcullis. Robbie explained his audience with the laird. "Will ye check in on my family for me?" he asked. "I leave in the morn."

"Aye," Brodie said. "Godspeed."

Robbie arrived home in time for the evening meal. He told them his plans of leaving on the morrow to look for Alex.

After the meal, the women retired to the parlor where they sipped tea. Anna kenned it was a way to get her out of the room in order for the men to talk about the best strategy to find Alex.

She had spent most of the day with Mary Ellen who insisted she go through her wardrobe and pick out a few dresses since she dinna come with many clothes. Anna had welcomed the distractions from her thoughts.

Now they were setting her up with quilting pieces as they talked and sipped their tea, which only made her miss her mother. It made her feel worse instead of better, but they meant well.

Once the men were finished, they said their good nights, and Anna and her da bid Godspeed to Robbie who gave Anna an extralong hug.

CHAPTER

Alex wore Anna's gemstone around his neck. He walked out of the woods into their campsite with his sword held in ready position.

There were five of them in total. They all got up, and one came at him. He stepped to the side and thrust, driving his blade into the man with a fatal strike. He jerked his sword out of his opponent as the man dropped to the ground.

Gregory held his hand out to stop another man from approaching Alex. He smiled as he saw the stone on his neck before his eyes locked onto Alex's.

"Come and get it," Alex said as his empty hand motioned him to come closer.

Gregory unsheathed his sword and walked over. They stood there in front of each other for a minute, each one waiting for the other to strike first. As Gregory's eyes drifted back down to the stone, Alex swung, slicing Gregory's arm due to his delayed block.

Gregory attacked back but was matched with Alex's fierce blocks. They went back and forth for a while until Gregory stepped back out of range of one of Alex's attacks before coming in low at Alex's thigh, causing him to stagger. Gregory kicked Alex in the stomach, knocking him down to a sitting position against a tree. Alex's sword hit the ground with his hand still firmly gripped on the hilt. As he went to lift the sword, Gregory stepped on his blade, trapping Alex's hand under the hilt.

Gregory smiled as he put the tip of his sword at Alex's throat under the ribbon holding the jewel. With a flick of his wrist, Gregory broke the ribbon, freeing the jewel, which he grabbed in his other hand just as Alex grabbed a dagger from his boot with his free hand and thrust it into Gregory's leg.

Gregory faltered, allowing Alex to regain control of his sword. While Gregory pocketed his treasure, Alex thrust his sword into Gregory's side. Gregory looked down at the bloodied laceration before swinging his sword.

They both pressed on without yielding. Gregory was able to keep Alex at bay despite his injuries. He thrust at Alex who dodged out of the way but tripped over something, putting him off-balance once again. Gregory swung his sword, slicing Alex from his chest down to his abdomen on his right side as Alex toppled over a log, landing on the ground. Once again, Gregory stepped on Alex's blade, trapping his hand as he placed the tip of his own sword at Alex's chest.

"Where are the rest of the jewels?" he asked. "The ruby brooch." Alex just looked at him. "The pearl necklace." Still no answer.

Gregory moved the sword to Alex's throat. "The diamond ring." With no answer, Gregory smiled. "Aah, the girl has it. I have no need of ye then." He called out to the other men. "We go find the girl!" he yelled as he lifted his sword to deliver a fatal strike.

"No!" Alex yelled, stopping Gregory in midstrike. "She doesna ken where they are."

The sword was back on Alex's throat. "Then where are they?"

"At a cottage on MacLeod land," Alex replied quietly, "near Dunvegan castle."

Gregory squinted his eyes as he drew closer to Alex. "Ye'd better pray they are still there."

He turned to the others and yelled, "Tie his hands and tie him to the horse." He put his sword back in the scabbard while one man grabbed Alex under his arm and pulled him up. The other man bound his hands.

Gregory looked down at his side. He untied his scarf, rolled it up, and put it on his gaping wound before adjusting his belt over it to secure it tightly to stop the bleeding.

"Let's go," he said as he mounted his horse, kicking it into motion with Alex in tow.

Alex kept pace with the horse despite his injuries. He gripped the rope with this left hand so when he lagged behind, it would not extend his right arm, putting more strain on his wound.

*****

They traveled for two days, only stopping to camp at night. At one point, Alex lost his footing and fell. Gregory turned in his saddle and smiled at him as he let the horse drag him for a minute before stopping to let Alex get up.

"If ye don't produce the jewels, I'll drag ye all day." Gregory said, before adding, "And if ye die on the way…well, I'll have to drag yer pretty lady all day then…after having my way with her, of course." Alex glared at him before Gregory turned back around in his saddle, kicking his horse back into motion.

The second night, they stopped early to set up camp. Gregory sent one of his men to acquire two small boats for the morn.

*****

They started before the sun was in the sky, the moon would be full in a day's time, and there was not a cloud in the sky, so there was enough light to guide them on the path.

By the time they got to the port, the sun was still rising. The port was too busy with fishermen making ready to set sail for the morn for anyone to take notice of someone tied and being pulled. They got on their boats and waited for the others to come back from taking care of the horses. As soon as the men were back, they began their journey toward Dunvegun castle.

They arrived in an alcove on MacLeod land a couple of hours before dusk. Alex recognized the place from his previous life. They could see the very tip of the tower of the castle in the distance. They waited as the sun set while eating the provisions Gregory's man had acquired at the port.

Alex watched, his hatred growing as Gregory looked at the lapis lazuli, holding it up to the last of the light before clasping it in his fist and clutching it to his chest.

"I can feel that we're close." He smiled at Alex who just glared back at him. Gregory picked up a large rock and flung it at Alex, who tipped his head out of the way, letting it hit the tree behind him. Gregory laughed.

"Where is this cottage?" Gregory asked.

Alex just stared. Gregory got up and put his sword to Alex's chest. Alex could tell from how slow Gregory had gotten up and the color of his face that he wouldna last more than a few days if he kept at the same pace they were going.

"A couple of hours on foot northeast of here," Alex replied.

"Did ye hear that boys?" Gregory said. "Let's be on our way."

They had the last bit of sun to start with before they traveled by moonlight. Finally, they came to the cottage, partly dug into the hillside. A glow from a fire within indicated that someone was inside. Gregory drew his sword, and as the men started to as well, Alex said, "Nay, 'tis not inside."

Gregory turned to Alex, "Where then?"

Alex lifted his tied hands and pointed to a ledge in the cliff behind the cottage.

"There's a crevice in the rock, above the ledge. It is in there," he said before adding, "or at least it was."

Gregory squinted his eyes at Alex, "It better be," he said before turning to his men. "Cut him loose," he ordered as he took the pistol from his belt and pointed it at Alex's head.

"Ye are going to fetch it. And if ye try anything, I'll shoot ye."

"I cannot pull out the rock covering the hole without a dagger to loosen it."

Gregory paused. He said to the man cutting the rope binding Alex's wrist, "Give him yer knife."

The man handed Alex his knife and stepped away from him. Alex turned and looked up at the ledge, studying the cliff before putting the knife in his boot.

Alex went to a tree at the base of the cliff. The tree was much larger now, so he would be able to climb most of the way up through the tree. Alex started climbing the tree. When he got as far as he could, he moved out onto a branch.

He studied the cliff to find the best footing before making his transition from the tree to the cliff.

Though the distance was shorter than the tree climb, it still took a long time as he had to ensure with every step he took that his foot was on a secure stone. The jagged rocks jutting out of the cliff dug into his cuts, tearing them up more with every step. Finally, he made it to the ledge and stepped onto it. It wasna too deep, just enough for someone to stand on.

He moved to the side and grabbed the knife from his boot. He worked at clearing the debris from around the stone. Once cleared, he wedged the blade into the crack and started to pry the rock out of the hole. Upon removing the rock, Alex reached inside and pulled out a small velvet pouch that he placed into his sporran before making the descent. Once on the ground, he handed the sack to Gregory whose eyes lit up, even in the darkness. He emptied the contents of the sack into his hands, revealing several rings, brooches, and necklaces.

He smiled as he put the jewelry back in the sack and into his sporran.

"Tie his wrists again," he ordered, then remembered he still had the knife. He pointed the pistol at him again, "and drop the knife."

Alex removed the knife from his boot and dropped it at his feet before holding his hands out.

They walked back to the shore, missing where they had started by a good bit, forcing them to walk another hour along the shoreline until they came back to their boats.

As they walked, Alex glanced at the moon. It would be completely full tomorrow night. He thought of Anna and her words. *It would have been better if we never found each other*. His heart melted knowing the pain he had caused her. All he could do was to right things in this life before Gregory killed him and then not search for her in the next.

She no longer had the stone, and Alex was sure from the looks of Gregory that he wouldna last but a couple more days. He seemed to be getting weaker and weaker with every step. She would be able to live out her life in peace.

In his next lifetime, there would be a big age difference between him and her. Who knows how long she would live? His head spun, thinking about it.

As soon as they got to the boats, they departed. Gregory ordered Alex to row.

After rowing for more than an hour, Alex dinna have the strength to continue rowing. He could feel his chest starting to tear open more and felt his shirt once again wet with blood. He could smell the blood. *I'm sorry, Anna. I'm so sorry*, he thought, wishing she could read his thoughts.

"Row!" Gregory yelled as he kicked him from behind, giving Alex a jolt. Alex shook his head but said nothing. He slouched, holding his arm to his chest to apply pressure on the cut.

Gregory called to the men in the other boat, who pulled up beside them. He ordered the man in front of Alex to get in the other boat. Once in, Gregory drew his sword and thrust it into the bottom of the boat a couple of times until finally the water slowly poured up through it. He sheathed his sword.

"I'll leave ye to the blue men of the Minch," Gregory said as he got up and smacked him on the back of his shoulder before getting into the other boat.

CHAPTER

31

Anna woke up, feeling somber. She got up and put a couple of logs on the fire and went to the window. She looked up at the moon. It would be full tomorrow night.

She thought about Alex and wished she would have said something to him before he left. She could sense that he was seriously injured. She had a pain in her chest and not just from a broken heart but pain as if the injuries were hers and not his. She wrapped her arms around her chest, holding it tight, and bent over in an attempt to ease the pain. She had a sense as if she were suffocating. She was so upset she thought she would throw up. She kenned she'd not see him again, at least not as Alex. A tear rolled down her cheek.

*****

Three days later, Brodie and Willie visited. Spending time with Willie was a good distraction from her thoughts and quilt work.

On the fifth day, when they came back, Brodie brought news that Jacob had left after a messenger arrived saying that his uncle had died due to injuries inflicted by a struggle.

He had explained that this Jacob had spent time with his uncle, Gregory MacDonald, often when growing up. They had suspected that he was the source, though innocently, of the trouble regarding the stone.

Brodie stated what was going through Anna's mind. "Certainly, Alex would not have left the man maimed," he said sadly. They all understood that if Alex couldna finish the job, it was because Gregory had killed him first.

Brodie's news had confirmed what she had already kenned in her heart, but the confirmation left her in despair nevertheless. They had been doomed from the start. How is it possible that she could go through the same thing time after time? It seemed to be worse each time.

The next few days ran together, a blur, as Anna took up going through the motions of living, indifferent as to what went on around her.

One would think that she would be happy since her captor was dead, but she was not. No one could understand at what cost it came to her. She would try to find time with Butterfly alone so she could release some of her feelings, if just to cry freely while riding for the love that was gone. Just meeting Alex a couple of months ago, there was no way that anyone could ken just how much he meant to her.

*****

Robbie came back on the tenth day while they were all at the evening meal. He had told them that he had found out that Gregory MacDonald was dead due to injuries induced from a fight. He had heard rumors that the man responsible was dumped into the Minch.

After traveling to the port, he had confirmed that several MacDonalds had rented two small boats, yet one was reported sunk.

Robbie stole a quick glance at Anna, who was in a dead stare.

"I am so sorry," her da said to Robbie. "I should've not let him get involved in our family affairs. I ken ye were close."

"Aye. He was like a brother to me," he said sadly, "but he also had dealings with this MacDonald. It's not yer fault."

Anna excused herself from the table. She thought she was going to be sick. "I'm going back to the cabin."

"Ye've hardly eaten," her da said. She looked down at her plate where she more or less just rearranged her food instead of eating it. "Stay a bit so we can visit." He turned to Robbie and said, "She's barely eaten all week."

He turned back to Anna. "Ye'll wither away to nothing."

"I'm not much hungry. I dinna sleep too well last night," she replied. "I just want to go to bed."

Her da took a deep breath and made to get up, but Robbie got up first and said, "I'll see her back to the cabin and come back so that we can talk."

Robbie noticed his hesitation. He put his hand on his da's and said, "She'll be fine by herself. The MacDonald is dead. No harm will come to her now."

Her da sat back down, his expression showed his hesitation to leave her alone but agreed nonetheless, "All right."

Robbie escorted her back to the cabin. "It's nice that ye are back safe," she said as they entered the cabin. Looking down at his feet, she said in a hoarse voice, "I'm sorry to hear about Alex."

"Anna," he said. He paused, waiting for her to lift her head and make eye contact. When she didn't move, he put his finger under her chin and gently lifted her head. Her eyes welled up with tears, just waiting to let loose.

"Alex told me," he said. She stopped breathing until he continued, "about the curse. I am so sorry."

He opened his arms, and she went into them and let the tears flow. They had never told anyone, ever. It was their burden to bear, but somehow having someone else know lessened the pain a bit.

A couple of minutes went by before she pulled away. "When did he tell ye?"

"When we were at our house," he replied. "When we encountered the MacDonalds on the road, ye gasped and stiffened. It was apparent that Alex and he had known each other, yet Alex had already told me that he had not met the man. Alex was not one to lie to me," he paused. "I questioned him later."

He pulled her back into his embrace and held her for a good minute. "He felt responsible for all the trouble ye'd been in."

"I dinna blame him," she whispered as she looked away leaving his embrace in an attempt to hold back the tears. "It's just that I had told him it'd been better if we'd never found each other."

She looked at him. "It has been so confusing as I've been figuring this all out in my head," she explained. "I wish I could take it back. Without him, it's like a piece of me is gone, but yet I had just met him. And I ken that I'll meet up with him someday, so there is always a need to search for him. He makes me whole." She shook her head. "I cannot explain it. It would be different if it was final, but for me and him, it's not." She went back into his arms and said, "But it helps that someone else knows…and even more…believes it. It was hard enough for me to comprehend it all. I was figuring it out in pieces as I remembered."

"I'll always be here for ye," Robbie said.

"In this lifetime," she whispered.

CHAPTER

D ue to the approaching winter, Anna and her da left two days later. The wind and the cold made for a long journey.

Anna did her best to act normal as not to draw any questions from him as they were with each other for the whole journey.

She was grateful once she got home, not just because of the tiresome trip but for the time she could spend alone, sorting out her thoughts.

The days dragged on. She felt like she was just surviving day to day, feeling numb no matter what she was doing, but she tried her best to appear cheerful. It was hard to go through life, knowing that the one that completes ye was gone but will be back decades later to do it all over again, to search, love, and be killed.

The holidays were not the same as neither Robbie nor William came home, though they had plenty to do as they made their rounds to their tenants, like they did every year, making sure all had enough food on their table for Christmas. It was a very hard time for her. Everyone was jolly, even the poorest of their tenants, yet she was hurting so much inside, and nobody kenned.

A couple of days after Christmas, a letter came from Robbie with the announcement of them expecting, which was a nice contrast to the bad times they had gone through.

In an attempt to snap out of her depression, she tried to do things she enjoyed doing. So despite the cold, Anna rode her horse almost every day. It was nice to have her quiet time with Butterfly, where she could get all her feeling out of her head.

At first, when riding, she was always looking in the sky and tree lines, as if she would spot the falcon. She would be saddened when she did not see it even though she kenned that he was gone. *Will I ever be able to do something without thinking of him?*

It had taken her a while, but finally, she got out of the habit as she kenned it had taken away from the enjoyment she had always had being in nature.

On one February day, Anna decided to go ice fishing while her da went to the village on business. She went to a spot in the stream where there was a deeper pool.

The sun was unusually warm that day. She dismounted and looked around before closing her eyes and turning her face to the sun. She could feel the warmth on her cheeks. She took her cloak off and draped it over the saddle. She nuzzled Butterfly's cheek and said, "It's a beautiful day."

She grabbed her gear and walked over to the frozen stream. Everything was quiet with the water frozen over except for the occasional sound of the snow and ice falling from the branches of the trees as the sun melted it a bit.

Taking her dagger out, she squatted down while thrusting it into the ice a couple of times making an arc.

She paused for a minute to study the dagger that bore Alex's crest. Every time she used it, it would suddenly bring back memories of him, but she could not seem to put it away for good. *God, how I miss him. This curse is too painful to bear. Haven't I suffered enough for my treachery?*

She wiped the lone tear from her face and returned to thrusting the dagger into the ice until a complete circle was formed. Using the dagger, she took the circle of ice out of the hole and tossed it onto the bank.

She watched the water flowing in the hole and an occasional fish swimming underneath for a while. "It's a wonder that the fish are still alive in this cold of water," she called out to Butterfly, not expecting an answer.

"Aye, it is," she heard.

Her heart skipped a beat as she froze. Slowly, she got up and turned around with the dagger in her fist. There he was, with her cloak tied around his waist. His chest was bare but for the mangled scar that ran all the way down it. It was not a straight clean scar but jagged, discolored, and bulged out a bit.

He had lost a lot of muscle weight, his chest and shoulders were not as broad as they once were, but he was a beautiful sight.

She raised her eyes from his chest to his eyes, which shone the uncertainty that she would want him.

She dropped the dagger and ran to him, throwing her arms around him and cried. He gently enclosed her into his embrace.

After several minutes of him just holding her while she cried, she finally pulled away, and she asked, "How?"

He had explained to her how they had left him to die in a sinking boat. "In the cover of the darkness, I…" He paused, not wanting to say the words out loud. She nodded that she understood, and he continued, "I ken that I couldna make it far, so I went to the barn of where the healer used to live. I took a chance that he still lived there, and I hid in the barn."

She stared at him, waiting for more.

"He found me the next morn, but I do not remember. Apparently, I barely made it, as my wounds were deep, and infected with debris from being dragged. He said I was fevered and out for three weeks before I ever woke up."

Alex looked down at his chest and then back at Anna. "He said the wound was so infected that he had to cut it back opened to drain it twice. The healer was surprised I woke up at all."

His eyes filled with such remorse as he gently brushed the hair off her face and curled it behind her ear. "I ken the problems I have caused ye, and I ken that I should not have come here, but…"

She put her finger to his lips and shook her head.

"No," she said as she went back into his embrace, and she buried her face in his chest. "I should never have said that. I've regretted saying those words to ye since ye left. If I could have taken them back…" She pulled away and looked back at him. "I dinna understand the little control I have over the intensity of my feelings. I dinna ken at that time, that I would have waited another twenty years to be with ye rather than give myself to someone else."

"Yes, but," he said then motioned to his chest, "look at me?"

"Aye," she said, smiling as she slowly traced the ragged scar down his chest. "Ye forget that I've seen ye as a beggar, a shriveled old man, and a slave with lash marks on yer back, and every time, I loved ye."

Her hand stopped where the scar met the cloak, and she looked back into his eyes. "But this scar," she said with a sparkle in her eyes, "this is the most beautiful thing I have ever seen because this is what freedom looks like to me." She kissed his scar and laid her cheek against it, holding him.

"Gregory MacDonald is dead. The spell is broken," she said. "We can finally be together."

Never had she felt such freedom. They were both alive, and Gregory MacDonald was dead. *Thank ye, God. Thank ye,* she prayed as she held him tight.

He kissed her on the top of her head. "I love ye, Anna."

"I love ye too, Alex."

After a couple of minutes of holding each other, he said, "I need to go."

She let out a deep breath and stepped back. "The healer went to the village and will not be gone verra long. I would have a hard time explaining my disappearance with my clothes on the bed."

"So Robbie does not know yet?"

"Nay," he said. "I leave tomorrow to go back to the MacKays. I will send word to my father." He took her hands into his and looked down at them before looking back into her eyes. It was as if he could see all the way down to her soul. "Will ye marry me, Anna?"

A smile slowly stretched across her lips. "Aye, Alex. Nothing would make me happier."

He leaned down and kissed her lips gently. Her body heated up and tingled all over. He smiled at her and kissed her more deeply before pulling her away.

He took a step back and paused. He smiled at her then took two more steps back as he untied the cloak but continued to hold the ends so it did not fall. As his eyes were locked on hers, he took a deep breath, letting the sensation come over him. Once more, he took a deep breath, and he let the phenomenon overtake him as he let go of the cloak just as the transformation completed. The burst of energy hit him, and he flew around Anna twice before taking up to the sky.

She put her fingers to her lips and blew a kiss to him then watched him fly away until she couldna see him anymore.

She was so happy the tears rolled down her face as all the years, the centuries, of fear and anxiety melted away. It was over…finally.

EPILOGUE

It felt like it was the longest winter she had ever experienced, but it finally gave way to much warmer days and a lot of rain. It was worse the farther they got into the Highlands, but she dinna care how much it rained as the horses slushed through the muddy trails.

She couldna wait to get there. Her da had received a letter from Robbie in March with news that Alex had returned. Robbie had invited them up for a visit to be there for the arrival of the baby.

She had spotted the falcon several times in the distance, which only intensified her excitement. She kenned he was checking on their progress. Their arrival couldn't happen soon enough for Anna.

They arrived at Robbie's in-laws and were greeted by Robbie and a very ripe Mary Ellen. As excited as she was to see them, the pleasantries seemed to drag on. The anticipation was more than she could bear. Her heart was beating so fast she thought it would burst.

Not wanting to blurt out, "Where is Alex?" Anna glance at Robbie with a questioning look. He just grinned, giving her playful eyes.

He stepped closer to her and put his hands on her shoulders and gently guided her around to face the door.

There he stood in the doorway. A steam of light came through the window, illuminating him. She stopped breathing as she watched him walk in. He was the most magnificent man she had ever seen. His long dark hair flowing as he walked into the room. His muscles had filled back in. He wore the Boswell kilt instead of his usual MacKays, which ceremoniously hung over his broad shoulders. His sword dangled at his side.

He walked up to her da and bowed low and long, tipping his head down. "Laird Duncan, it is an honor to see ye again."

"Get up! Get up!" her da said as he embraced him. "Please do not bow to me," he said as he pulled away and bowed to Alex, "I am forever in yer debt."

Alex sidestepped so he was in front of Anna. He took her hand in his and kissed it while bowing to her. "My lady, it is a pleasure to see ye again."

His touch sent sparks through her whole body. It took everything she had not to run into his arms and hold him.

She had not realized until that moment that she had been holding her breath this whole time. She slowly took a breath in and said, "The pleasure's all mine."

*****

The baby arrived one week after they arrived. Alex spent every possible moment with Anna.

The eve before they were to leave for home, they were all assembled in the parlor. Mary Ellen and her mother were doting over the baby as the men traded stories. Alex and Anna played chess.

"Checkmate," Alex said.

She just stared at the board, sure she had another move.

Robbie looked over at them to confirm the words he had heard truly came from Alex instead of Anna and let out a laugh as he slapped his knee. "Aah, I think ye've met yer match!" He looked at her. She looked up to him with a smile and twinkling eyes.

She watched Alex get up with a big grin, all proud of himself. He gave her a small bow. "Milady." She gave him a smug look.

He turned and walked over to her da and knelt on one knee in front of him. "Sir," he began, "I would like to marry yer daughter and would like yer blessing."

Her da stood up, pulling Alex up gently by his shoulders. "There is no one else I would want to see my daughter marry," he said as he embraced Alex.

The End

D enise Lupinacci has always been fascinated with anything old-fashion. As a child, she sewed her own colonial peasant dress and spent her days in the woods behind her house on the American frontier. As an adult, she enjoys going to Victorian teahouses and has hosted several afternoon teas herself.

Denise draws inspiration from nature, and it is not uncommon to find her writing in the quiet of the woods while camping or along the side of the lake in her kayak.

Denise lives in the suburbs of Pittsburgh with her husband and her youngest two of her four children. Please see her website, Deniselupinacci.com.

CPSIA information can be obtained
at www.ICGtesting.com
Printed in the USA
BVHW081833201121
622059BV00001B/4

9 781649 529220